Nick Russo's Tips On How To Discover If You Are About To Become A Daddy:

1) Does the entire town stare at you and inquire as to your whereabouts precisely nine months ago?

2) When you think back to your last visit through town, do you recall waking up in a strange bed?

3) Have you caused any pregnant women to suddenly faint at the mere sight of you?

4) And does a certain beautiful, single mom-to-be ignite flashes of remembered desire?

Dear Reader,

Our lead title this month hardly needs an introduction, nor does the author. Nora Roberts is a multiple *New York Times* bestseller, and *Megan's Mate* follows her extremely popular cross-line miniseries THE CALHOUN WOMEN. Megan O'Riley isn't a Calhoun by birth, but they consider her and her young son family just the same. And who better to teach her how to love again than longtime family friend Nate Fury?

Our newest cross-line miniseries is DADDY KNOWS LAST, and this month it reaches its irresistible climax right here in Intimate Moments. In *Discovered: Daddy*, bestselling author Marilyn Pappano finally lets everyone know who's the father of Faith Harper's baby. Everyone, that is, except dad-to-be Nick Russo. Seems there's something Nick doesn't remember about that night nine months ago!

The rest of the month is terrific, too, with new books by Marion Smith Collins, Elane Osborn, Vella Munn and Margaret Watson. You'll want to read them all, then come back next month for more of the best books in the business—right here at Silhouette Intimate Moments.

Enjoy!

Leslie Wainger
Senior Editor and Editorial Coordinator

Please address questions and book requests to:
Silhouette Reader Service
U.S.: 3010 Walden Ave., P.O. Box 1325, Buffalo, NY 14269
Canadian: P.O. Box 609, Fort Erie, Ont. L2A 5X3

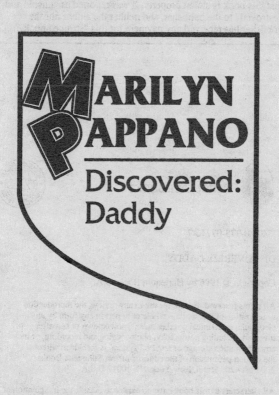

MARILYN PAPPANO

Discovered: Daddy

Silhouette®
INTIMATE™MOMENTS®

Published by Silhouette Books

America's Publisher of Contemporary Romance

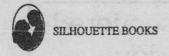

SILHOUETTE BOOKS

ISBN 0-373-07746-7

DISCOVERED: DADDY

Printed in U.S.A.

Books by Marilyn Pappano

Silhouette Intimate Moments

Within Reach #182
The Lights of Home #214
Guilt by Association #233
Cody Daniels' Return #258
Room at the Inn #268
Something of Heaven #294
Somebody's Baby #310
Not Without Honor #338
Safe Haven #363
A Dangerous Man #381
Probable Cause #405
Operation Homefront #424
Somebody's Lady #437
No Retreat #469
Memories of Laura #486
Sweet Annie's Pass #512
Finally a Father #542
*Michael's Gift #583
*Regarding Remy #609
*A Man Like Smith #626
Survive the Night #703
†Discovered: Daddy #746

Silhouette Books

Silhouette Christmas Stories 1989
"The Greatest Gift"

Silhouette Summer Sizzlers 1991
"Loving Abby"

*Southern Knights
†Daddy Knows Last

MARILYN PAPPANO

has been writing as long as she can remember, just for the fun of it, but a few years ago she decided to take her lifelong hobby seriously. She was encouraging a friend to write a romance novel and ended up writing one herself. It was accepted, and she plans to continue as an author for a long time. When she's not involved in writing, she enjoys camping, quilting, sewing and, most of all, reading. Not surprisingly, her favorite books are romance novels.

Her husband is in the navy, and in the course of her marriage she has lived all over the U.S. Currently she lives in Oklahoma with her husband and son.

Meet The Soon-To-Be Moms
of New Hope, Texas!

"I'll do anything to have a baby—even if it means
going to the sperm bank. Unless sexy cowboy
Jake Spencer is willing to be a daddy...
the natural way."
—*Priscilla Barrington, hopeful mom-to-be.*

THE BABY NOTION
by Dixie Browning (Desire 7/96)

"I'm more than willing to help Mitch McCord take care
of the baby he found on his doorstep. After all, I've been
in love with that confirmed bachelor for years."
—*Jenny Stevens, maternal girl-next-door.*

BABY IN A BASKET
by Helen R. Myers (Romance 8/96)

"My soon-to-be ex-husband and I are soon-to-be
parents! Can our new arrivals also bless us with a
second chance at marriage?"
—*Valerie Kincaid, married new mom.*

MARRIED...WITH TWINS!
by Jennifer Mikels (Special Edition 9/96)

"I have vowed to be married by the time I turn thirty.
But the only man who interests me is single dad
Travis Donovan—and he doesn't know I'm alive...yet!"
—*Wendy Wilcox,
biological-clock-counting bachelorette.*

HOW TO HOOK A HUSBAND (AND A BABY)
by Carolyn Zane (Yours Truly 10/96)

"Everybody wants me to name the father of my baby.
But I can't tell anyone—even the expectant daddy!"
—*Faith Harper, prim, proper—and very pregnant.*

DISCOVERED: DADDY
by Marilyn Pappano (Intimate Moments 11/96)

Chapter 1

Though her feet were sore, her ankles swollen as usual at the end of the day, Faith Harper ignored the chair behind the counter and paced restlessly around the shop. It was the day before Thanksgiving, and the store was quiet. She had sent Beth Reynolds, her part-time help, home early to help her mother with preparations for tomorrow's dinner, and she had promised the girl that she would close up and go home early herself. After all, it promised to be a busy evening for most people in New Hope, especially those with families. It wasn't likely that anyone would suddenly remember an urgent need requiring a last-minute preholiday visit to the Baby Boutique.

But it was five-fifteen, only fifteen minutes before her regular closing time, and Faith was still there. She hadn't had a customer in more than an hour. She'd done the usual closing up chores—returned misplaced merchandise to its proper location, run the sweeper, balanced the cash drawer and prepared the bank deposit. All she had to do was flip the sign on the door from Open to Closed, shut off all but the softly tinted lights that shone on the displays filling both front windows, lock up and leave. Still she waited. She thought, believed—hoped—he would come. She was sure of it—if not to the shop, then this evening to her house. But just in case he chose the shop, she had to stay until closing time. She had to give him every minute of opportunity.

He. Him. Nick Russo.

She had been with her good friend Wendy when he'd walked into the shop more than four hours ago. Wendy had stopped by to compare notes on gifts for Michelle Parker's wedding this weekend to Michael Russo when the bell over the door had rung. "I'll be right with you," Faith had called out without even looking, and an achingly familiar male voice had responded. "No hurry. I just need directions to the formal wear place..."

He had said more, but Faith hadn't heard it. Those few words had been enough to stir long-ago memories, enough to make her whirl around—*whirl,* she thought with a grim smile, in the condition she was in—and face for the first time in months the man who had spoken them. Nearly nine months, to be exact. She'd gotten only a glimpse of him, only enough to see that memory hadn't embellished fact, that he *was* as handsome as she'd thought, as dark and tough and sexy as she'd remembered.

And then she had fainted.

Even now, four hours later, her face burned at the memory. Fainting was such a weak thing to do. She'd never done it before, not once in her life.

But she'd never come face-to-face with Nick Russo after he'd removed himself so thoroughly from her life. She'd never been nearly nine months pregnant and seeing the baby's father again for the first time since they'd done the deed. She'd never felt so vulnerable, so lost, so utterly unwanted—and, after a lifetime of living with Great-aunt Lydia, that was saying something.

By the time she'd come to again, he had been gone. She was lying on the couch in her office—where *he,* according to Wendy, had carried her before he'd taken off again without waiting for those directions he had asked about. He seemed to be very, very good at making quick exits.

But he would be back. She was sure of it.

Stopping in front of a rack of infant dresses, she picked up a hanger and admired the dress it held. It was hunter green velvet, with a pristine white collar edged with eyelet lace, a white satin sash and a narrow ruffle of eyelet lace peeking out from beneath the hem. It was beautiful, expensive and totally impractical. She had bought one for Amelia Rose for her first Christmas service and her first baby portrait. Once those big events were past, she intended to wrap the dress in tissue paper and carefully pack it away for Amelia Rose to give to *her* first daughter. With care, it could become a Harper family tradition, something that was sorely lacking in Faith's life—both family *and* traditions.

With a sigh, she returned the hanger to the rack, then glanced at her watch. Five twenty-five. Maybe she'd been wrong in thinking Nick would prefer a meeting at the shop, where he could always claim he'd simply been asking directions or considering a purchase for one of his myriad nieces and nephews. Maybe he would prefer the privacy of her house, where there would be no prying eyes and little chance for interruption. Maybe he wouldn't come at all but would ignore her for the next few days until his brother Michael's wedding was over, and then return to Houston without saying so much as a word to her, the same way he'd left before. Maybe....

The bell rang, a soft, melodic tone that wouldn't disturb even the weariest of sleeping babies, and she went cold inside. It was him. She didn't have to turn to face the door to know it. She could *feel* it.

The door closed with a quiet whoosh, and slowly, gathering her courage, she turned to face him. He had come only as far as the ceramic tile. Where it gave way to plush carpet, he had stopped, hands in his jacket pockets, shoulders squared, his expression not quite a scowl. Grateful for the racks of clothing between them, she clasped her hands together underneath her belly, her way of connecting with

Amelia Rose, of reassuring her daughter that everything would be all right.

For a time, they simply looked at each other. He looked like his brother Michael, only harder. Like his father Antonio, only rougher. He had his mother's big dark eyes and his father's square-cut jaw, had the same thick, black hair that all the Russos shared. He lacked their softness, though, their friendliness and their warmth. He looked at this moment like a mean son of a bitch, but Faith knew he could be tender. He could be gentle, warm and generous.

And he could be cold. Hostile. Aloof. Like now.

After one moment had dragged into another, then another, he finally broke the silence. "How are you?" The question was grudgingly polite, the concern minimal, the sincerity nonexistent. Luisa Russo's manners had just barely stuck with her oldest child.

"I'm fine." She sounded no friendlier, not even as polite.

"Do you often faint like that?"

"No, but I'm pregnant. I do all sorts of things that I don't ordinarily do."

With a vague nod, he glanced around the shop. Checking to make sure they were alone? she wondered. Was he afraid of someone seeing him there? Did he fear that when he sat down to dinner tonight with his parents and Michael—or, worse, tomorrow with the entire Russo clan, all forty or fifty of them—that someone would say, "Hey, Nick, I heard you were at the Baby Boutique. What were you doing there?" Maybe he could brush off the family's curiosity, but more than likely, his wife wouldn't be so easily put off. She would wonder what business Nick, the tough-guy cop, might have in a baby shop.

Faith would love to tell her—but, of course, she wouldn't. Except for blurting out her secret to Wendy in this afternoon's weak moment, she'd told no one. Not one other soul in town knew or even suspected that Nick Russo was the father of her baby...except, judging from his hostility, Nick himself. What, she wondered, would he do about it?

He moved a few steps closer, his boots making no sound on the pale gray carpet. Taking up a position directly in front of her, with a rack of miniature winter coats between them, he glanced away, then back again. Like that, a fair bit of his antagonism disappeared and was replaced with bewilderment. "Who are you?"

For a moment she simply stared at him. Then she became aware of a sinking sensation in her stomach. It was disappointment, she realized. She was incredibly disappointed. "I expected better from you than that," she said flatly. "If we weren't alone, if somebody else were around to hear.... But we *are* alone. There's no one else here."

"I know your name is Faith—the woman here earlier told me that. Faith Hunter."

"Harper."

He acknowledged her correction with another of those curt little nods. "Have we met? Did I know you when I lived here?"

Made restless by her disillusionment, Faith turned away and walked to the counter. He followed. "I knew I would see you this week," she said. "I knew you'd come back for Michael and Michelle's wedding. I even knew you wouldn't be too pleased by what you saw. But I never imagined that you would be so cowardly that you would pretend not to know me."

"Lady, if I knew you, I wouldn't be here," he said sharply. "I only came back because—" Breaking off, he grimaced, then went on. "Apparently, you think we *have* met before. Pardon me for not remembering, but when was it? When I lived here? When I was in school? One of the times I came back to visit my family?"

"We met at your brother's engagement party." Her voice was soft, her words as cold as the ice inside her as she locked gazes with him and waited for some response, some recognition, some hint that this was just a cruel, stupid game he was playing, but she found no such hint in his eyes. Maybe if she told him that he needn't pretend, that the whole thing—the whole mistake—was New Hope's best-kept secret. That she had no desire to share that secret, that night and, most especially, the product of that night with him or anyone else. Maybe if she told him all that, he would quit playing and act at least remotely similar to the man she'd thought he was.

"Michael's engagement party?" He shook his head. "I don't remember."

"Oh, please," she said scornfully.

"Look, I admit I got drunk that night. There's not a whole lot about it that I *do* remember. Did something happen? Is that why you're acting this way?"

She studied him for a long time, searching once again for some evidence of his deceit. Again, she found nothing. He looked confused, curious, a little chagrined by his admission of drunkenness and a whole lot blank. He wasn't playing a game. He wasn't pretending. *He didn't remember her.*

Abruptly, before he could see the shock she was feeling steal across her face, Faith turned away. First she retrieved her coat and purse from the storeroom, tugged the coat on, lapped it over her stomach and belted it. Next she tucked the deposit bag under one arm, along with her handbag, and began turning off the lights. The only ones she left burning were at the front. There she flipped the Open sign over, pulled the door open and finally looked at him. He still stood halfway across the dimly lit store.

"No," she said at last, feeling about a hundred years old. "Nothing happened. Now, if you don't mind, I'd like to go home. It's been a long day."

He hesitated as if he wanted to argue. She suspected that he did. People didn't often give Nick Russo orders—*he* was usually the one in charge. But, after a moment, he came to the door, passing close to her as he stepped out into the chilly evening. She followed him out, waited for the door to swing shut, then locked it.

"Where are you parked?" The grudgingly offered politeness was back in his voice.

"In the lot out back."

"I'll walk you—"

Perversely, she interrupted. "I've got to go to the bank first." She turned toward the bank, less than two blocks away down New Hope's main street, and he fell into step beside her. When she stopped, so did he, and he matched the ferocity of her scowl degree by degree. "I don't need an escort."

"Only a fool would carry a bag of cash down the street by herself after dark when most of the businesses downtown, including the bank, are already closed for the day. And, you, Ms. Hunt—Ms. Harper—don't look like a fool."

Faith felt the strangest urge to both laugh and cry at that. "You're wrong, Mr. Russo," she said, giving in just for a moment to bitter laughter. "I'm the biggest fool New Hope has ever seen." Pulling the bank bag from under her arm, she pushed it against his chest. "You want to play Good Samaritan? Here. *You* make the deposit. *I'm* going home."

Quickly, before he could respond, she turned and headed back the way they'd come, turning the corner, walking as quickly as Amelia Rose would allow. Once she reached her car, she fumbled with the lock before finally getting the door open and sliding inside. She was halfway home before the trembling in her hands stopped, before the tightness in her chest eased enough to allow her to draw a deep breath, before the emptiness inside her started to disappear, before her heart calmed enough to deal with the disillusionment and hurt.

He didn't remember her.

In the last nine months or so, she had come up with a dozen reasons to explain why Nick had left the way he did, with ten times that number to explain why he'd never called her, never come to see her, never made any attempt whatsoever to contact her. But she had never thought of that particular reason. She had never considered the possibility that he simply didn't remember her. That he had found her utterly forgettable. That what they had shared had meant so little to him that he'd put it immediately out of his mind.

She'd thought he'd felt awkward, maybe a little guilty, maybe even a little overwhelmed by the intensity of it all.

She'd thought his job with the Houston Police Department was keeping him busy, that maybe he had some personal problems in his life, or that possibly he didn't know how to handle what had happened between them. Later, of course, had come his marriage, only a month later. It was a surprise to his friends and family and a real shocker to *her*.

But she had been wrong, *so* wrong. He hadn't felt awkward or guilty or overwhelmed. He had *forgotten* her. Forgotten meeting her. Forgotten talking to her. Forgotten making love to her. Forgotten saying such sweet, sweet things to her. The most special, most memorable, most important night of her life and, as far as he was concerned, it had never happened.

She pulled into the driveway of the big Victorian house Great-aunt Lydia had left her and shut off the engine. For a time she simply sat there, listening to the settling sounds as the motor cooled. When finally the car was silent and all she could hear was her own uneven breathing, she got out and headed for the steps to the wide veranda. It was only when the cold air hit her face that she realized she was crying.

And why shouldn't she cry? She was twenty-five years old, soon to be a mother, and she was alone in a way that she hadn't been even just this morning. At least this morning she'd still had a few secret hopes, a few treasured dreams. She had believed that once Nick saw her he would realize the significance between her pregnancy and last February's party, would acknowledge his paternity and accept his responsibility. She had believed that Amelia Rose would have a mother *and* a father—even if they weren't married, even if he was married to someone else. She had believed that her baby would have a family to love her—grandparents and great-grandparents, aunts and uncles and a full two dozen cousins.

Though her head had known better, in her heart she had believed—had *pretended* that that late February night had been as important to him as it was to her. But he didn't remember it. He didn't remember the magic. He didn't remember the words. He didn't remember *her.*

So much for hopes and dreams.

So much for magic.

She had lied to him.

As he made the short walk from the bank, where he'd dropped Faith Harper's vinyl bag into the night depository, to his truck, Nick considered her denial. Obviously something *had* happened at Michael's party, otherwise, she wouldn't be acting as if he were her sworn enemy. Had he been rude to her? Made a pass at her? Somehow offended her?

He couldn't remember. She had seemed disbelieving, and it wasn't something he was proud of, but he really had been drunk that night. He'd had too little sleep and too little food and Michelle's demon nephews had kept him supplied with punch doctored with far too much booze. He remembered drinking a third cup—or had it been his fourth?—and the next thing he'd known it was morning. He had thought about asking Michael to supply the missing details, but there had been something just a little embarrassing about admitting to his kid brother that he'd gotten drunk enough to lose eight hours. Besides, it had just been a simple little party—all the Russos and the Parkers, Michelle's family, some out-of-town relatives and a host of friends. With his mother and all his little nieces and nephews there, it was guaranteed that he hadn't done anything too awful. And so he had forgotten about it, had put it out of his mind.

Or had he?

She said they'd met then and, on his earlier stop at the Baby Boutique this afternoon, he had been stunned to see her. He had been seeing her in his mind—even, damn it, in his dreams—off and on for months. He had thought that surely here in New Hope, surrounded by his loud, boisterous family and caught up in wedding plans, he would be safe from her. But there she'd been, exactly the way he had imagined her. Well, except for the pregnancy. He had *never* imagined that.

But the rest of her had been the same. The long brown hair that he knew was as soft and silky as a baby's—not guessed, not suspected, but *knew*. The voice sweeter than honey. The eyes as blue as any Texas sky. He had been absolutely shocked. Here he'd thought she was merely a figment of his imagination, a temptation of the only sort—during those long months on the Sanchez case—that he'd been able to succumb to, an elusive, ethereal angel come to haunt his nights. Sometimes he had awakened to the lingering touch of her fingers, cool and soft, on his skin. Other times he had sworn her scent clung to him in those first fragile moments of awakening, and his dreams of her had left him hot and flushed, his breathing labored, his body hard and his arousal almost—*almost* satisfied.

Climbing into the truck, Nick slammed the door harder than necessary and started the engine, but he didn't pull away from the curb. Instead he found himself staring at the Baby Boutique, at the tiny little doll-like clothes spotlighted in the window by pale pink bulbs overhead. He had convinced himself that the woman in his dreams wasn't real, easy enough to do since he *knew* he'd never met her before. He never would have forgotten a face like that...or eyes like that...or a desire like that. He had a damned good memory for faces and names, for places and details. It was one of the tools of his trade...and he was good at his trade.

But Faith Harper was very definitely real—and, if she was to be believed, very definitely someone he'd met before. Someone he had offended before? Or, considering the erotic nature of his dreams, someone he had—

Swearing aloud, he refused to complete the sentence. Shifting into gear, he released the brake and, after a quick look over his shoulder, gunned the engine and pulled into the street. He was in fourth gear and approaching fifty miles an hour before he reached the end of the block, where he brought the truck to a screeching halt beside the phone booth on the corner.

Telling himself to leave well enough alone—hadn't she insisted that nothing had happened between them?—and that even looking was a waste of time, he got out and flipped open the ragged-eared book hanging from a chain inside the booth. Faith Harper might very well be married—New Hope was the sort of place where women still got married before getting pregnant. Even if, by some chance, she *wasn't* married, single women who lived alone didn't have their names and addresses listed in the phone book for security reasons, not even in New Hope.

But there it was: Harper Faith 411 Sycamore.

Four hundred eleven Sycamore. That was the corner of Sycamore and Lee Streets. The house there was old, built around the turn of the century, dominating its lot. It was a Victorian, with lots of gingerbread and a big porch, a wrought-iron fence enclosing a big lawn, plenty of trees and a curving brick driveway. He had lived away from New Hope for sixteen years, but he remembered that old house well because the last time he'd come back, he had gone there. Michael and Michelle's party had been held at Faith Harper's house on the night she said they'd met and he absolutely couldn't remember.

The night about nine months ago.

The night . . .

Oh, God.

The phone book slipped from his hands, banging against the glass on the way down before the chain stopped its fall and set it on a slow pendulum sway. Nick stared at it, imagining he could hear each creak of the fine chain, but all he could really hear was his own breathing and, barely audible somewhere deep down inside him, a tiny little voice, one that had been silent more years than he cared to remember, softly praying, *Please, God, no.*

Please don't let it be my baby.

Please don't trap me that way.

Please let this be a bad dream.

Please, please, please . . .

"Hey, Nick, you okay?"

It took a moment for the question to register, a moment longer to realize that it was directed to him and that it was his brother speaking. Turning slowly, he saw that Michael had pulled to a stop just through the intersection and rolled down the window of his battered old Chevy. The gray suit and black overcoat he wore presented an amusing contrast to the fifteen-year-old sedan, but Nick wasn't in the mood to be amused.

"Nick? What's wrong?"

He gave a shake of his head to clear it. "Nothing. Nothing's wrong."

Michael glanced from him to the phone booth behind him. "You get some bad news?"

The worst, Nick thought grimly. He couldn't imagine anything he wanted to hear less right now than that he was about to become a father. He didn't want to get married, had never wanted to get married, and he certainly had no intentions of ever bringing a child into the world. But he might have done just that in a night he couldn't even remember.

"Mama's going to have dinner on the table in about ten minutes. We'd both better get moving."

Nick glanced down the street where a lighted sign flush against the stone building marked Faith Harper's store, and he thought about going home, about sitting down to dinner with his parents and Michael. About eating and talking and pretending that everything was okay when he'd just found out that he might have royally screwed up his life. He thought about facing his father, who had passed on to Nick his own rather strict code governing the behavior of an honorable man, and he knew he couldn't do it. Not without a few answers from Faith Harper.

And if her answers were the wrong answers, he just might never be able to face his father without shame again.

"Listen, Mike, tell Mom and Pop that I had to take care of some business. I won't be able to make it to dinner, but I'll be back tonight."

"Aw, come on, Nick. You know Mama's been cooking all day. She's made all your favorite foods."

"It's important, Mike."

His brother sighed, then nodded. "All right. I'm sure she'll understand. See you later." He rolled the window up as he drove away.

His comment about their mother made Nick feel guilty. No doubt she would understand. Since he'd made detective eight years ago, business had always come first with him. She didn't approve—didn't believe that a man should let a job be more important to him than his family—but she understood.

But this business tonight wasn't business at all. It was personal. But if he tried hard enough, he could make it business. He could keep his emotions out of it. He could hide the sick feeling of doom that was already settling in his stomach. He could be very logical, very reasonable and detached. And he could find some way—besides the obvious—of resolving this problem.

His truck was warm, the heater blowing on high, when he returned to it. He fastened his seat belt, then made a left turn. Lee Street was a couple of blocks over from Main, and the four hundred block of Sycamore was a mile or so north. Pulling up to the stop sign at the intersection of the two streets, he sat for a moment and simply stared at 411.

He'd been right. It was definitely the house where the engagement party had been held. He had come late, and the broad curving driveway had been filled with cars. He had parked on the street at the opposite end of the block and walked to the house through the cold and a light layer of snow. His entire family had been there when he'd arrived, along with every old friend he'd had in high school, all of Michelle's family, people he'd known growing up and plenty of strangers. He had been introduced to so many people by the time Michelle's nephews had offered him the first cup of spiked punch that he'd lost track of them all.

What man in his right mind could forget meeting a woman like Faith Harper? But he had already established that he hadn't been in his right mind. After those few drinks, he had been drunker than he could remember ever being, and he had paid for it the rest of the weekend with one hellacious hangover. It had been almost enough to make him swear off booze for the rest of his life.

If his fears were on target, he might be paying for those few drinks for much longer than one weekend. He might spend the rest of his life paying for his sins.

The tap of a horn behind him made him realize how long he'd been sitting there. He crossed the intersection and continued down Lee, then, after a few blocks, turned to the right, again to the right and back down to Sycamore. This time he parked in front of the house.

It was a big place for a woman all alone...but maybe she didn't live alone. Maybe she was married after all. So what if she hadn't worn a wedding ring? She was pregnant—pregnant women had problems with swelling and weight gain. Maybe the wedding band didn't fit anymore.

But he didn't think she had a husband tucked inside. He had nothing to base the presumption on, just instinct... and he had good instincts. That was part of what made him such a good cop.

There was a car parked in the driveway and lights on inside—in several rooms on the first floor and upstairs. He wondered what she was doing that required such illumination, wondered if all those empty rooms ever bothered her, if she ever wished for the security of a compact, easily secured apartment or condo like his in Houston. In this white elephant of a house, he could count three sets of French doors in addition to the main entrance, countless ground-floor windows, trellises leading to the porch roof and plenty of other windows above, and that was only from the front.

After a time, he got out of the truck and shoved the door shut. It sounded loud on the quiet street. There was a gate in the iron fence just a few steps away and a brick path that led across the lawn to the driveway and the porch beyond. He listened to his boots echo on the brick, the sound slowing the closer he drew to the house. He didn't want to be there, didn't want to see her again, didn't want to ask the questions that he had to ask, and he damned well didn't want to hear the answers he fully expected her to give. He wanted to turn around, get in his truck and drive all the way back to Houston. He wanted to exorcise those dreams, forget those blue eyes, wipe all record of today from his memory as thoroughly as the alcohol had erased that February night. He wanted to return tomorrow, once again blissfully unaware of Faith Harper's existence, to spend the holiday with his family. He wanted to attend Michael's wedding on Saturday and leave again without any obligations, without any responsibilities following him back home.

But he couldn't leave. He couldn't stop the dreams or forget those eyes. He'd been trying for months. He couldn't forget today, either, and as long as he had even the slightest suspicion, even the slightest doubt, he couldn't face his family.

Hell, he wouldn't even be able to face himself if he left here without knowing—and once knowing, if he left without doing something. Without accepting those obligations and responsibilities the way his father had taught him.

Crossing the porch, he rang the doorbell, then waited impatiently. Resisting the urge to ring it again only seconds later, he shoved his hands into his pockets to warm them. To hide the fists they immediately clenched into.

Through the frosted sidelight, he watched a shadow approach. A moment later the lock clicked and the door slowly opened inward. Faith Harper stood there, one hand on the cut-crystal knob, the other gripping the wooden door as she frowned at him. Unable to form the important questions into words, he asked the first unimportant one that came to mind. "What kind of idiot gives her cash deposit to a stranger and tells him to take it to the bank while she goes home?"

She tilted her head back until those damnably blue eyes were locked with his, and she offered him a cool smile. "You may not know me, but *I* know you. You're a cop in Houston. You're Assistant District Attorney Michael Russo's brother. Most importantly, you're Antonio Russo's son. If you can't be trusted with a few dollars' cash, who can?''

She had a good point. Most importantly, he *was* Antonio Russo's son, and Antonio Russo's son didn't steal. He didn't cheat, he didn't lie—except in the course of his job—and he didn't shirk his responsibilities. Antonio's son couldn't simply go back to Houston and forget her. Antonio's son had to ask the difficult questions, and he had to live with the unwelcome answers.

He exhaled heavily, then grudgingly asked, ''Can I come in?''

''Why?''

''There are some things I need to know.''

She glanced over her shoulder at something out of his line of sight, then back at him. ''This isn't a good time.''

''Are you alone?''

Her answer came after a brief hesitation. ''Yes.''

''Are you expecting a husband home soon?''

''No. There's no husband.'' She waited a moment, then continued. ''What? No shock? But of course not. You live in the big city of Houston. You people down there aren't as easily shocked as the small-town minds of New Hope.'' After another brief silence, she stepped back, opened the door wider, and gestured for him to come into a foyer cluttered with cardboard and parts of a crib.

As she closed the door, Nick edged the box back a few inches with his foot, then took a long look around—at the stairs that made a long, straight journey to the second floor, at the living room on the right, the study opening on the left and the family room straight back. He remembered this place from February. It had been filled with people—every room on the first floor and spilling outside in huddled groups, smokers on the front porch, drinkers out back. There had been such a crowd that, when he'd felt the first real punch from the doctored fruit drink, he'd had to look long and hard to find a quiet, cool place where he could sit down, be alone and draw a breath for the first time all evening.

He remembered coming to her house, remembered talking there to just about everyone he'd ever known. He remembered a room with an iron bed whose rails were cold to the touch, a room with little tables and a little glass lamp. He even—God help him—remembered coming down these stairs in the dark sometime before dawn. But he still didn't remember her. Damn it, just how drunk had he been?

Looking down, he studied the box, cut open with a paring knife discarded on the runner beneath it. A few pieces of the crib were gone, probably already carried upstairs where she planned to assemble it. "Did I interrupt something?"

"It can wait. Isn't your family expecting you for dinner?"

"I saw Mike. He'll make excuses for me. Mom and Pop won't mind."

"And what about your wife? Won't she mind? Or is she used to your excuses?"

He gave her a quizzical look, opened his mouth to reply, then recalled one of the less enjoyable aspects of his undercover work on the Sanchez case: his so-called marriage. His relationship with Phoebe had been strictly business. As an FBI agent, she'd needed entrée into Sanchez's inner circle. Since Emilio Sanchez had already known and trusted Nick, the bureau and the department together had come up with the idea of marriage. Unfortunately, the tale had made its way back home to New Hope and to his family, who had been shocked, surprised, excited, hurt and pleased, all at once. Nearly four months had passed before he was able to explain it all to them, emphasizing that he'd never been married and never intended to get married.

Apparently that part of the gossip had failed to make its way to Faith.

"I don't have a wife," he said quietly. "That was part of the cover I was using for the case I was working on." He thought he saw relief pass through her eyes, but it was gone so quickly that he couldn't be sure. "Is that why you never got in touch with me? Because you thought I was married?''

Her cheeks red, she bent to pick up one of the honey-finished side rails and tried to bluff her way through. "Why would your marital status matter to me? I hardly know you, and you don't know me at all, so why in the world would I want to get in touch with you?''

"To tell me that you're pregnant. To tell me that you're going to have a baby. To tell me..." Hating the words, he swallowed hard and forced them out anyway. "To tell me that I'm going to be a father.''

In the room Great-aunt Lydia had always called the parlor, Faith used a brass poker to jab at the logs burning on the grate, thankful for any means to alleviate even a little of the tension that made her body feel like a rubber band wound too tightly. Any minute now she just might fray and explode, everything inside her bursting free. All the anger. All the shame. All the hopes, the dreams, the need. The hurt, the sorrow and the fear.

After months of praying for Nick's return, she wished now that he would simply go away. It seemed that each time she saw him, things just got worse. First she fainted, then he told her that he didn't remember her. Now he might as well have come right out and said that he found the idea of being a father totally repugnant. It had been in his face. It had been in his eyes. It had been in his voice when he'd said those dreaded words—*I'm going to be a father.*

She had expected other reactions. That he might actually be happy about it. After all, he came from a large family, and his sisters were doing their best to make it a whole lot bigger. Was it so farfetched to think that the Russo sons might value family as much as the Russo daughters did? She had thought that he might not be thrilled, but at least not put off by the idea. She had thought that he might look forward to fatherhood even if he didn't care at all for Amelia Rose's mother. She had even thought that he might not care.

But she hadn't expected him to find the idea so objectionable.

She had been prepared for him not to want *her*. She was nothing special, after all. Her own father hadn't wanted her. Heavens, even her mother had had better things to do than raise her daughter, and Great-aunt Lydia had taken her in only out of a sense of duty. But for Nick not to want Amelia Rose, not to want a child who was a part of him...

It didn't matter, she insisted as she poked at the fire one last time. She had come this far alone and she could continue that way. She could love her baby more than enough for two people, could love her so much that she would never miss her father or any of the family that he could have provided.

The floorboards in the center of the double door creaked under Nick's weight as he came into the room. Faith had hoped, when she'd brushed past him a moment ago, that he would have the courtesy to leave, simply to walk out. She wouldn't have blamed him and wouldn't have minded. In fact, she probably would have been relieved. But he couldn't make it that easy for her.

"I deserve an answer one way or the other," Nick demanded.

She sat down in the rocker where she spent many of her evenings. It was a massive piece, more than a hundred years old, certifiably antique according to the owner of the shop where she'd bought it five months ago. She didn't care about its age or how that affected its value. She had liked that it was big and solidly made, that the rockers were just the slightest bit warped from a hundred years of rocking, that the arms were worn smooth, that the slats curved against her back just so. She had sat down in it in that dusty store, had set it in motion and had sworn for an instant that she could actually feel her baby in her arms. She had bought it, not even blinking at the price, and had used it every day since. It brought her peace and made her feel secure.

But not tonight. Not with Nick Russo in her house.

"What answer do you want?" she asked, folding one foot beneath her, clasping her hands together, using her slippered toes to start the chair moving.

He came closer. "I want you to tell me that I'm wrong. That it's not my baby. That you and I didn't—" He had the grace to look ashamed of his response. "But we did, didn't we?"

She drew a fortifying breath, then blithely answered with the untruths he wanted. "You're wrong. She's not your baby. You and I never even spoke the night of the party."

"Speaking is hardly a necessary part of the act," he said dryly, then abruptly he locked in on her earlier words, on one in particular. "She? It's a girl?"

"I think so. I believe so." She hadn't been tested, but she had been convinced in her heart since the day the doctor had confirmed what her body—and the home pregnancy kit—had already told her. Of course she would have loved a son equally as much, but she had *known* that this first child was a daughter. A sweet little baby girl by the name of Amelia Rose.

He moved still closer, circling around the sofa, taking a seat on the edge of the overstuffed cushions. "We did, didn't we?" he asked again, looking as grim and unhappy as anyone Faith had ever seen.

"I gave you your answer, so please leave."

"I want the truth."

"You have your truth," she said stubbornly. "You don't remember ever seeing me, ever meeting me, ever—" Breaking off, she shrugged. "That's the only truth you need."

"Damn it, don't play games!" he snapped, making her flinch. "Is this my baby?"

Her fingers knotted tightly together, she took another deep breath and lied. "No. It's *my* baby. This isn't a game, Nick, it's my *life*. It's my daughter's life. Any idiot can see that you don't want a daughter, and every daughter in the world is better off with no father at all than with a father who doesn't want her. Don't worry about it. Amelia Rose and I have gotten along just fine without you, and we'll continue to do so. We neither want nor need anything from you, so go back to Houston and forget all about us. You did it once before. You can do it again.''

For a moment he stared at her, his eyes dark and angry. Then he leaned back against the cushions, tilted his head back and lifted his gaze to the ceiling. "Oh, God," he muttered, whispered, prayed. "I had been working some damned long hours. I hadn't had much sleep that week, hadn't eaten anything that day. When I got here, someone gave me a cup of punch—plain fruit punch. I hadn't taken more than a drink or two when Michelle's nephews, the redheaded kids, brought me another cup. This one came from the back porch, they said."

Because of all the children at the party, the punch had been strictly nonalcoholic. Faith had made it herself. But she'd spent enough time in the kitchen—most of the evening, in fact—to see the steady stream of men cutting through on their way to the back porch. She hadn't thought anything of it. That was the way things were done in New Hope.

She hadn't had a clue at the time what impact that back-porch stash was going to have on her life.

"I don't know who was supplying it, but the stuff would have stripped paint," he went on. "I was trying to work my way around to the dining room, because I damned sure didn't need to be drinking on an empty stomach, but I kept getting sidetracked. There were a lot of people to meet, a lot of people I hadn't seen in a long time. Finally, I was feeling pretty lousy, so I went into the kitchen—it was the only quiet place I could find—and..." He shrugged. "Then it was morning."

The party had ended, and everyone else had gone home. Faith's friends—Valerie and Wendy—who had shared hostess duties while she hid in the kitchen had offered to stay and help with the cleanup, but she had sent them home. It had been late, and she had been tired, and there was always Saturday for cleaning. Once they left, she had gone into the kitchen with an armful of dishes, and there he'd sat, arms on the table, head on his arms, eyes closed. Asleep, she'd thought. Knowing what she knew now, "passed out" seemed more likely.

"What happened next?"

Faith mimicked his shrug and stubbornly continued the lie that he so obviously wanted to believe but couldn't quite buy. "Nothing. Everyone left and I locked up and went to bed. My friends came over around ten the next morning, and we cleaned up. If you spent the night here, I didn't know it." At her lie, Amelia Rose gave a kick, swift and unexpected, making Faith catch her breath. Never in her life had she felt as close to anyone as she had to her baby the past eight months, but she was seriously looking forward to the next phase of their relationship. No more heartburn, no more backaches, no more swollen hands and feet and, most especially, no more strong and well-placed kicks.

He leveled his gaze on her. "I spent the night," he said stiffly. "I remember coming down those stairs the next morning. I remember waking up naked."

She remembered waking up naked, too, and leaving the bed while he still slept. Even better, she remembered seeing him naked. As inexperienced as any grown woman could possibly be, she had been favorably impressed by her first up-close-and-personal encounter with a man. "Didn't that set off some sort of alarm? Didn't you wonder how you'd gone from fully clothed at the kitchen table to naked in a bed upstairs?"

"I always sleep naked," he said with a scowl. "I wake up that way every morning."

"In a strange bed? In a strange house?"

The expression that crossed his face was eloquent in its regret. "I've experienced my share of mornings in a strange bed in a strange place."

Just what she needed to know, she thought bitterly. He didn't remember her at all when he was sober, and even drunk he hadn't thought she was anything special. She'd just been one more in a long line of anonymous women in unfamiliar beds. This man had a tremendous effect on her ego.

Last February he had made her feel like the most important, most fascinating woman in the world. Now she felt insignificant. Ashamed. Dirty.

He ran his fingers through his hair in a gesture that spoke of frustration. "Jeez, weren't you using birth control pills or condoms? Don't you believe in safe sex?"

Trying to hide the stiffness spreading through her, Faith kept her voice soft and level as she turned the question back on him. "You think it's entirely possible that you had sex with a complete stranger and that she's now pregnant. Don't *you* believe in safe sex?"

Standing, he shoved his fingers deep into the pocket of his jeans, pulled out an old wallet, dug around inside for a few seconds then tossed two small, square packets on the table in front of him. "I never leave home without 'em," he said sarcastically.

"Then you don't need to worry, do you? Obviously, this isn't your baby." Taking a deep breath, Faith got to her feet, and the chair rocked forward one last time, bumping the backs of her knees. "Go home. Spend some time with your family. Leave me alone."

She was on her way out of the room, fully intending to carry the rest of the crib upstairs to see if she could make any sense of the instructions that came with it, when he grudgingly spoke again. "When is she due?"

She stopped without turning. "Next week." She had no doubt that, in the silence that followed, he was mentally counting—and not liking the numbers he was coming up with.

"If I'm not the father, who is?" The question was asked with a faint hopefulness, she suspected, that she would name another man, tempered by near certainty that any name she might give besides his own would be a lie.

With a cool, mocking smile, she faced him one last time. *"That,"* she said softly, "is the best-kept secret in town." Then, with a broad, sweeping gesture, she motioned toward the front door. "Good night, Mr. Russo. Enjoy your visit. Have a good time at Michael's wedding. And don't feel that you need to speak to me again."

For a long moment he ignored her invitation to leave, then, with an audible sigh of frustration, he moved past her. He stepped over the crib rails to reach the door, then stopped and looked back.

Faith kept her expression cool and mocking as she waited without moving, without even breathing. Whatever he'd been about to say, though, remained unsaid. His mouth settling into a thin line, he turned once more, opened the door and walked through it. The click when the door closed behind him seemed to echo through the entire house.

Faith stood where she was, still smiling. "Cool" had now turned to downright icy, and rubbing her hands up and down her arms did nothing to ease the chill. With a forlorn sigh, she turned away from the closed door and the hallway scattered with crib pieces, and she went into the parlor, settling in the rocker, snuggling under one of Amelia Rose's quilts. She didn't have the energy tonight to lug the crib upstairs, much less put it together. Tonight she was tired and cold. Tonight she needed to simply sit here. Tonight, when she was feeling emptier and lonelier than she'd ever been before, she really needed to dream.

But if she had any dreams left, she couldn't think of them.

Chapter 2

Nick climbed the steps to the porch, moving at a reluctant pace toward the front door and, behind the carved wood, his parents and their questions. They would want to know what had come up, where he'd gone, why he'd taken so long, and they were certainly entitled to the answers. He just couldn't give them.

It was amazing how things could change. Six hours ago he couldn't have asked for a better mood. He'd had a few badly needed days off. He was home to spend Thanksgiving with his family for the first time in years. In a couple more days he was going to stand up next to Michael and watch his kid brother get married. Then he was going back to his carefree and responsibility-free life in Houston.

At least, that had been his plan. Until Faith Harper had shot it all to hell.

Zipping his coat against the wind, he turned toward the north end of the porch and its wooden swing. He had helped his father hang it more than twenty years ago—and had helped him *re*hang it only a few months later, after all eight kids, along with half a dozen cousins and friends, had piled on, resulting in a hole in the ceiling where the anchor bolt had been. Antonio had scowled and fussed, but he hadn't yelled, hadn't punished them. He had hardly ever punished them, but it had rarely been necessary. All of them would have died rather than defy or disappoint their father.

How disappointed was he going to be in Nick?

Tremendously.

Unless his eldest son did the right thing and married a complete stranger whom he couldn't even remember meeting—who was, unfortunately, about to give birth to his child.

His child. He was about to become a father.

Sinking onto the swing, he examined the emotions roiling inside, searching for even the faintest hint of something paternal. He was a Russo, for God's sake. They loved kids, every last one of them. Shouldn't he feel even a little pleasure, a little happiness, a little pride that he was following tradition and continuing the line? Of course he should. But he didn't. All he felt was despair. Dejection. Hopelessness.

He had never wanted to get married in the first place, but he sure as hell didn't want to enter into a marriage that was destined from the start to fail. It *had* to fail. Faith Harper was a stranger to him. He knew nothing about her...except that she had pretty blue eyes, was soft to the touch, and that she'd given him more pleasure in his dreams than most women had managed in reality. But it was easy to want a dream, to obsess over something that disappeared within seconds of awakening. The woman he'd met today was far more substantial—and far more dangerous—than any dream.

Hell, he didn't even know if the baby—if Amelia Rose— was his daughter. Faith could be playing him for a fool. It could simply be a bizarre coincidence that he'd gotten drunk and passed out at her house about the same time she got pregnant. She could even see him as a way out of what were obviously uncomfortable circumstances for her. Being single and pregnant in a town like New Hope couldn't be particularly easy. What was it she had said when she'd commented that she had no husband? *You live in the big city of Houston. You people down there aren't as easily shocked as the small-town minds of New Hope.*

Small-town minds? Or small-minded town? He remembered enough from his years in New Hope to know the answer to that one. While many of the town's residents couldn't care less, there would be a substantial number who could. Hell, his own parents probably disapproved. They wouldn't blame Faith, wouldn't let it color how they felt about her, but they undoubtedly believed that she should have had a husband before she had a baby.

But he didn't believe that she was trying to fool him into believing that her child was his when it wasn't. And he didn't believe that the timing was mere coincidence. In the three times he'd seen her today, not once had she looked at him as a welcome rescue. The first time she had fainted, and the other two times "hostile" was the first word that came to mind. And she had denied that he was the baby's father, had demanded that he go away and leave them alone.

There was also that sick feeling in his gut, the one that had appeared as soon as he'd made the connection between his erotic dreams, the party nine months ago and Faith's pregnancy. It was the same sense of inevitable doom that he'd felt when he'd seen his partner shot by Diego Sanchez, when he'd known in the passing of a heartbeat that it was bad, in spite of the protection of Dave's body armor. Even if Faith Harper was a complete stranger to him, Amelia Rose *was* his daughter, and he had to do something about it.

A dozen feet away the door opened, splashing yellow light onto the gray boards. Michael called his goodbyes, then closed the door, walked to the top step and paused there to button up his overcoat. He was about to take the first step down when he turned slowly toward Nick. "You hiding out here or just soaking up the atmosphere?"

"Just thinking."

His brother came closer, moving through the shadows, then into the light filtering through lace window curtains. "Everything okay?"

Nick's answer was noncommittal, a simple grunt. If he told the truth, Michael would want to help, which would require details he wasn't ready to offer. If he didn't tell the truth—well, he would be lying, and he tried to avoid that off the job.

"Mama kept a plate warm for you. I hope you got your tux a size too big, 'cause she's planning on feeding you until you leave." After a moment he asked, "You did pick up the tux today, didn't you?"

"Yeah, I got it." That damned tux had been the start of a long downhill slide. If he'd gotten the address of the formal wear shop from the phone book instead of thinking he could just stop in somewhere and ask, or if he'd chosen to ask at the bank or the post office or any of the other stores on Main, he never would have gone into the Baby Boutique. Faith would probably be at the wedding Saturday, but so would everyone else in New Hope and every Russo relative within a thousand miles. He could have easily missed running into her. He could have gone back to Houston still a stranger, completely in the dark about her and her baby, and she, still believing that he had a wife, would have let him.

Thoughts of his temporary marriage of convenience made him rise from the swing and find a spot on the rail to lean back against. "Hey, Mike, did you guys tell a lot of people that I'd gotten married?"

"Not a lot. Mostly just family. Mama wanted to wait until you brought her home to meet everyone before she broke the news. She was planning a big party for the whole town." He shrugged. "Then you told her that it wasn't for real, and everyone just put it out of their minds."

But someone had shared the news with Faith and then had forgotten to put it out of *her* mind. Would she have contacted him if she'd known? Would he have come home from work some evening to find a message from her on his answering machine, or worse, to find her standing on his doorstep? If she hadn't believed that he was already married, would she have wanted him to know she was pregnant? Or would her sentiments—*Go back to Houston and forget all about us*—have remained the same?

"Hey, Nick, are you okay?"

He exhaled heavily. "Yeah, just tired."

"Then you'd better get inside, eat and get to bed. Tomorrow morning the hungry hordes will descend on the house, and you won't have a moment's peace."

Nick smiled a bit. His brother wasn't exaggerating. A family gathering at the Russo house was as crowded and as noisy as—although less profane than—a drunk tank on a Saturday night. Space would be at a premium, mere paths that meandered through the crowd. The men would congregate around the television in the living room, the women at the dining table and in the kitchen, and the children would be everywhere. It would be minimally controlled chaos, and, ordinarily, he would love every minute of it.

But this wasn't turning out to be an ordinary Thanksgiving. With each passing moment, it seemed he was finding less and less to be thankful for.

And he could thank Faith for that.

Tired as he was, though, he didn't head for the door. He needed another moment to get his feelings under control, to find a mask that he could hide behind, to find some dark, secret place inside him where Faith, Amelia Rose and his incredible dismay would be safe from his father's sharp eyes and his mother's prying questions.

Turning, he focused his gaze on the moonlit yard. The grass was yellow, most of the trees bare. The stark light illuminated a tire swing hanging from a sturdy oak and washed over a platform, either all that was left of an old tree house or the beginnings of a new one, six feet above the ground in the next tree over. Twenty-five years ago it had seemed that all the kids in the neighborhood had played in the Russo yard—not because they had the most or best or newest toys. They hadn't. But they had had the most kids in the widest range of ages, the best-loved mother and the most tolerant father. Neither Luisa nor Antonio had ever complained about the chalk drawings on the sidewalk or the dying grass flattened in the shape of a baseball diamond. They hadn't minded the constant shrieks and laughter or the regular thump-thump-thump of a basketball dribbling down the driveway and rebounding off the garage wall. They hadn't even cared how many of those kids who had come to play managed to find their way to the dinner table. Luisa just always cooked extra, expecting company.

His parents were good parents. So were his sisters and their husbands. Michael and Michelle would be, too. It seemed that he was the only one of the bunch who didn't feel the urge.

"Nervous about the wedding?"

He glanced his brother's way. "It's your wedding. Why would I be nervous?"

"Because I'm the last single sibling. Because now Mama's going to turn all her attention to getting you married."

Nick ignored Michael's all-too-true prediction. "Are you nervous?"

"Michelle and I have been dating nine years," he dryly reminded Nick. "This is something we decided on right at the beginning."

"You were sixteen—just kids. How could you know then that you wanted to get married?"

"The same way you knew when you were eighteen that you *didn't* want to get married. I can remember you coming home from college to go to Dan Wilson's wedding. When you came home from the bachelor party the night before the wedding, you were more than a little bit drunk, and you insisted that you were never, ever going to get married."

Nick could recall the same memory—most of it, at least. Dan had been one of his best friends. From grade school on, they had studied together, played together and, in high school, double-dated the Harland twins together. They had intended to go on to the University of Texas together, but only a few weeks before classes were scheduled to begin, Dan had broken the news that he wouldn't be going. Instead he was staying home, going to work full-time on his father's ranch outside town and marry Tammy Harland, who was three months pregnant and kicking up a fuss. The last Nick had heard, they had four kids, spoke to each other only to fight and generally made each other miserable.

He could all too easily imagine himself in the same situation—minus the extra three kids. If he had to get married, if he had to make that kind of sacrifice, there was no way in hell he would bring any other kids into it to suffer along with them.

"Come to think of it," Michael continued, his tone teasing, "you got more than a little plastered when Tim Bailey got married, too. And Brent Owens. What is it? An uncontrollable response to the prospect of wedding vows?"

"They all got married within a year of finishing high school. I was a dumb kid. I didn't know better," Nick said in his own defense. But he hadn't been a kid when he'd overindulged at Michael's engagement party. He'd been within a month of turning thirty-four—old enough to know better. For damned sure old enough to avoid what had followed.

"This time just make sure you stay sober at least until Saturday evening. By then, Michelle and I will be on our way to the Caribbean. I won't care about your sobriety." Grinning, he pulled his car keys from his pocket and started toward the steps. "See you tomorrow."

Nick watched him leave, then drew a few deep breaths of sweet-scented night air. Prepared the best he could be for the interrogation to come, he walked to the door, wrapped his fingers around the cold metal knob, twisted it and pushed the door open. "Hey, Mom, Pop," he greeted with a smile that was as phony as they came. "Is it too late to get some food around here?"

Thursday was a beautiful day for Thanksgiving—chilly enough for a sweater but warm enough for a stroll through fallen leaves to enjoy the sights and especially the scents of autumn. Faith could use the exercise, but for some reason she couldn't find the energy to leave the rocker, put on her shoes and head out the door.

It was the shoes that were stopping her, she decided, stretching her feet out and wiggling her toes in soft ragg socks. Walking on a day like this required comfortable shoes. She had a pair of green suede hiking boots that she loved, but it was doubtful that she could squeeze her swollen feet into their well-worn confines. Even if she somehow succeeded, how would she ever get the laces crisscrossed over the hooks and tied in tight bows? Her belly was too big, or her arms and legs too short, to manage anything other than slip-on shoes.

And so she would simply sit here, alone in her big house with Amelia Rose and...

And what? Initially, when she had turned down the Thanksgiving dinner invitations that had come from all her friends, she had intended to spend the day exactly the way she was: alone with Amelia Rose. She had intended to make it a special day, to fix a special dinner for herself, to make plans and daydream and simply treasure the peace, the quiet and the specialness of the day.

Then Nick Russo had shown up.

Most men who found themselves in his situation would have been more than happy to hear her absolve them of any responsibility. Most men would have listened to her first denial, and then gratefully run from her life, without a backward glance. Why couldn't Nick be like them? Like her father?

Yet some small part of her was happy that he wasn't. Some small part was grateful that Amelia Rose's father wasn't quick to turn his back on her and run away. It might still happen, she knew. After all, he'd made it clear that the prospect of fatherhood didn't thrill him at all. But he could always change his mind. Once she was here, once he held her and saw how sweet and innocent she was, he might well decide that part-time parenthood wasn't so bad. He might even acknowledge her to his family, and they would welcome her and love her even if he didn't.

Or he might take Faith's last words to heart. He might enjoy his visit, have a good time at Saturday's wedding and never speak to her again. He might never acknowledge his daughter to his family. He might never give her anything more than dark hair or dark eyes or a wickedly sweet smile.

Across the room the television was tuned to a Thanksgiving Day parade broadcast from New York. Next year Amelia Rose might give the giant balloons a wide-eyed moment of her attention, but it would be several years before she could truly enjoy the hoopla. Today it was simply depressing, too strong a reminder of Thanksgivings past. There had never been any joyous holidays celebrated in this house, not while Great-aunt Lydia had lived, and Thanksgiving had been no exception. Every year they had arisen at their usual 6:00 a.m.—Lydia hadn't believed in wasting God's mornings in bed—and had eaten their usual breakfast of oatmeal and toast. They had passed the morning quietly before sharing a dinner for two. The afternoons had been spent in quiet, too—no visitors, no playing outside, no television. The only diversion allowed the entire day had been the Macy's parade—one half hour of it and not one minute more.

Once, when she was fifteen, Faith had suggested inviting guests for dinner—friends of her great-aunt's who were alone, a couple from church whose children had moved too far away to visit—but Lydia had refused. Thanksgiving was a holiday for family, she had decreed, and that was how they would observe it. Even though they had no family but each other. Even though, regardless of the weather outside, the day was always dreary and bleak. Even though they gave thanks for little.

Lydia had died four years ago, only one week away from her seventy-eighth birthday. She had left Faith this old house, enough money to start the business and a lifetime of teachings, rules and judgments. It had taken Faith less than four years to break the most important rule, to commit the gravest sin. If Lydia were alive to see her now, the old lady would be full of righteous anger. She would profess great shame, would induce great guilt and exact daily penance from her great-niece and even from Amelia Rose. She would make them suffer, the way she had tried to make Faith's mother suffer, the way she had made Faith herself suffer for twenty-one years.

But she wouldn't throw them out. She wouldn't wash her hands of them. No matter how great the burden, no matter how deep the shame, Lydia would do her Christian duty. She would accept her responsibilities, would carry out her obligations.

Was it possible that Nick Russo had a little of her great-aunt Lydia in him?

The thought made her scowl. It didn't matter if he did. Faith had lived most of her life not as Lydia Harper's great-niece but as her duty, her family obligation. She was never going to be anyone's responsibility again. She was never going to be anyone's burden.

Pushing the subject to the back of her mind, she slid to the edge of the big scooped seat, then awkwardly got to her feet. Some days she forgot how her body had changed and remembered only after trying to do something that was once routine—stand up or sit down, pick up a box, bend to take something from a low cabinet. Other days, like today, she couldn't forget the changes even when she was sitting and doing nothing. Her back ached. Her feet ached. Her hands were swollen. The twenty-nine pounds she'd gained threw off her center of gravity and made grace and easy movement things of the past. Some days she felt she had been this way forever, feared that she might stay this way forever.

Walking—waddling—across the room, she shut off the television, then gave the parlor a slow, thorough study, searching for something to do. There was little enough cleaning when she lived alone and had learned by the time she was three to put things away as soon as she finished with them. The only things out of place in the room were her fuzzy house slippers that she'd kicked off once the central heat had warmed the room this morning and the two small packets that last night's visitor had left behind.

Condoms. What would Wendy or one of the others say if they dropped by to try to change her mind about sharing their Thanksgiving dinners and found the condoms so prominently displayed there? Probably point out that she was, oh, about nine months late in acquiring them. "I never leave home without 'em," Nick had proclaimed, which meant that he'd probably had a few tucked in his wallet that cold February night, if only he had been sober enough—or she had been rational enough, knowledgeable enough or smart enough—to look. If either of them had checked, he would have been saved the discomfort of having only eight days' or so notice that he was having a baby with a woman he didn't know, and she would have been spared the shock, the gossip, the whispers and about six months of incessant questioning.

But she also would have been robbed of the sheer joy and pleasure of the past nine months. She would have missed out on the thrill of feeling her baby growing and moving within her. She wouldn't have experienced the miracle—oh, yes, no matter how sappy it sounded, it definitely was a miracle—of life. She would have missed out on feeling, for the first time in her life, all this love—hers now, of course, but sure to be returned by Amelia Rose in full measure.

Bending at an odd angle, she scooped up the two packets, intending to take them straight into the kitchen and the wastebasket there. Instead, though, with the curiosity of the near-virgin that she was, she studied them carefully. The packets were white plastic with blue writing that had been scratched off in places. They had been bent and creased and treated with no care at all. There was a tear in one that went all the way through both layers of plastic and the latex inside, and the crimped edges of the other were coated with what looked like grease, from an engine, maybe, or a tool that had been used to work on one.

She was no expert, but she expected that a single man intent on protecting himself—a man like Nick, handsome, sexy, always popular with the ladies—would take better care of his protection than this. The plastic packs looked as if they'd endured a long, rough period of neglect. They didn't look suitable for anything but their eventual destination: the trash.

But she was no expert, and she never would be. Her one and only experience with that aspect of life, although supremely successful at the time, had turned into a disappointing failure. She had no need of a man in her life, and, once Amelia Rose was born, she would have no desire for one, either.

Not even one like Nick.

Carrying stacks of dirty dishes in both hands, Nick made his way through a maze of dining chairs and through the open door into the kitchen, where his mother and two of his sisters had begun the after-dinner cleanup. It was a job as big, it seemed, as the dinner preparation. Every bit of counter space was filled with dishes, pots and pans, serving platters and bowls. The kitchen table all but groaned under its load of leftovers and desserts, and a folding table pushed against the far wall held stacks of clean dishes, sorted by owner. He recognized his grandmother's glazed pottery and, at the opposite end, Aunt Marguerita's good china. The plain white dishes in the middle came from the family restaurant that bore his father's name. His father the chef created mouth-watering dishes at the restaurant five days a week, but he rarely set foot in this kitchen. This was the women's domain. Even Nick felt like an interloper, but he stayed after adding the dishes he carried to the stack... especially once he heard an all-too-familiar name.

"I saw the cutest little sleeper down at Faith's store," the oldest of his sisters, Anna, remarked. "But I couldn't think of anyone to buy it for."

"She does stock some of the neatest things," Lucia, the youngest, agreed. "Don't you know her baby is going to be the best-dressed, best-provided-for baby New Hope has ever seen? It's awfully convenient for her, owning the Baby Boutique."

"I was in there yesterday," Nick remarked, pretending innocence when he felt none. "I needed directions to the formal wear place."

His mother lifted her hands from the water, sending a soap bubble drifting into the air, and turned toward him. "Then you met Faith. Pretty, brown hair, very sweet?"

"And very pregnant?" he added dryly.

"That's her." Anna dried a large oval serving platter, then shoved it into Nick's hands. "Put that over there with Aunt Marguerita's dishes, would you? Isn't Faith a sweetheart?"

Lucia didn't give him a chance to answer, which was just as well. Of all the things he'd thought Faith Harper might be in the last twenty-four hours, "sweetheart" wasn't one of them. "She provides New Hope with all their baby needs, along with much of their food for gossip. Half the town spends half its time trying to figure out who the father of her baby is." She gave a disgusted snort. "As if it's any of their business."

Nick very carefully laid the platter down, then remained where he was, his back to the women, his gaze on the kids playing outside.

"Come on, Lucia, don't be self-righteous," Anna chided. "We've spent enough of *our* time trying to solve the mystery. People can't help but be curious. She hardly ever dated, and she was never serious about any man. She never left town, so it couldn't have been a romance in Dallas or elsewhere. No man in town is looking guilty when he sees her or stepping forward to accept responsibility or—"

"Or hanging his head in shame," their mother interrupted. "Which is exactly what he should be doing—exactly what they both should be doing."

"Oh, Mama, no more talk about shame, please," Lucia pleaded. "She made a mistake. She got pregnant. At least she's doing the right thing. She's having her baby. She's going to make a home for him, and she's going to love him and be the best mother he could ever want. She's got nothing to be ashamed of."

Luisa returned to washing the dishes, the splashes punctuating her words. "I just don't understand her. Being raised the way she was, she knew people would talk. She knew certain people would blame her baby for what she's done the same way she was blamed for her mother's choices. Why didn't she take precautions?"

An uncomfortable sensation that he knew all too well as guilt crept down Nick's spine. He wished he had never come into the kitchen, wished he had never mentioned meeting Faith. Still, he forced himself to ask the question his mother's words had prompted. "What do you mean, being raised the way she was?"

"Why, Faith is illegitimate herself."

"And no one's ever let her forget it," Lucia grumbled under her breath.

Before his mother could return to the subject—one Nick found himself wanting to know more about—Anna stepped in once more. "What good does being ashamed do, Mama? What were her options, anyway? Have the baby and—according to you—live her life in shame? Or have an abortion and live with the regret?"

"She could have told the man no," Luisa retorted.

"Maybe he didn't ask. Maybe for once in her life she got to act like a typical, normal person and get swept away. Maybe she loved the guy. Maybe she was forced."

Nick turned around, silently protesting Anna's last suggestion before grudgingly conceding a very small chance that she could be right. He didn't think he would ever force a woman to submit to something she didn't want. It went against everything he believed in. But the simple fact was that he had been stinking drunk that night. He didn't remember what he did. He couldn't swear that he hadn't forced Faith, couldn't swear that he hadn't hurt her—even though the mere idea that he might have—that he could have—made him sick.

"What do you mean, she could have told the man no?" Lucia rinsed two handfuls of silver, gave it a shake, then dumped it in a colander. "The last time we had this conversation, you said the person who did this to Faith wasn't deserving of being called a man.''

Feeling queasy and not wanting to hear his mother's response, Nick edged toward the back door. He didn't get there quickly enough, though. Her vehement words filtered out seconds before he closed the door that would cut them off.

''And I meant it. If he can't accept responsibility for what he's done, then he's no man at all. I would be ashamed to know him.''

Shoving his hands into his pockets, he made his way around the house and onto the sidewalk. He had his keys in his pocket. He could get in his truck and go anywhere—to visit old friends, to see how the town had changed or simply for a long drive. But instead of going to his truck, he turned down the sidewalk. He didn't question the wisdom of where he was going, didn't even acknowledge to himself where he was going until he was standing on the sidewalk at one end of the broad brick drive.

It was foolish to come here. He was in New Hope to spend time with his family, not Faith Harper. She didn't want to see him. She had made that clear enough last night. Hell, he didn't even want to see her. He wanted to pretend that she didn't exist.

But she did exist, and he couldn't deny it.

He also couldn't deny her baby. His baby.

He crossed the lawn to the veranda steps. Maybe she wouldn't be home. It was Thanksgiving, after all. Surely she, like everyone else in the country, spent it with family whenever she could. But from the top of the steps, he could see her car parked in the same spot where she'd left it last night. That in itself meant nothing, but that odd, wary feeling in the pit of his stomach suggested that she was home, that any moment now she was going to answer his ring and fix that cold, blue gaze on him.

He gave her what he thought was plenty of time to reach the door before ringing the bell a second time. Almost immediately the lock clicked and the door swung open.

Somehow she managed to look more fragile in the bright afternoon sunlight than she had yesterday, even when she had fainted right in front of him. Maybe it was because she hadn't expected him, and so the hostility wasn't yet in place. Maybe it was the silly teddy bear, big enough to make her seem small, that she was holding in one arm. Maybe it was the way her hair hung loose, curling around her face before falling to brush her shirt, instead of being secured in a snug, no-nonsense braid, as it had been yesterday.

Maybe she seemed fragile because he knew that she was illegitimate, just like her baby. Because he had helped make her the subject of cruel gossip. Because people blamed her for indulging in something—sex—that other women did every day and for something she didn't do at all. She didn't choose to get pregnant, didn't choose to have the father of her baby disappear from her life without so much as a word.

Faith didn't offer a greeting, didn't pretend to be gracious or even remotely pleased to see him. She simply stood in the doorway, hugging the ridiculous teddy bear, and waited.

Nick combed his fingers through his hair. "Can I come in?"

"Why?"

"We've been through this before, haven't we?" He offered the best smile he could muster—a pretty sickly one—but she didn't return it. She didn't reveal any expression at all. "Do you have company?"

"No." After a moment, clutching the bear tighter, she stepped back and allowed him entry, but not without a warning. "I don't have much time."

The house smelled exactly as it had the night before—of old wood and spicy potpourri. There was no aroma of roasted turkey, no freshly baked bread, no tempting pies. He wondered if she'd gone to a relative's for dinner and returned early or if she'd spent the day alone. Thanksgiving Day alone, he knew from his own experience, was a lonely place to be. "Do you have plans for this evening?"

"I have plans right now, and they don't include standing in the hallway pretending to be sociable."

"Do they involve your friend?" He reached out to straighten the bear's droopy ear, and she took a hasty step back. She didn't want him even coming close to touching her, he realized, and the sick feeling in his stomach intensified. Withdrawing, he shoved both hands into his pockets, then abruptly, without any warning even for himself, asked, "That night—did I hurt you?"

Faith stared at him. Had he hurt her? Oh, yes, that was very definitely pain she'd felt when she had gone upstairs to wake him for breakfast and discovered that he'd slipped out sometime in the early morning hours. It had hurt to find out the next day from Michelle that he'd returned to Houston, to realize that he had gone back home halfway across the state without so much as an "It was fun." It had really hurt later when she'd found out, in the space of a few days, that she was pregnant and he was married. Reaching the understanding that her baby would have no father and no family other than her had been particularly painful, too.

The biggest pain of all, though, had begun as a fear early that morning in February, and it had grown, as surely as Amelia Rose had grown, over the following weeks. It was her overwhelming bad judgment, her unforgivable mistake. After years of Great-aunt Lydia's warnings, after years of promising herself that she wouldn't turn out like her mother, she had done exactly that. She had let a man sweet-talk her into throwing caution to the wind—along with good sense, morality and a few other qualities Lydia held dear— just as her mother had done, and she had found herself pregnant and alone, just as her mother had been. Her only consolation was that at least she had waited until she was twenty-five, when she was grown, had a job and a home and could care for her baby. Her sixteen-year-old mother hadn't had those advantages.

Yes, Nick had hurt her—but only because she'd been foolish and naive. Because she had believed in magic, in princes and knights in shining armor, in love at first sight, soul mates and happily-ever-after. She'd been hurt because of her dreams, her expectations, her loneliness and her incredible need for love.

And those were answers she would never share with him or anyone else.

In front of her he shifted uncomfortably. "I realize I was drunk, that I might have . . . might not have . . ." He looked away, muttered a curse, then looked back. "Did you want . . . Did I force you . . ."

Understanding dawned, bringing with it a bitter amusement at her own naiveté. He wasn't interested in any emotional pain he might have caused. For some reason it had occurred to him that his behavior that night might have been less than honorable. Silently she scoffed at the notion. She would bet money that Antonio Russo's son had never behaved dishonorably in his life. That was the whole reason he was here. Honor. Making things right. Accepting responsibility for his actions.

How far would honor require him to go? Would he ask for a paternity test to prove that Amelia Rose was his daughter? Would he offer money to help support her? Would he play the role of part-time father?

Would he introduce Amelia Rose to his family, give her grandparents and great-grandparents, aunts and uncles and dozens of cousins? Would he want her with him on weekends, holidays and summer vacations down there in Houston?

Would he even suggest marriage?

Deep in her heart Faith hoped not and said a whispered prayer to that effect. There was no way in the world she could ever marry Nick Russo, no way she could take his name, live in his house and be a part of his family, knowing all along that it was only because he felt obligated, that it wasn't *her* he wanted but rather only to make things right. There was no way after four sweet years on her own that she could return to being someone else's burden, no way she could live with anyone for any reason less than love. She couldn't endure that sort of marriage, even though it would give her everything else in the world that she'd ever dreamed of. A husband, a home, a family. Ever since she was old enough to realize that she didn't have one, she'd wanted a family so badly she had ached with it. Ever since she'd been befriended in fourth grade by Lucia Russo, she'd wanted *that* family, or at least one just like it.

Please don't let him offer it for all the wrong reasons.

"No," she answered at last on a sigh. "You didn't do anything."

He looked pointedly at her stomach, then offered a hesitantly teasing disagreement. "Unless this is New Hope's first virgin birth, I'd say I did *something.*"

The first part of his statement was too close to the truth for her to be amused. She'd heard more than a few similar jokes around town when her pregnancy had first become obvious. Even Nick's brother Michael, an old friend, had laughingly remarked—not knowing that Faith was only a few feet behind him—that when it came to virtue, it was well known that hers was intact. She had forgotten until then just how much guys talked. She had been warned—repeatedly, from the time she was ten years old and ignorant of the subject matter—that boys always talked about girls who did, and she had learned in high school that they also talked—with the same adolescent humor—about girls who didn't.

"So what are your plans?"

"What plans?"

"The ones that don't include standing here pretending to be sociable."

"I was moving some things upstairs."

"I'll help."

"I don't need help."

"Then they must be very small things. Baby things?"

She answered with a shrug.

"Where are they?"

With a sigh, she gestured toward the living room. Everything was in pastel bags and boxes marked with the shop's logo and dumped on Lydia's petit point couch. They provided the one bright spot in a room that could best be de-

scribed as cheerless. It was one of the few rooms in the
house that Faith hadn't redecorated yet. She had intended
to do it before Michael and Michelle's engagement party,
but business had picked up at the shop, and afterward . . .
Well, she'd had other, more important things on her mind
since then.

Nick crossed the few yards into the room, gathered up an
armload of boxes and filled his free hand with bags, then
joined her at the stairs. Heaving a sigh that was transpar-
ently reluctant, she led the way up the long staircase, holding the bear around the middle, feeling the fat padded feet
bump her legs with each step.

At the top was a broad hallway, wider than most rooms,
with two rooms on either side. Her room was at the back of
the house, looking down on the yard and over the tall privacy fence into the Nicholsons' yard behind her. The nursery was across the hall, and farther down, facing the front,
were the two remaining bedrooms. One had been Great-aunt
Lydia's. The other had an iron bed, marble-topped tables
and lace curtains. She had been seriously tempted to turn
that room into the nursery, to cut the bed into pieces, take
a sledgehammer to the marble tables and use the curtains for
kitchen scrubbers, but in the end, reason had prevailed. She
wanted Amelia Rose closer to her own room, and Lydia's
teachings on thrift couldn't be so easily discarded.

Although it seemed she'd had no trouble at all ignoring
the old lady's warnings about chastity.

Turning into the nursery, Faith settled the bear on the
chaise longue underneath the side windows, then watched
uneasily as Nick gave the room a thorough study. She didn't
need or care about his approval of the room. She knew it
wasn't exactly traditional. The woodwork—moldings and
doors, window frames and shelves—was dark, and one
pretty, breezy day last spring, she had painted the walls a
deep coral. The chaise was one of Lydia's antiques, thickly
padded and elegantly curved, reupholstered in an ivory-on-
ivory floral-patterned fabric. The changing table was a mahogany dresser with a hand-quilted pad draped over the top,

and the nearby lamp shaded with creamy glass was as Victorian—and as old—as the house itself.

But there were softer touches, too. A herd of pastel-hued carousel horses pranced across one shelf. Baby-oriented planters in front of the windows held ivies and fragrant jasmines. The wooden quilt rack was stacked with quilts in shades of pink and sky blue, peach and palest yellow, along with vibrant primary colors. A crescent-shaped night-light formed a sleeping moon with a star or two dangling from its tip, and the chimes in front of one window offered the sweetest, softest musical tones.

She didn't care about Nick's opinion. She reminded herself of that as his gaze circled the room and reached her. "Where do you want this?"

Moving forward, she took the boxes from him and stacked them on the foot of the chaise. He set the bags on the floor nearby, then turned his attention to the crib that lay in pieces on the floor. "Are you working on this?"

"I'm thinking about it." Actually, she had started on it that morning, before discovering that putting rails, slats and legs together so that the resulting product was straight, sturdy and square was a two-person job, one that she would save for a visit from a friend—provided that a friend came visiting soon. She was going to need this in another week or so.

Nick crouched down, examining the few pieces she had succeeded with, then picked up a corner of the box the crib had come in. The directions for assembly, skewered to the box with the screwdriver she'd been using, came off the floor with it. "That's no way to treat a precision tool," he remarked, his tone mild and barely hiding amusement. He worked the screwdriver free of the box, then offered the directions to her. "Read them to me."

She clutched the paper tightly. "Why?"

"So I don't have to take the time to read them myself." Sitting, he located the hardware bag and sorted through the myriad screws, nuts and bolts, putting them in some sort of order. That done, he looked at her. "What's first?"

His tone might be mild, even amused, she acknowledged, but his expression was determined. It would be easier to let him do this—to fulfill some displaced sense of responsibility—than to make him believe that she really didn't want his help. Accepting that, she folded the directions to the place where she'd quit—Step 2—and read out loud. "Align holes in middle and bottom rails of Side A with corresponding holes in End C . . ."

Nick didn't really need the directions. The crib was a pretty simple piece—sides, ends and a bottom to support the mattress. He didn't mind her reading them out loud, though. She had a nice voice—soft and Texan. Sometimes it seemed that, thanks to the oil industry, practically everyone he met in Houston had come there from someplace else, but Faith was very definitely a Lone Star native.

"Can you balance this?" he asked when he moved closer to her to secure the opposite end to the side rail.

She gave the pieces a wary look. Still afraid to get too close? he wondered. But that wasn't her concern at all, he realized. It was the actual physical process that slowed her. Bending was awkward. Crouching was out of the question, and sitting meant getting clumsily down to the floor and accepting help to get clumsily back to her feet when they were done. Finally, with a rueful glance at the pieces yet to be assembled, she very carefully lowered herself to the carpeted floor, managing without looking clumsy at all.

Nick secured the screws while she steadied the rail, then turned the entire section around so she wouldn't have to move for the next part. "Where does your family live?" he asked as he leaned across to get the hardware.

For a time he thought she wasn't going to answer, then, at last, her reply came in a flat tone. "I don't know."

He carefully controlled his surprise—and his curiosity. "They don't live around here?"

"My mother grew up in Fort Worth. I guess her family is still there. I don't know where she is. I haven't seen her in years."

"What about your father?"

"I don't know where he is, either. He took off before I was born." Her voice took on a dry, faintly sarcastic quality. "Evidently he wasn't pleased by the prospect of impending fatherhood."

Nick kept his gaze tightly focused on the screw he was tightening. So history had repeated itself. *Like mother, like daughter.* She'd probably heard that more than once, with just the right holier-than-thou touch. "I wouldn't have run off," he said evenly, "if you had bothered to tell me."

There was a moment of utter stillness in which he couldn't bring himself to look at her. Then, her voice stiff and unforgiving, she asked, "And when would have been a good time for me to get in touch with you? When your brother was telling me about your new wife?"

Finally he did look at her. Her mouth was unsmiling, the look in her eyes distant and cold. "I told you, the marriage wasn't—"

"Wasn't real," she finished for him. "Yes, you told me last night. Not six months ago when I needed to know it. Not three months ago when it might have made a difference."

The screwdriver slipped and scraped a furrow of skin from his thumb. Sitting back on his heels, he scowled at her. "Okay, so you believed I was married. You still should have told me."

"Yes, it would have been great fun. I could have driven all the way down to Houston, found a way to see you without seeing your wife and said, 'Hey, remember me? Oh, you don't?'" Her cool, taunting smile faded, and her expression shifted to match his own. "Has it occurred to you that maybe I didn't tell you because I didn't want you to know? Women do not need men to have babies and raise families. They do it by themselves all the time."

"Not women like you," he said softly. "Not if you have a choice."

Letting go of the rail now that one screw supported it, she scooted back a few inches to lean against the chaise. Her measuring, calculating gaze never left his face. "Women like me," she repeated. "What does that mean?"

"Tell me you wouldn't have preferred to do this the traditional way—to have a husband at least nine months before you have a baby. Convince me that you wouldn't have done anything in your power to keep this baby from being subjected to the same sort of gossip that you grew up with. Make me believe that, being illegitimate yourself, you don't have the slightest qualm about bringing your own illegitimate child into this town."

Once again she became frozen, then, abruptly, she laughed, a harsh, humorless sound. "You've been in town—what, twenty-four hours?—and you've already picked up all the gossip. Is that why you were asking about my family?"

"I was curious."

"Why?"

"It's normal, I believe, to want to know something about the mother of your child." He matched her earlier sarcasm degree for degree.

"It's normal to know the mother of your child before you create that child," she scoffed. "Besides, I never said you were her father. I told you last night—"

"You lied."

She stared at him for a long moment, then softly challenged, "Prove it."

He gave it a moment's thought. He was used to providing proof—district attorneys asked for it all the time. All he had now, though, was circumstantial. Coincidence. Possibilities. Suspicions. He was in the same position he'd often found himself in in the past. He knew the truth. He just couldn't prove it. "The room next door has an iron bed in it. It's a double. The rails get really cold in the winter." Briefly he wondered about that last part. He didn't remember touching the rails that morning when he'd gotten dressed and slipped out. He had been so intent on leaving quietly, on not drawing anyone's attention, especially on not facing a scene that could only be uncomfortable once it became apparent that he only vaguely remembered the party and nothing about what had happened afterward.

After a moment he went on. "There's a little lamp—glass, heavy. I knocked it over when I was leaving that morning. And curtains that let in a lot of light." Thanks to them, he hadn't found it necessary to turn on the lamp he'd knocked over. There had been enough light filtering through the windows to allow him to dress and find his way out. If he had turned on the lamp, what would he have seen besides a rumpled bed? Further details, of course—the color of the sheets, the walls, whether the lamp shade was ruffled, pleated or plain. He wouldn't have seen Faith, though. One other memory he recalled was the sense of having been alone for some time.

She looked away, her gaze focusing on the chimes that hung above an empty space where, Nick assumed, the crib would go. The thin glass shapes—starfish, sea horses and sand dollars—stirred gently, but not enough to collide, not enough to make music. He shifted his gaze back to her face only an instant before she looked once more at him. "All that proves is that you've been in my guest room."

"I spent the night in your guest room almost exactly nine months prior to the date your baby is due. There's no other possible candidate around—"

"Who told you that?"

He started to answer, then closed his mouth. Was he reluctant to answer because he didn't want her to know that he'd been asking about her? Or was it that he didn't want her to know that his family had been gossiping about her?

In spite of his silence, she guessed where the information had come from. It showed in the sudden weariness that shadowed her eyes, in the slight droop to the set of her mouth. She probably liked his family, and they—at least, his mother, Anna and Lucia—professed to like her, but they still found it easy enough to talk about her, to discuss, judge or defend her choices. How much easier was it for people who weren't particularly fond of her? How much harder did their talk make the situation for her? How much of the blame for that was his?

He hadn't *known*, he reminded himself. If she'd told him, they could have done something sooner, could have put a stop to all but the worst of the gossips. At least, he would like to think so. But if she'd told him in the beginning, back at the time that he was pretending to be married to Phoebe, there was little he could have done for her. The case had taken much of his time, most of his energy and all of his attention. He couldn't have married her, not when he was already "married." He couldn't have given her the time necessary to work out some sort of solution. Hell, last spring he couldn't even have spared a thought for her and her baby. If she had told him then, he would have denied it, would have turned his back on her and convinced himself that it wasn't true. Or he would have brooded over it to the point of distraction, screwing up months of intensive undercover work and putting his own life and Phoebe's in danger.

But the case was over—except for the upcoming trial—the sham marriage was dissolved, and he had all the time he needed to work things out.

Choosing a handful of hardware, he fastened the last screw to the side rail, then reached for the remaining rail. Faith automatically leaned forward to brace it while he fastened the screws at the opposite end, then scooted aside when he moved to the end nearest her. Once that was finished, he stopped working again and fixed his attention on her. He didn't move a safe distance away, but remained where he was, close enough to touch her. "Why are you trying to convince me that I'm not the father?"

Rubbing at a worn place on the knee of her faded jeans, she answered without looking at him. "Why are you so willing to believe that you are?"

Hazy memories. Erotic visions. A certainty that came from places unknown. "Call it instinct."

Then she did look at him, scowling. The fierceness of her expression made her eyes bluer, her mouth poutier, her cheeks brighter. "Most men would need convincing. Most men would demand blood tests, and even when they had the proof, they would say it wasn't their problem. Even with proof, they would require court orders before they offered any financial support and acts of God before they gave any emotional support."

"Are you an expert on most men?"

The flush coloring her face heightened, making him wonder just how much experience she did have. Not enough to make her come looking for justice—damn the wife she'd believed he had or anything else that got in her way. Not enough to allow her to lie believably, to control those hot flushes and unsteady gazes when she offered untruths. Certainly not enough for her to be taking birth control pills nine months ago or to have her own stash of condoms, like most of the single women he knew.

If she'd been the kind of woman who indulged in affairs, the people in town wouldn't have been so shocked by her pregnancy and her decision to go through with it. She wouldn't be so vulnerable to their talk. She wouldn't have fainted when he'd walked into the shop yesterday. If she were an easy sort of woman, most likely she would have been at least vaguely amused by his earlier reference to a virgin birth.

But she wasn't that sort of woman, and maybe his remark had hit too close to home.

She'd hardly ever dated, Anna had said, and she had never been serious about any man. She had never left town, so it couldn't have been a romance elsewhere. No man in town was looking guilty, stepping forward to accept responsibility or hanging his head in shame. She was probably as innocent as she looked...and she looked more innocent than any other woman he'd ever met.

God help him, what had he done?

His hands trembled just a little as he reached for the bottom that would connect to the four sides of the crib frame and support the mattress. "I'm a good cop," he said, his voice even. "I have good instincts. I get this feeling when someone's lying to me, and I've had it practically from the moment I saw you yesterday. So—" He drew a deep breath, but it didn't fill his lungs and it didn't quiet the uneasiness inside him. It didn't prepare him for the question he was about to ask, but he asked it anyway. "What are we going to do about Amelia Rose?"

Chapter 3

The question hung in the air between them, an annoyance, a patience-draining frustration. Faith held on to her temper, though. She always did. Losing control, according to Great-aunt Lydia, was to be avoided at all costs. When a woman lost control, she was vulnerable to outside forces. It was an open invitation to sin, sorrow and heartache. Faith was walking proof of that. If she had remained in control that February night when Nick had first touched her, she never would have let him kiss her. She never would have let him undress her, carry her to the bed and, oh, so sweetly seduce her. She never would have allowed passion—and desire, need and a lifetime's hunger for love—sweep her away, and she never would have found herself in the situation she was now in.

But, she acknowledged with a little nudge from Amelia Rose, losing control that night was the single best thing that had ever happened to her. No matter how sordid it sounded—and she could think of little that sounded worse than a few hours' fling with a drunken stranger who would remember nothing of his passion the next morning—it was still the best, sweetest, most important night of her life. It had given her a child, and that was worth all the disillusionment, all the gossip, all the relinquished dreams.

Now that child had brought the source of those dreams back into her life. He was kneeling only a few feet away, asking questions that she didn't want answered, heading in directions that she couldn't bear to go.

What are we going to do? he wanted to know, and she had only one answer. She was just afraid that it was an answer he couldn't accept. "*We* aren't going to do anything," she said quietly. "*I* am going to have my baby, take care of her, love her and be the only family she'll ever need. *You* can go back to Houston and forget that we exist. We're not your responsibility. You don't owe her or me anything. She won't need your money or your time or your attention. I've got plenty of all that to give her."

"You can't be a father to her." His voice was just as quiet, just as determined, as hers had been. "You can't replace her grandparents, aunts and uncles. You're her mother. You can take care of her and love her, but you can't be her family. You can't give her—" he faltered, only slightly but enough for her to notice "—what I can."

She knew he was right. It was one of her greatest regrets that all she could offer her sweet little girl was herself when Amelia Rose deserved more. All babies deserved more—a father who welcomed them, grandparents who spoiled them, siblings to play with, stand up for and torment them. They needed aunts and uncles at the Thanksgiving table and cousins by the score around the Christmas tree. Amelia Rose deserved all of that, but she would have to make the best of what fate had given her. "I can give her enough."

"Was it enough for you—living alone with your mother? Never knowing your father?" He asked the questions as if he already knew the answers. Probably he did. He'd grown up in the largest, loudest, most loving family in all of New Hope. No matter what else, family came first with the Russos. While Nick didn't seem to feel the connection as intensely as the others—he had, after all, moved half a state away—he still felt it. That was why he'd driven nearly three hundred miles at the end of a long week when he'd been working damned hard and sleeping too little, just so he could attend his brother's engagement party. That was why he was in town now, for the holiday and Michael's wedding.

That was why he was *here* now.

"For the record, I didn't live with my mother." Her upbringing wasn't a topic Faith would choose to discuss with Nick, but she suspected it would distract him—momentarily, at least—from the more important subject of Amelia Rose.

She was right. "Then who did you live with?" he asked, his look a little puzzled.

"Lydia Harper was my mother's aunt. She was fifty-seven years old when I came to live here."

"How old were you?"

She exhaled softly. "Three and a half weeks." This was the only home she'd ever known, Lydia the closest thing to a mother she'd ever had—even though the old lady had never let her forget the sinner who *was* her mother. Her reminders had been so frequent that they had seemed part of her daily admonitions: stand up straight, be good, don't get your clothes dirty, eat all your vegetables, brush your teeth, say your prayers, and don't turn into a harlot like your mother. *Harlot* had been Lydia's second-favorite way of referring to Sally Harper; her favorite had simply been *that girl*, offered in a judgmental tone that suggested she found Sally's name too abhorrent to cross her lips.

For all her reliance on the Bible and all her proclamations of being a good Christian woman, Lydia had never been strong on forgiveness.

"Why did your mother bring you here?"

She sighed again, a soft puff of air that eased none of the tension inside her. "I imagine she was no more eager to be a mother than her former boyfriend was to be a father." But that wasn't true. On her rare visits, Sally had assured her of that. She'd been sixteen and trying to make it on her own with no one to turn to for help except her aunt, whose sense of Christian duty demanded that she assist her niece in her time of trouble. Sally had wanted Faith, she promised her. She had always intended to come back, as soon as things got better. As soon as she got a job and a decent place to live. As soon as she got rid of the current boyfriend. As soon as she paid off her bills or got out of some little bit of trouble.

There had been a dozen visits over fifteen years, a dozen farewells with Faith left behind in Lydia's care, and more than a dozen excuses for it. By the time of Sally's last visit, Faith had accepted that her mother was never going to rescue her from the strict, sterile environment of Lydia's guardianship. Even at fifteen, she had accepted that there would be only one escape for her: her great-aunt's death. Even at eighteen, when she was legally free to leave, she hadn't. She couldn't have. Family duty and obligation had been too deeply ingrained in her. Lydia had taken her in and raised her. Faith owed her for it. She had been repaying her right up to the day the old lady had died.

"How old was your mother?"

She glanced at Nick, giving all the screws, nuts and bolts one last check in preparation for setting the crib upright and in its place. She was anxious for that moment, she realized. That one small piece of furniture would truly, finally, transform the room from just another bedroom into a nursery. It brought home how close her time was, how few empty nights remained. "She was sixteen."

"Jeez, she was just a baby herself."

"She was old enough to have a boyfriend, old enough to go out on dates alone with him. She was old enough to have sex with him." There was a weary tone to her words, and a familiarity that brought Lydia, in all her self-righteousness, vividly to mind. They were *her* words, and she had believed them with a ferocity. Once Faith had timidly tried to dispute them, but her great-aunt had shown such disbelief and offense that she had never tried again.

"Hell, I had sex with my girlfriend when I was sixteen, but that didn't mean either of us was ready to become a parent."

Faith felt a faint twinge of jealousy at his comment. She wondered which lucky girl had caught his attention eighteen years ago. In a moment of weakness last spring, she had gone to the library and looked up his high school yearbooks. He had been cute, cocky, a so-so student and an outstanding athlete. He had been starting quarterback, played basketball and been the school's fastest miler before trading track to become the championship-winning baseball team's pitcher. He had escorted the homecoming queen and been elected junior class vice president. No doubt his girlfriend had been the prettiest girl in school, a cheerleader, probably, or that homecoming queen. The closest Faith had come to cheerleader or queen of anything had been passing them in the hall.

"Some people are never ready to become parents," she said softly. That was another understanding her mother had helped her reach.

Nick took the remark personally. "I was surprised," he said impatiently. "You had nine months to get used to the idea. I had a couple of hours."

"There's nothing wrong with not wanting children."

Carefully he turned the crib over, then moved it to the place she'd chosen. There were other suitable locations in the room. She wondered how he'd known that was where it belonged, then warned herself that it didn't matter. He'd made a lucky guess. Considering the way things had gone for him since his arrival in town yesterday afternoon, he was entitled to a little bit of luck.

Once it was in place, he came back, stopping in front of her, extending his hand. She didn't mind that she needed help to get up from the floor. It was a temporary condition. A few more weeks and she would be in as good shape as ever. She did mind, though, that he was the one offering the help. She had always known that simple touching could be a powerful thing. She'd heard of the studies showing that babies deprived of human touch suffered for it in the long run, and she knew from her own experience how empty and unloved a person could feel when there was no one to offer a hug or a kiss or even a casual touch of a hand. She knew what it was like to crave that contact, to feel as if you just might shrivel up and die without it.

But not from Nick. It was his touch—just a casual brush at first that had ignited instantly into something more, something raw, something incredibly breath-stealing—that had tumbled her into bed with him. She had believed at the time that it was magic. She knew now that it had been weakness—and she was already feeling pretty vulnerable this afternoon.

Moment followed moment, until finally he withdrew his offer of help and turned away to study the books on the shelf beneath the carousel horses. He didn't turn quickly enough, though, to hide the grimace that tightened his jaw.

"You're right," he agreed, a sharp, angry sound to his voice that hadn't been there earlier. "There's nothing wrong with not wanting children, as long as you make that decision before you have the kids."

She moved onto her knees, took a breath, then used the chaise and every muscle in her body to lumber slowly to her feet, like some great bear coming out of hibernation. "And when did you make that decision?" she asked, only slightly winded from her exertion.

"Back before I started sleeping with my girlfriend when I was sixteen."

"So you're free and clear."

He faced her, the anger audible in his voice now apparent also on his face. "No, Faith, I'm not. If you don't want kids, then you have to be careful, and obviously I wasn't careful enough."

Pushing her hair back from her face, she found a wide window ledge to lean against. "Answer one question for me honestly. Do you *want* this baby? Do you *want* to be a father, to make the changes having a child entails? Do you want that kind of responsibility in your life? Before you do anything you used to do—go to work, go out on a date, plan a trip—do you want to stop and think how it might affect your daughter?''

He looked at her with such dismay, such incredible regret, that it broke her heart. He wanted to say yes. She knew it as surely as she knew that, for her, the answer was and always had been yes. But he couldn't, not honestly. He couldn't say that he wanted this child he had helped create, but his sense of honor wouldn't let him admit that he didn't.

''Thank you for your help, Nick,'' she said softly. ''Thank you for your concern. Now please just do one thing for us. Stay out of our lives. Forget about us, and we'll forget about you.''

Nick had been given a gift that most men in his situation would treasure: absolution. All he had to do was go home and keep his mouth shut, and no one would ever know the difference. Even if Amelia Rose looked exactly like him, no one would make the connection between them. No one would look at Faith and see the sort of woman he'd always preferred. No one would look at him and think that she might possibly give him the time of day. He would be—as she had put it—free and clear.

So, if he'd been given such a great gift, he wondered morosely as he closed Faith's door behind him, why didn't he feel better about it?

Because there was no freedom from his own conscience, no clearance from his sense of right and wrong. Doing what Faith was asking would be wrong, and even if no one else ever knew it, *he* would know. Walking away would cost him more than he could bear to lose—things like honor, self-respect, dignity, pride. But staying would cost his freedom. He would have to give up his job, his home, his friends. He would have to return to New Hope, right back into the center of his family. He would have to somehow manage marriage to a woman he hardly knew, a woman who clearly didn't want to marry him. He would have to fulfill the two roles he'd hoped never to experience—husband and father—and he would have to do it under the watchful eye of his family and the entire town.

He could learn the father part. God knew, he had the best example in the world in his own father. He could approach it as he did his covert police assignments, as a challenge of successfully pretending to be something he wasn't. The stakes wouldn't be as high, not life or death, but close. And who knew? Maybe a few years down the line, he might start to enjoy the pretense. He might even actually become what he was pretending to be.

The marriage part, though.... Faith was pretty. Under better circumstances, she was no doubt a real sweetheart, as his sister had described her. She was bright and obviously capable. Her shop seemed prosperous, and everything was in order at her house. For someone who wanted to settle down, get married and raise a family in a place like New Hope, she would be perfect. There were just a few small problems. He was as settled as he wanted to get. He didn't want to get married. He didn't want to raise a family. And he didn't want to live in New Hope.

But, courtesy of one forgotten night's overindulgence, those choices might be lost to him forever. He might not—probably didn't—have any other options that he could live with.

Walking to the porch railing, he rested his hands on it and sighed. He should head home. He'd been gone from his parents' house for nearly two hours. Someone had surely missed him by now. He didn't move, though. He simply stood where he was, his gaze directed to the lawn in front of him, his thoughts still on the woman in the house behind him.

It was a great house, much too big for Faith and Amelia Rose, to say nothing of Faith alone. He wondered if it had been her great-aunt's house. It looked like the sort of place where someone named Lydia Harper might live. What had the old woman been like? Motherly, he hoped, for Faith's sake. Generous, apparently, taking in an infant at an age when most women were slowing down and taking it easy.

No matter how motherly and generous Lydia might have been, it couldn't have been easy for Faith, abandoned by her father, given up by her mother, evidently rejected by her grandparents. While Nick, as a kid, had sometimes wished there were fewer Russos around, Faith must have been wondering where her family was and why none of them wanted her. It was easy enough to understand why her mother had left her with Lydia in the first place—at sixteen, she'd probably had all she could handle taking care of herself—but why hadn't she reclaimed her? Why hadn't she gotten herself straightened out, then come back for the daughter she'd left behind?

Maybe Faith had been right. Maybe her mother had been no more thrilled by the prospect of parenthood than her father was. Than Nick himself was.

But he wasn't like them, either of them. He might not have chosen to become a father, but once the decision had been made, he would certainly never turn his back on his child.

Would he?

The breeze that had been pleasantly cool on his walk over rustled along the veranda, colder now, penetrating his sweater and chilling his skin. He liked days like this, liked the evenings they turned into, and missed them in the warmer climate of Houston. Back in school, he and Dan had often taken the Harland twins out to the lake five miles out of town on nights like this one promised to be. There they'd built campfires, drunk the beer Dan had smuggled from his folks' refrigerator and…well, done what kids did. He had been young and foolish—but always prepared. Theresa Harland hadn't trapped him the way Tammy had caught Dan. The way fate had caught him now.

Who had Faith Harper been young and foolish with? Back when she was sixteen—and possibly not much more innocent than she was now—which teenage boy had tempted her at Hardison Lake? Had she gone skinny-dipping when it was warm enough or cuddled in a sleeping bag when it was cold?

The unlikely image made him grin at the same time it sparked a little discomfort. What Faith had done before last February—and especially with whom she had done it—was none of his business. Technically, he supposed, neither was what she did now, except for one small matter: Amelia Rose. The baby made her mother's life and everything in it his concern.

He walked down the steps, got to the bottom and paused between two brick-bordered shrub beds. He should go on home, he counseled himself, and spend what was left of the holiday with his family. Wasn't family the reason he'd come here?

And wasn't it possible—likely—that, in the future, "family" would include Faith?

Wishing that he wasn't doing this, that somewhere inside he didn't feel obligated to do this, he pivoted around, climbed the stairs once more and, for the third time in two days, found himself ringing the doorbell. When she opened the door, he didn't give her a chance to speak or react in any way. He simply, quickly asked, "Want to get some dinner?"

Her gaze was steady and patient. "There's no place to get dinner in New Hope on Thanksgiving evening."

"We could go to Dallas. Plenty of places will be open there." And the chances of being seen by anyone either of them knew were nil. That seemed fair payment for a sixty-mile round trip.

"Look, Nick..." It wasn't the first time she'd used his name, but somehow it felt like it. It felt different. Softer. Less hostile. "It's been a long day, and I—"

"Don't feel much like cooking. You've both got to eat." He tried a smile and was surprised to find that it felt almost natural. "We'll drive into the city, find a place to eat, and then I'll bring you home."

"I have to work tomorrow."

"The shop doesn't open until ten." He wasn't sure where he'd picked up that little bit of information. The hours posted on the door must have stuck in his subconscious.

"It's not even five yet. You'll be home in plenty of time."
When she still hesitated, he tried once more. "Don't you
know you can't spend the entire Thanksgiving Day alone in
your house? It's un-American."

She stood there a moment longer, one hand clasping the
cut-glass doorknob, one socked foot braced atop the other.
Finally she sighed. "Is this how you catch crooks down there
in Houston? You badger them until they say whatever you
want just to get rid of you?"

"I take it that's a yes?"

Reluctantly she nodded. "I need to change."

"While you're doing that, I'll go home and get my
truck."

Her gaze slipped past him to the empty driveway and the
street beyond. "Give me five minutes, and I'll walk with
you." As soon as the last words were out, a look of discomfort stole across her face. "That is, unless you don't
want...your parents..."

Did he mind his family knowing that he was taking her to
dinner? He was ashamed to admit that some part of him
did. They would be so damned curious. They would realize
that he hadn't known Faith when he lived at home—she'd
been probably about eight or ten years old when he'd left for
college. They would wonder when he'd met her. They would
want to know what interest he had in a sweet, innocent, un-
married, pregnant woman. They would remind him that she
wasn't his type, that he certainly wasn't her type. They
would probably even warn him away from her.

When he didn't speak, she gave him a thin, faintly sour
smile. "I wasn't thinking. Go on. I'll be ready when you get
back."

"Listen, it's not—"

She cut him off with a wave of her hand. "I'm already the
subject of gossip in most households. I'd prefer not to give
your family any further reason to talk about me." With
that, she closed the door in his face with a quiet click.

It seemed he'd taken one step forward—and two steps
back. He had convinced her to go to dinner with him, only

to insult her by silently admitting that he didn't want his family to see him with her. He would have to be more careful than that in the future, or Amelia Rose would be graduating from high school before he and Faith ever resolved their problem of what to do about her.

It was a quick walk back to his folks' house, where he had to go inside to retrieve his jacket from the coat tree in the hall. It took a few minutes to say goodbye to everyone, to explain to his mother that he was having dinner with a friend. It wasn't a lie, he reminded himself as he headed out the door. If she chose to assume that it was an old friend—probably an old male friend—that was her problem, not his.

Less than five minutes after that, he was pulling into Faith's driveway. She was ready, as she had promised, and sitting in a wicker rocker on the porch. She still wore jeans, but had changed from the big chambray shirt into a white, pleated and tucked tuxedo-style shirt tied at the neck with a narrow black ribbon. The oversize shirts were necessary, of course, to fit over her swollen stomach, but instead of accentuating her size, they downplayed it. They made her look small and delicate.

As he pulled to a stop, she rose from the chair, picked up a jacket and her handbag from the matching footstool and carefully made her way down the steps. He knew he should be polite and get out, go around the truck and help her with the tall step up. He also knew that she would be no more willing to accept his help now than she had been upstairs in the nursery. He just wished he knew why.

It took her a moment to climb in, another moment to settle back and adjust the seat belt. He took advantage of her preoccupation to study her, to notice that her hair shone from a recent brushing, that large sections were drawn back from each side and tied in back with another black velvet ribbon. She'd added simple black hoop earrings and a spritz of floral-scented fragrance. A black-banded wristwatch circled her left wrist, and around her neck, only a few links visible underneath the shirt collar, was a thin silver chain. He remembered catching a glimpse of it earlier, and he thought, but wasn't sure, that she'd worn it yesterday, too. He wondered idly if it was simply a chain or if held a pendant, maybe something of sentimental value—a gift from her absent mother, a piece inherited from her great-aunt Lydia.

At last he realized that she was settled and waiting, and he straightened in his seat, shifted into gear and pulled onto the street. "Do you have any preferences on restaurants?"

"I hardly ever go to Dallas. I'm not familiar with many of its restaurants."

He gave her a sidelong look. "You live thirty miles from one of the biggest cities in the country, and you hardly ever go there?"

"I rarely need anything that I can't find with a lot less hassle right here in New Hope."

"So you're not a big-city person."

"No." She glanced his way. "I guess you are, since Houston is... what? Twice the size of Dallas?"

"Not quite, but we're working on it. Yeah, I like the city. There's always something going on. You never get bored."

"I like being bored. I like quiet times. I like knowing all my neighbors and my customers. I can't imagine any place I'd rather live than New Hope."

That confirmed one of his earlier thoughts. If he handled this situation the way his family would want, the way his father's teachings decreed, he would have to give up his job. He liked the city, but he could live in a town, while giving up New Hope for the city apparently wasn't even open for Faith's consideration. With his experience, he could probably get a job with the New Hope Police Department, and he might even someday learn to enjoy it. But he would miss the excitement, the varied cases, the complex investigations. He would especially miss the people he worked with. In the twelve years that he'd been in Houston, they had become his family.

But some families were more important than others.

As they left the city limits, Main Street became a highway, two lanes, winding, not heavily traveled this early in the evening. In a few more hours traffic would pick up on all the roads as people headed home from their Thanksgiving celebrations. Tomorrow some of them would go to work, while most would go shopping. It would be a busy day in Houston, and probably in New Hope, too. He wondered if Faith's shop would be busy, if there was much demand for expensive baby clothes and fancy toys. With Christmas coming up, he imagined there was. Doting relatives liked— and could often afford—the best.

"Have you lived all your life in New Hope?"

"Except for the first three and a half weeks. I spent those in Dallas."

"And your grandparents live in Fort Worth."

"That's where they were living when they threw my mother out. I don't know whether they're still there."

She spoke casually, as if parents abandoning their teenage daughter because she got into trouble was an everyday occurrence. Unfortunately, he knew from the job that it did happen all too often. Sometimes the kids really were problems—unmanageable, out of control, violent or self-destructive. Sometimes, though, it was the parents who were the problem. Which was the case with the Harpers?

"Do you know their names? Have you ever tried to find them?"

"Yes, I know their names. No, I've never tried to locate them. I've never even called Information." She had turned her head away from him, but he saw the reflection of her taut little smile in the window.

"I was under the impression that family was important to you."

"They're not my family. They wanted nothing to do with my mother when she was pregnant. They wanted nothing to do with me when I was born." She faced front again, then turned slightly toward him. "Great-aunt Lydia called them periodically and told them what was going on in my life, but they were never interested. As far as they were concerned, they had no daughter, and if they had no daughter, then they couldn't possibly have a granddaughter."

For a moment he tried to think of anything he might do that would cause his parents to disown him, but not a single act came to mind. In their view, love could overcome anything. Every mistake could be made right. Nothing was unforgivable. He couldn't comprehend parents who could remove their child from their lives simply for making a mistake, for being careless—hell, for being a teenager. He knew such people existed, but they were so far outside the realm of his experience with his own and his friends' parents that he couldn't understand them.

"You know, it's been a long time. People change as they get older. They become more forgiving, easier to get along with. Maybe if you called them—"

The cold, steady look she gave him stopped him midsentence. "What have my baby and I done that requires forgiveness?"

Chastened by that look, he directed his gaze to the highway in front of him. "Nothing," he said quietly. "I just meant—"

"I know what you meant. Maybe they can forgive my mother. Maybe she can forgive them. But I have no place in my life for them. Amelia Rose has no place for them. All she needs is me."

He was beginning to understand the importance this baby held for her. Not only was she getting a child, whom she obviously wanted and already loved, but she was also getting a family. It would be a very small, very close family, possibly with no room for anyone else. Faith was possessive. She'd waited much longer than nine months for this baby. "*My* baby," she'd said. *His,* too, he wanted to point out. Amelia Rose was his daughter every bit as much as Faith's—except in love. Nothing her mother could do could change the fact that she was half Russo. Her Italian heritage would likely be dominant over Faith's fairer skin, her lighter hair, her blue eyes. The Russo personality would probably smother Faith's quieter, shyer characteristics. Nature would eventually come to the fore. Put Amelia Rose

in the midst of the Russo family and she would know instinctively that she belonged.

But that exception—the love—kept him quiet. Faith had
been in love with her baby probably from the instant her
subconscious mind realized she was pregnant, while he was
in love with neither of them. While he, to his great shame,
would be much happier if they vanished from his life, leaving not even a hint of a suggestion of a memory that they'd
ever been a part of it.

But that would be too easy, and life, he knew well, was
rarely easy. In fact, thanks to Faith, Amelia Rose and his
own incredible carelessness, he suspected that his life was
never going to be easy again.

The restaurant was a matter of fate rather than choice: it
was the first one on a long boulevard of restaurants open for
dinner. Nick had offered to find something else, but Faith
had declined. She liked Chinese well enough. Besides, she
figured that the sooner they ate, the sooner he would take
her back to New Hope, and the sooner she could retreat into
the peace and privacy of her house. The sooner she could be
alone. The sooner she wouldn't have to look at him and occasionally find herself wondering why things couldn't be
different. Everyone she knew was married or getting married. Practically all of them had babies of their own or
stepchildren or adopted kids that they adored. Why was *she*
still alone? Why couldn't she get married and have babies?
Why hadn't she found someone to love, someone who
would love her, too? Why did she have to be different?

She had thought—nine months ago when she was stupid
and foolish—that Nick might actually be that someone.
He'd been everything she'd ever wanted in a man, and he
had a big family, and, where no other man she'd been out
with before had managed, he had created the magic. In
those few sweet hours, she had believed that she'd found
Mr. Right. Instead, he'd been Mr. Not-in-a-Million-Years.

But he'd given her something better than his love, commitment and devotion. He'd given her Amelia Rose, a

treasure far more precious than any man's love could ever be. Faith was usually satisfied with that, but she still occasionally suffered little attacks of greed. Other women had husbands to love them *and* babies to love. What was wrong with her that she got only one but not the other?

Before she could get too blue, the waitress set platters of food in front of them, refilled their glasses, offered chopsticks, then left. Faith picked up her fork and speared a piece of chicken as Nick slid his chopsticks from their paper wrapper. "Does New Hope have a Chinese restaurant?"

She nodded. "Chinatown. It's a couple of blocks from the shop."

"I like Chinese. And Vietnamese. Korean. Greek. Middle Eastern."

"And Italian?" she asked dryly. She couldn't imagine anyone who had ever sampled Antonio Russo's cooking not liking it. Apparently, Nick couldn't either, because he laughed.

"Pop's a great cook, but Mom's even better. He cooks for the whole town, but *she* cooks for the family. When I first went to college, I didn't know how to eat a meal that didn't include pasta, olive oil or cheese."

"Your father always hoped that one of you would want to follow him into the restaurant business."

A little of the good humor disappeared from his face. "I know. I cook occasionally, but I couldn't face doing it for a living. It's a tough business."

"And being a cop isn't tough?"

In the space of an instant, the grin returned. "It's fun. I like my job. I can't remember ever waking up in the morning and thinking, 'Oh, God, I have to go to work today.'"

"Then you're a lucky man." She was lucky, too. She liked her job, liked attending to all the details of running a business, even if the dealing-with-customers part wasn't always easy. But she could give it up if other opportunities presented themselves—like being a stay-at-home mother and wife, which was never going to happen. If she hadn't met the right man yet, when everything was in her favor, what were the odds of meeting him after Amelia Rose was born? How many men wanted to take responsibility for another man's child? How many men wouldn't mind the whispers or the gossip that was sure to pop up just when everyone thought it was forgotten?

Besides, she wouldn't have time for a man after Amelia Rose was born. Beginning a romance, building a relationship, falling in love and getting married were all time-consuming processes, and she would be too busy being the perfect mother to bother. She would devote herself to ensuring that her foolish mistake nine months ago didn't come back to haunt her daughter. She would be the best mother, the best father—the best *everything*—a child could ever want. She would surround her baby with such love, such happiness, that Amelia Rose would never notice that something was missing.

"I always have been lucky," Nick said, drawing her attention back to him.

"Until yesterday," she noted pointedly, then corrected herself. "Until nine months ago."

"Careful there. You're coming close to admitting that I'm her father." His warning was soft and teasing, but it seemed ominous to Faith. He was a threat to her—to her peace of mind, to her future and, most especially, to her daughter.

What if he persisted in this? What if he insisted not only on claiming paternity but on actually being a father to Amelia Rose? And what if someday down the line, he decided that he *liked* being a father, that he wanted to do it on a full-time basis? What if he offered their daughter the option of going to live with him? How hard a decision could it be: stay with the mother who ran a clothing store for babies, whose idea of a pleasant evening was curling up on the couch with a book, who had nothing to offer but love, or go live with the father she was sure to adore, the father who lived in a big city and held an exciting job and could provide her with a family the size of some small towns, every single one of whom was sure to adore her?

"I'm not admitting anything," she said coolly, twisting noodles around and around on her fork but never lifting it to her mouth. "You have no obligation to my daughter."

"I'm getting that feeling again," he remarked. "You're not a very good liar, are you?"

"Lying is the work of the devil."

"From the Bible or Great-aunt Lydia?"

She smiled just a little. "Probably both."

"What was she like?"

"Why do you want to know?"

"I'm curious."

"You're curious about a lot of things."

With a grin, he shrugged. "I'm a cop, and I'm Italian. I can't help being nosy. Tell me about her."

She studied him a moment, then mimicked his shrug. "She was a sweet old lady—very loving, very well liked, much admired. If I couldn't be with my mother, I couldn't have asked for a better home to be raised in. She was kind, generous, caring." The slow sharpening of his gaze made her uncomfortable, but she tried to ignore it, fiddling instead with her napkin as she went on. "She never made me feel like a burden or an imposition. She did her best to give me a normal, happy, healthy environment to grow up in. She was a wonderful woman. I only wish—"

Finally, under the full weight of his stare, she broke off. He knew she was lying—*knew* it—and he suspected the worst. Shifting uneasily, her gaze locked on her plate, she mumbled words she hadn't intended to say, words that had provided scant comfort when she growing up. "She never hit me."

"How long did you live with her?" His voice was cold, distant, sounding more like a stranger than the man she had spent the better part of the afternoon with.

"She died when I was twenty-one."

"You lived with this woman for twenty-one years, and the best thing you can say about her is that she never physically abused you?"

Shame burned her face. She should have given a closer version of the truth. She should have admitted that Lydia hadn't been an easy woman to live with, but, hey, it hadn't been easy for a fifty-seven-year-old woman to take in a three-week-old infant, either. She could have told him that she didn't want to talk about Lydia, could have changed the subject to something less important, less personal.

She hadn't wanted him to know what her upbringing was like. She didn't want to give him cause to wonder about her emotional fitness to raise his child, didn't want to tell him anything that might bring to mind subjects like custody and Amelia Rose's best interests.

She especially didn't want him to pity her. All her life all her friends had felt sorry for her. She had been the only kid in first grade, and second and third, who didn't live with both a mother and a father. She'd been the kid who couldn't play outside after school, the one who couldn't go to their birthday parties, the one who had never had a birthday party of her own until she turned twenty-two. She'd worn plain, modest dresses when everyone else was in shorts or jeans. She'd had long, feminine curls when all the other girls had short, stylish haircuts. She hadn't known how to play, hadn't been permitted to get dirty, had never slept over at a friend's house or had a friend spend the night with her. She hadn't been allowed to date until she was eighteen, hadn't been kissed until she was nineteen and hadn't dared venture beyond that until she was twenty-five.

If she were a man like Nick Russo, she would certainly never pick herself as a good candidate to be the mother of his child.

"Faith—"

Carefully laying her fork on the plate, she pushed it back a few inches. "I really need to be getting home soon," she said, trying to ignore the quaver in her voice. She half expected him to argue—he seemed to find it so easy—but instead he laid the chopsticks aside and maneuvered his wallet from his hip pocket. Part of her felt guilty for not letting him finish his meal, but, heavens, he was going home to the

Russos. If he was still hungry, Luisa would feed him and be happy to do it.

They sat in silence until the waitress took the check, then brought back Nick's change. He left a tip, then, with nothing more than an impatient gesture, suggested that they leave.

They were back in New Hope, passing the shop on Main Street, before he broke the silence. "Do you think you're the only person to grow up in a bad home with a bad guardian?" he asked quietly, then answered for her. "Because you're not. A lot of people come from dysfunctional families. A lot of kids are raised by people who see them as nothing more than an ordeal to endure until they can get rid of them. Believe me, I see a lot of them at work. It's unfortunate, but it's nothing to be ashamed of."

"I'm not ashamed," she lied. "Lydia did the best she could, which was better than my mother could do, better than my grandmother *would* do." It wasn't Faith's fault that the old woman's best wasn't enough. It wasn't Faith's fault that Lydia had never been able to see her as the result of Sally's sin and not somehow the partner in it, as a child in need of love and affection as well as stern guidance and strict discipline. It certainly wasn't her fault that life had disappointed Lydia, had turned her into a sour, unforgiving, bitter old woman unable to find pleasure or joy in anything.

None of it was her fault, but it *was* her shame. She was ashamed that her father hadn't wanted her, her mother hadn't loved her, and her great-aunt had only tolerated her. It was her fear that maybe something had been so wrong with her that the people who were supposed to love and treasure her couldn't. Maybe whatever it was, was still wrong. Maybe even Amelia Rose would find it impossible to love her.

Or maybe Nick wouldn't give her the chance to try. Maybe he would assert his paternal rights and take her away from Faith. Maybe he had someone back home in Houston he thought would make a better mother. Maybe he would figure that no mother at all would be better than one who'd grown up the way Faith had, who even as a child had somehow alienated everyone, had caused her parents and grandparents to abandon her.

Taking a deep breath, she waited until he turned onto her street, until only a few blocks remained, before she spoke again. "Things will be different for Amelia Rose. She'll know that she was always wanted, from the very beginning. She'll know that, for the last nine months and for the rest of my life, she has been and always will be the most important thing in my life. You don't have to worry about that."

"I'm not worried about that," he said flatly, but she wasn't sure she believed him.

He passed the house, then turned into the driveway and brought the truck to a stop right in front of the steps. She unbuckled the seat belt and unlocked the door as he reached for the key in the ignition. "No," she said, startling both herself and, she suspected, him by laying her hand on his. "Don't come in with me."

"Just to check—"

"This is New Hope, not Houston. The house is locked up, and the lights are on. If anything suspicious had happened, one of my neighbors would have noticed. Trust me." She managed a faint smile that quickly disappeared. "Thank you for dinner. I'm sorry it wasn't a more pleasant evening."

"We'll try again sometime."

With a shake of her head, she opened the door. "No, I don't think so." Holding on to the door, she ignored the step and slid to the ground. With the familiar, uneven brick surface under her feet, she turned back and looked at him for a moment. He didn't look any too pleased with the way the evening had turned out... and yet, in the dim light of the cab, there was a hint of uncomfortable relief. He looked as if he wanted to say something but wasn't quite sure what. She knew exactly what she wanted—what she had—to say.

She said the words, closed the door and climbed the steps to the veranda. It took only a moment to find her keys in her purse, a moment to slide the right one into the lock and turn it, and yet another to stand there, eyes closed, while her last words echoed silently around her. They were short, not too sweet, and if she let them, they could break her heart.

Goodbye, Nick.

Not, "Good night." Not, "See you later." Not even, "See you again." *Goodbye.* For the last time. For all time.

Goodbye.

After the chaos of the preceding day, the Russo house was quiet when Nick finally made his way downstairs late Friday morning. He was tired and feeling irritable. While he'd fallen asleep easily enough, he'd found little peace and less rest. It was those visions or dreams or whatever the hell they were. It was Faith, damn her blue eyes.

In the kitchen he found a pot of strong coffee on the stove and a note from his mother. She'd gone shopping and his father was at the restaurant, preparing for the lunch crowd. There were leftovers in the refrigerator, Dan Wilson had called, and, oh, don't forget the rehearsal dinner this evening at eight. He tasted the coffee, grimaced and poured it down the sink, then took the makings for a turkey sandwich from the refrigerator. Instead of settling at the kitchen table, he wandered through the downstairs while he ate.

It wasn't a fancy house by any means, and there was nothing remarkable about the style. It was two stories, painted white, with a big porch, a big yard and even bigger trees. A detached garage had once stood at the back of the lot, with big doors that opened out from the middle, but it had been torn down years ago to give his mother more room for her garden. There were flower beds close to the house and lots of grass for running and playing. It resembled most of the other houses in the neighborhood—a little bigger, maybe, and for the better part of the last thirty-some years, definitely more crowded.

The four bedrooms upstairs had meant precious little space for anyone. The girls had slept three to a room, and Nick had shared his room with Michael. It hadn't been such a problem when his little brother _was_ still little, but by the time Nick had reached sixteen, having a seven-year-old squirt around all the time hadn't been fun—especially when that squirt had developed a fondness for going through Nick's things whenever he wasn't around. The kid had gotten quite an education before Nick left for college.

His meandering brought him to the door of the living room. The big square room was dimly lit, the bright autumn sun blocked from the lace-curtained windows until midafternoon. The area was crammed with furniture—two sofas, a love seat, four armchairs. Even with all the kids moved out, his parents still entertained a lot—family, friends, business associates, grandchildren. It would be crowded again tonight, for it was tradition, one of his nephews had informed him yesterday, that all the grandkids slept over on Friday nights, and not even Michael's rehearsal dinner or wedding could interfere with it.

Maybe, he thought sourly, _he_ could sleep over someplace, too. Surely Michael had a couch in that cramped apartment of his. His sisters would all have empty bedrooms ... unless they were putting up the out-of-town relatives who would begin arriving today.

Faith had two guest rooms.

The mere thought made him scowl. Using Faith's guest room had gotten him into more trouble than he knew how to deal with. It wasn't something to joke about.

Reluctantly, because he'd avoided it since he'd gotten home, he walked through the double-wide door and approached the wall his sisters teasingly referred to as the rogues' gallery. Framed photographs, some more than seventy years old, filled every available inch of space. There were his father's parents, who lived four streets over, and his mother's parents, who had never left Italy except for rare visits to their youngest daughter. There were pictures of ba-

bies, weddings and more babies, school pictures, graduation portraits and just-for-fun snapshots.

In a row together, in matching frames, were the most recent photographs: his parents celebrating their thirty-eighth
anniversary, Michael and Michelle, each of his sisters with
her husband and children. He didn't mind that there wasn't
a recent photo of himself. After all, he had no family,
nothing worthy of celebrating on this wall. It didn't make
him feel a little left out, a little distant from the others. It
had been his choice, after all, not to marry, not to have a
family.

His choice—but, ultimately, not his fate. He just might be
the first Russo to marry for any reason other than love. The
first Russo to find himself not helped by the teachings of
honor but trapped instead.

His mouth thinning, he studied his sisters' families. All
those kids—an even two dozen—dressed in their Sunday
best for the camera, as neat and polished as their mothers'
determination could make them. Whether siblings or cousins, they all looked alike, with only minor variations thanks
to their non-Russo fathers. They all had the same manners,
the same attitudes, the same smiles, the same eyes. Big, dark
brown eyes were the family hallmark.

And he was being haunted by the bluest eyes in Texas.

"We're a handsome bunch, aren't we?"

Startled, Nick looked over his shoulder to find his father
standing in the doorway. "Mom left a note saying that you
were at work."

Antonio shrugged. "Maurice is putting the finishing
touches on tomorrow's cake, and he said I made him nervous, so I came home to pick up the changes to the menu
that Michelle dropped off yesterday."

"Are you doing all the food for the reception?"

"Of course," Antonio replied in a voice that said naturally no one else could be entrusted to the job.

Of course, Nick silently echoed. For his sisters' weddings, his mother had fussed over invitations, dresses, pho-
tographers, guests and a million other things, and his father

had fussed over the cake, the food, the champagne. Michael's wedding was a little different for their mother, at least—as mother of the groom, she got to take it easier while Michelle's mother dealt with the lion's share of responsibility. But his father was still in charge of the cake, the food and the champagne, and very likely making everyone down at Antonio's nervous.

His father came to join him in front of the photos. "Look at that. A man couldn't ask for a better family."

"Or a bigger one," Nick conceded.

"We're counting on you and Mike to make it bigger."

Nick gave him a look of feigned annoyance. "He and Michelle aren't even married yet and you're pushing them for more grandkids? Don't you know that newly married couples need time to get to know each other before they bring babies into their lives?"

"I think they should know each other *before* they get married. Besides, Mike and Michelle have been dating all of their lives. What could they possibly not know about each other?"

Probably nothing, Nick agreed. Although he'd put much effort into avoiding it, he suspected that there was a real satisfaction in having that kind of intimacy with another person, in sharing thoughts and feelings, in facing situations where no language was needed, where a certain look could communicate everything. It could be—and probably was—very comforting.

He hadn't felt comforted—or comfortable—in nearly forty-eight hours. It seemed like forever.

"So how about it?"

He looked questioningly at his father.

"When are you going to settle down?"

"Pop, I've had the same job for twelve years. I've lived in the same city those twelve years. I own my own place. I pay my own bills. I don't think I can get any more settled than that."

"What about women?"

With a grimace Nick faced the photographs again. "What about them?"

"Are you seeing anyone?"

"No," he answered reluctantly. "Not right now." Not *seeing* her...but damned if he couldn't stop thinking about her.

"You're thirty-four years old. Don't you have any desire to get married? To have a son? To have a family to go home to every night instead of that empty little apartment?"

Two days ago his answer would have been an automatic no. He liked being single, liked having no responsibility for other people. He liked living alone, knowing that his condo was his to do with what he would. He liked coming in late, sleeping till noon on his days off, having the guys over for Sunday's football games and cleaning only when he felt like it. He liked answering to no one, owing consideration to no one. He liked his life exactly the way it was, and, no, he had no desire to change it.

But in the last two days it *had* changed, and not for the better.

"People are different, Pop. You grew up always planning to get married and have kids, and I—"

His father's burst of laughter stopped him in midsentence. "Where did you get an idea like that? I was different, too. I was never going to marry. I was going to be the first lifelong bachelor the Russo family had ever seen." Antonio's amusement softened into a smile. "But then I went back to Italy for a visit and I met your mother. She was a vision—the most beautiful girl in the entire world. I took one look at her and I knew. It was fate."

Nick thought of Faith, pregnant and determined to go through it alone, and scowled. "Fate isn't always so kind, Pop."

Sliding his arm around Nick's shoulders, Antonio hugged him tightly. "One day you'll meet the right woman, and when you do, you'll know."

And when he did, he wondered morosely, would he already be irrevocably bound to Faith by the fragile link of a

child? "Until that happens, do you and Mom plan to continue badgering me about getting married and adding to the
brood?"

Antonio's regretful sigh was as phony as Nick's earlier
annoyance. "I wish I could say the answer was no, that we
would simply have faith."

Nick tried to hide the stiffening his father's last word sent
through him. It was a sad day when a simple word like *faith*
could bring a man such guilt and discomfort.

With another of those expressive shrugs, Antonio continued. "Sometimes fate needs a little push, you know. You
might need us to give it."

A little push. Did a secret-until-now pregnancy and the
impending birth of a daughter constitute "a little push"?
Was this fate's way of forcing him into the role his parents—and probably their parents before them—had long
ago planned for him?

Without waiting for a response, Antonio moved to the
desk on the far wall, where he collected a handful of notes
before turning toward the door. "I'd better get back to the
restaurant and make sure everything is in order. Why don't
you come by this afternoon? Things get quiet after two
o'clock."

Neither accepting nor declining the invitation, Nick said
goodbye, then watched his father leave. After silence settled over the house, he turned once more to the photos.
There weren't any babies, he noticed. Lucia's last one was
the youngest of them all, and she was about four now. All
those kids, and he'd missed their births, their birthdays,
their lives. The older kids remembered him from visit to rare
visit, but to the younger ones, he was a stranger, and they
were all strangers to him. He sent birthday cards and paid
for gifts provided by his mother, but he didn't really know
any of them. He didn't know what sports they played, what
shows they watched on TV, who liked to read and who preferred video games or what they wanted to be when they
grew up. Sometimes he couldn't even keep straight exactly

who belonged to whom. He didn't have any real sense of having twenty-four nieces and nephews.

He bet, if they belonged to her family, Faith would know them. She would know each one's dreams, their fears, their hopes and insecurities. Of course, it wasn't surprising that family was so important to her, since she'd never had one. But she had one now in Amelia Rose.

He hoped that wasn't too big a burden for that six- or seven-pound baby girl to bear.

Chapter 4

"*Well?* What happened?"

Faith didn't look up from the unpacking she was doing in the storeroom, not that unloading a box of soft, woven blankets in subdued pastels required much of her attention. It was just easier—safer—than looking Wendy in the eye while she lied to her. "Nothing's happened. I had a quiet, peaceful Thanksgiving. This morning has been busy, though. The biggest shopping day of the year, you know."

"Did he come back?"

"Who?"

Wendy tugged the last blanket from Faith's hands and added it to the haphazard pile on the worktable. "Has Nick Russo come to see you since Wednesday? Has he asked about the baby? Did you tell him the truth? What is he going to do about it?"

Hushing her, Faith glanced into the shop. Ten minutes ago she had escaped into the storeroom, just seconds ahead of the arrival of Miss Agnes, Miss Ethel and Miss Minny. The widows were best of friends and the Three Musketeers of the silver-haired set. They were also the nosiest, gossipiest old biddies Texas had ever seen. Nothing escaped their scrutiny and, for the past nine months, Faith had felt the ceaseless sting of their curiosity and their wagging tongues. They had spread the news of her pregnancy and her apparent abandonment by the baby's father more efficiently than blaring headlines and trumpeting newscasts ever could have done, and not one of them had missed a chance to state her disapproval loud and clear. The last thing Faith wanted was to give them something more to gossip about.

With a sigh, she closed the door and faced Wendy. "Yes, he came back."

"And?"

Wendy was a good friend, one of her best, Faith acknowledged, but did that mean she had to know the whole truth? Could Faith's pride endure telling her everything? It was bad enough that every soul in town thought Amelia Rose's father had run out on her because he didn't love her, didn't want her or the responsibility of a baby, but did she also have to admit, even to her best friend, that, in truth, he simply didn't remember her? That he'd found her utterly forgettable? That, if he hadn't been drunk, he never would have touched her?

"We talked."

"Did you tell him?"

"He guessed."

"What was his reaction?"

Faith picked up the empty carton the blankets had been shipped in and used a box cutter to slit the tape on both sides, then broke it down flat. She added it to the stack in the corner then, twisting the cutter in nervous circles, replied, "He doesn't want a baby." Her voice, meant to be flat, unemotional and uncaring, wobbled on the last word. No tears, she warned herself. So Nick didn't want Amelia Rose. She didn't need him.

"Well, honey, it's a little late for him to be deciding that, isn't it?" her friend asked, dismay that he even thought he might have a choice clear in her expression. "The time to make that decision is *before* you do the deed, not after. He can't just walk away from you two because he's decided that he doesn't want a baby."

"Why can't he?" Faith demanded. "Why can't he just go back to Houston and forget about us?"

Wendy stared at her, more than a little surprised.

Her friend knew her so well, Faith lamented. Wendy knew she was conservative, even old-fashioned. She knew that this—single, alone and open to gossip—was the last way in the world Faith would have chosen to have a baby and that Faith was the last person to voluntarily do something outrageous, something nonconforming. Of course Wendy expected that Faith would want the father of her baby to do what fathers were supposed to do.

Wendy would be a hundred percent right if Faith loved Nick, if he loved her. Heavens, she wasn't so greedy. If he just liked her. If he wanted her. If he saw her as *something*—friend, partner, lover—other than an obligation.

"I don't need his money," she insisted. "Thanks to Lydia and the shop, I'm more than able to meet all of Amelia Rose's needs. He can't provide any sort of assistance from three hundred miles away. He can't baby-sit if I have to work late or take care of her if I get sick. He can't be a regular part of her life. All he can do is take her away from me on holidays, and I certainly don't want that."

"But he's her *father*," Wendy gently disagreed. "Don't you think that someday she'll want to know him? That she'll wonder why he's not a part of her life? What if she finds out someday that he was willing to be there—even if it was long-distance or only on holidays—but *you* wouldn't let him?"

Her argument sent a shiver down Faith's spine. She knew better than Wendy, better than anyone in her circle of friends, what it was like to grow up without a father. How would she feel if she discovered that her father had wanted her all along, but someone had kept him away? How much anger, how much hatred, would that create?

She couldn't bear the idea of Amelia Rose hating her—so she would have to make sure it didn't happen.

She just wasn't sure how.

"Is he going to tell his family?"

The possibility brought her such longing. Legitimate or not, surely Amelia Rose would be welcomed by the Russos. They would love her the same as they loved all their other grandchildren. They would spoil her and fill her life with joy, exuberance and love. They would give her everything Faith wanted her to have and couldn't give herself.

If Nick chose to tell them. She couldn't venture a guess whether he would. On the one hand, he seemed to feel an obligation to their daughter, but on the other…well, he had made it clear yesterday that he hadn't wanted her to accompany him to his parents' house. He hadn't wanted to be seen with her, hadn't wanted to give anyone cause for speculation. He'd made it abundantly clear that he didn't want a daughter. More than anything in the world, he wanted this problem to go away and leave him untouched.

Telling his parents might give Amelia Rose a family, but it wouldn't be easy for him. They would disapprove of his actions, would probably push him to do the "right" thing. They would pressure him and probably Faith, too, and that was the last thing in the world she needed.

"I don't know. It would be so much easier," she said, opening another box, "if he would just go back to Houston and never tell anyone anything. He could live his life the way he wants, and I could have Amelia Rose…" Her words trailing off, she stiffened.

Wendy waited through a moment or two of silence, then prompted her. "You could have Amelia Rose…"

Faith covered her face with both hands, then, with a sigh, pulled them away. "I just caught a glimpse of how selfish I've become," she said with a crooked smile. "I was going to say that I could have Amelia Rose all to myself. I wouldn't have to share her time or her love or her life with anyone. She could be all mine."

"That's not selfish, honey," Wendy said, then allowed, "Well, a little. But it's understandable."

Understandable because of the way she was raised. Faith scowled as she folded back the box's flaps. There were no secrets in a town like New Hope, other than the one she, Wendy and Nick shared, and it was anyone's guess how long that would stay private. She didn't intend to tell, and she knew she could trust Wendy not to. Nick was the wild card. With his good-Italian-son, good-Catholic upbringing, guilt or some ridiculous sense of duty might prompt him to confess all. If his role in her pregnancy became common knowledge, those three batty old ladies out there in the shop would teach her a new meaning for the word gossip. Prim, proper, virginal Faith Harper pregnant? Shocking. Prim, proper, virginal Faith pregnant by that oldest Russo boy? Scandalous. *Why, she didn't even know him. Seducing strangers...and after all Miss Lydia did for her. She's turned into a harlot like her mother, after all.*

Realizing that she was staring dumbly at the box she'd opened, Faith forced her attention to its contents—booties, sneakers, sandals and walkers. She loved all baby things, but shoes in particular fascinated her. They were so small, perfect tiny replicas of their adult-size counterparts. She withdrew a pair of white satin booties from their clear plastic box and balanced them in the palm of her hand. They were soft, only a few inches long, designed to slide easily onto a wiggly baby's little feet. They would be perfect for Amelia Rose's first portrait, to go with the green velvet dress with the white lace collar and the satin sash.

Her first portrait. It was an event Faith anticipated and, at the same time, found sad. She would dress her daughter in a lovely dress, lace socks and these booties, and Amelia Rose would smile for the photographer, and when the portraits were ready, Faith would buy one. *One.* She would have no need of the package deals that everyone else chose, because she would have no relatives to share the occasion with.

Returning the shoes to their box, she set them aside on the shelf next to her purse, then looked up to find Wendy watching her with a smile that eased her blues—a little teasing, a little wistful and a lot tender. ''You know, this baby is going to be the best-dressed kid in all of Texas. You've already selected an entire wardrobe for her, and you've got all the toys, stuffed animals and books a child could possibly need. Can't you leave something for us to buy when we have her shower?''

"I don't need a shower," Faith replied. She intended to provide for her daughter herself.

"It's not for you. It's for the baby, and she's getting it whether you want it or not." Wendy reached up to pluck down the box. "Thank you for the gift idea. I'll get Beth to help me find something else." Raising a hand to her recently-turned-blond hair, she smiled smugly. "After all, she's helped me with so much already."

Beth had been a lot of help to Wendy, Faith knew, and the transformation had been nothing less than miraculous. With her thirtieth birthday approaching and her maternal instincts growing stronger, Wendy had decided that it was time to find a husband and have a baby. With guidance from Beth and Sue Ellen over at the diner, she had gone from drab to knock-out.

But with all the outside changes, inside she was still the same Wendy Wilcox, still and always one of Faith's best friends.

With a sigh, Wendy rose from the stool where she'd perched. "I'd better get back to work. Need some help carrying these things out?"

"If you'd grab an armload of blankets—" Faith picked up the large box of shoes, but Wendy immediately relieved her of it.

"You get the blankets, honey. I'll take this."

Faith opened the door, then scooped up as many blankets as Amelia Rose would allow. Steeling herself for an encounter with the three old ladies, she followed Wendy out of the storeroom. "Good afternoon, Miss Agnes, Miss Ethel, Miss Minny," she greeted politely.

Each of the women subjected her to a measuring look. "Still working, I see," Miss Agnes remarked disapprovingly. "You should stay off your feet."

"Take better care of yourself," Miss Ethel added.

"Be kinder to that baby," Miss Minny admonished.

Faith drew a patience-supplying breath. "Dr. Austin says it's perfectly all right for me to continue working."

"Dr. Austin." Miss Ethel tsked. "What kind of doctor wears long hair like that and rushes all over town on a motorcycle like he does? Why, in my day, women didn't need doctors to help them birth their babies. Today they want fancy hospitals and fancy doctors and as little inconvenience as possible."

"I gave birth to four children in my own bed with no one but my sister there to help," Miss Minny put in. "Women today are spoiled."

Miss Agnes agreed. "Spoiled. They think they should do whatever they want and no one should blink an eye."

"Like having a baby without a husband?" Faith's smile was thin and cool, prompting Wendy to step in.

"Excuse us, Miss Agnes. We'll let you ladies get back to shopping while we tend to our own business." Wendy put a definite emphasis on the last three words, causing the women to turn away in a concerted huff. She maneuvered Faith in the direction of the blanket display near the front of the shop. There she set the box down and offered encouragement in a low voice. "Don't let them get to you, Faith. They're just nosy old women."

"I know. It's just that sometimes I get so tired of their looks, their comments and their finger-pointing that I get this incredible urge to really shock them."

"Let me know if you decide to give in to it. I'd like a front-row seat." Wendy glanced at her watch, then headed for the door. "I'm going to be late. See you tomorrow?" At Faith's blank look, she explained, "The wedding?"

The wedding. Other than her occasional mentions of it to Nick, she had managed to more or less forget Saturday's nuptials. As happy as she was for Michael and Michelle, she wasn't anxious to attend their wedding. She wasn't sure she could bear seeing the incredibly happy and deeply in love couple when her own situation was so far from ideal. She didn't want to witness their marriage when she was alone, as she'd been all her life, and often lonely. She didn't want to tarnish their joy by wondering greedily why she couldn't have it, too.

She didn't want to see Nick, and especially not at a wedding.

"Oh, honey, you are going to come, aren't you?" Wendy asked worriedly.

"Yeah, I'll be there."

"Travis and I can pick you up if you'd like. It's right on our way."

Faith forced a smile. "I can still fit behind the steering wheel of my car. I'll get myself to the church on time."

"If you change your mind, give me a call. Gotta go now."

The bell rang, then quieted as the door closed behind Wendy. Faith stood motionless, still clutching half a dozen blankets, and watched until her friend was out of sight. Only then, as she prepared to get back to work, did she see Nick standing on the sidewalk in front of the office supplies store next door, talking to friends.

It wasn't pleasure that made her palms grow damp and her heart pick up its tempo, she insisted, but nerves and an awful feeling of dread. *Please don't come in,* she silently prayed, not with the biggest mouths in Texas still searching for just the right purchase.

In spite of her brain's commands, she couldn't turn away, couldn't pull her gaze away. She stood there, feeling relatively safe inside her shop, and simply looked at him. He was dressed in boots, jeans and a dark blue shirt with the sleeves pushed up his forearms. He was so handsome, so appealing, and he had a smile that could sweep a woman right off her feet. He had smiled at her that night in February, and she had felt like the most important woman in his world.

How foolish she had been.

His attention wandered her way, his gaze making contact before she had a chance to turn away or pretend that she didn't see him. His good mood seemed to darken a bit, and his only acknowledgment of her was a nod of his head so slight that no one else would have noticed. Then he pointedly shifted so that his back was to her before continuing the conversation with his friends.

That was what she wanted, she reminded herself as she dumped the load of blankets on the table, then began arranging them by color. She wanted him to ignore her, wanted not to exist in his life. She wanted it for herself and especially for Amelia Rose. He was only giving her what she had asked for, what she had demanded.

Why, then, did she suddenly feel so betrayed?

"Why don't we go out tonight and have a few drinks? It'll be just like old times."

Nick turned his head just enough to see the corner of the nearest window at the Baby Boutique before refusing Dan Wilson's invitation. "I can't. I'm under strict orders from Michael not to do any drinking until after the wedding. Besides, we've got the rehearsal and the dinner tonight."

"You remember that the rehearsal is traditionally the night before the wedding, don't you, Danny?" Tammy's catty tone made Nick's nerves tauten. "Of course you don't, because when we got married, *you* insisted on skipping the rehearsal and went out drinking with the boys instead."

"One mistake. I made one mistake sixteen years ago, and she's never gonna let me forget it," he muttered.

Which mistake was he referring to? Nick wondered. Getting drunk the night before the wedding? Or the pregnancy that led to the wedding?

"One mistake?" Tammy echoed. "Darlin', I can't even remember the last time you did something right."

Nick shifted uncomfortably. He'd had his doubts about the success of his friend's marriage from the start. Dan had been forced to give up his dream of college and Tammy had been faced with the reality that there was nothing romantic about being barely eighteen, married, living with your in-laws, and having a baby. Hard luck had turned disappointment to anger, frustration to resentment, and the easiest target for venting those bitter emotions was apparently—naturally—each other.

Was that what the future held for him and Faith? Would he blame her for taking his freedom? Would she be bitter over the circumstances that had brought them together, resentful of the obligations that kept them together? Would they become like Dan and Tammy, sniping at each other on a downtown sidewalk in front of an old friend, so miserable that they didn't care who knew it?

That wasn't a future he could face. It sure as hell wasn't one he could willingly accept.

"It's been good seeing you, Nick, but we'd better get going." Tammy's smile was so strained that it looked as if it surely must hurt. "We don't want to keep Dr. Austin waiting."

Austin. Nick had never heard the name before Wednesday afternoon, but he remembered it. He was Faith's doctor—her obstetrician. Maybe Tammy was just having a checkup. But one look at his friend's face confirmed Nick's suspicions.

"Yeah," Dan said glumly after she headed for their truck with long strides. "She's pregnant again."

"You know," Nick said, his voice soft and carefully blank, "there are ways to prevent that." And who the hell was he to point that out, when his own mistake was only a few dozen feet away?

"Yeah, but the only one that's a hundred percent foolproof with Tammy is abstinence, and I'm not that strong." His smile was halfhearted. "You're a lucky man, Nick. You got out of this place. You got an education, a good job, no strings to tie you down. I wound up with a ranch I don't want, a wife who blames me for every disappointment in her life, four whiny kids and another one on the way. There are times I just want to walk away." He heaved a sigh, then stuck his hand out. "See you, buddy."

As he watched Dan leave, Nick wondered why his friend didn't just walk away. He could get a divorce, get Tammy out of his life, still be a father to the kids and maybe do something for himself. Why stay with a wife he didn't even like, much less love, in a town he hated, on a ranch whose dust he'd been dying to shake from his boots since he was twelve years old? He had accepted his responsibilities. He had married Tammy all those years ago, had given their baby the respectability of a name. His duties now were to the kids, not her, and fulfilling those duties had nothing to do with being married. Why not put an end to his misery now before it got any worse?

Dan gave one last wave as he drove by. Nick returned it, then turned toward Antonio's. He'd met his brother for lunch—sandwiches from the deli in Michael's office—and now he was on his way to the restaurant. He had almost talked himself out of going—the temptation to confide in his father, the way he always had when he was troubled, would likely be strong—but he had little enough time to spend with Antonio, especially without the rest of the family vying for his attention. Nick would just have to watch what he said and resist those old urges.

His steps slowed as he came even with the display window for Faith's shop. There were a number of customers inside, mostly browsing, one being helped by a blond-haired teenager. Faith was in the same place where he'd first seen her, fussing over a display, making adjustments here and there and keeping her eyes down.

He hadn't missed the finality of her farewell last night. *Goodbye,* said the way she'd said it, most definitely *meant* goodbye. She didn't want to see him again, didn't want to talk to him again. She expected him to spend the rest of the weekend here, to go to Michael's wedding and not speak to her. She expected him to go home Sunday, just as he'd planned, without trying once more to resolve this problem between them. And she expected him to let Amelia Rose's due date pass without a call, without even a little curiosity about whether he was yet a father.

She didn't think much of him, and it pained him that she was entitled to her low opinion.

He didn't mean to stop in the store, but before he realized it, the bell was ringing overhead and three of the customers, elderly women examining a selection of storybooks, turned as one to look at him.

Faith didn't look up, but she knew it was him. Scowling deeply, she moved around the display of blankets so that her back was to everyone else, and when he stopped across from her, she whispered a heated demand. "Go away."

"Having a busy day?"

"Yes, too busy to bother with you."

She'd taken one of the blankets out of its protective packaging and fixed it so that the folds draped from the top shelf. He ran his palm over it. It was softer than anything he'd ever imagined, warm and enveloping. It could chase away the coldest of chills and make a baby feel snug and safe. He wondered if Faith had already collected one for Amelia Rose and figured she had. All those boxes and bags that he'd carried upstairs for her yesterday had been filled with clothing and blankets. Amelia Rose probably had everything she could possibly need. There wasn't anything that Nick could give her...except his name, and Faith was convinced she had no need of that.

"Would you please leave?" she asked. "I don't want my customers to wonder."

"You mean the old women. Are they still the biggest gossips in town?"

"Yes, and I don't want to give them anything new to talk about." Finally she looked at him. Her eyes were unusually bright, and there was a look in them that he couldn't begin to describe. Sadness, pain, disillusionment, weariness—it was a little of bit of everything and it touched him, making him feel somehow as fragile as she looked.

"What's wrong?" he demanded, his voice low so no one else could hear.

"Nothing."

But she glanced over her shoulder as she replied, and he followed her gaze to the three old women who were watching them. Agnes, Ethel and Minny had always loved to gossip and he had always thought they were harmless—but that was before their gossip concerned him. What right did they have to spread talk about Faith and her baby?

And what right did he have getting angry with the old women when he was as much responsible for the gossip about Faith as they were? "Did they say something?"

"No. But please go before they get suspicious. Please..." Turning abruptly, she saw the women heading their way. "Excuse me," she blurted before making a beeline for the storeroom in back.

"Why, if it isn't Nick Russo," Agnes said. "Your mama told us you would be home for the wedding."

Nick gave the three women a cool smile. Years ago they had been easy to tell apart. One had been handsome, as his father put it. One had been a redhead, one a blonde, one a brunette. One had been plump, one thin and one in-between. Now age and too much of each other's company had created a resemblance where before there had been none. The three had come to look, dress, act, think and speak as one.

"We didn't know you and Faith were friends," Agnes continued. "She's much closer to your brother's age than yours."

"We didn't know you two even knew each other," Ethel added. "What with her being so young when you moved away and you hardly ever coming back for visits."

"Of course I know Faith. The whole family does," he said, and hoped he was right about that. "We were just discussing Michael's wedding tomorrow."

"Oh, dear, the wedding." Minny sorrowfully shook her head. "It won't be easy for poor Faith, having to sit through the festivities."

"What won't be easy about it?" he asked, his gaze narrowing as he looked at each woman.

"Why, her condition, of course," Ethel replied.

Next to her, Agnes leaned forward conspiratorially. "Being pregnant and alone. The father ran out on her, you know. At least, that's the story. It's possible—" she looked from one woman to the other, then lowered her voice "—she might not even know who he is."

Ethel took over then, sidling around the table closer to him. "We didn't want to believe it at first, what with her seeming so sweet and shy. We thought that surely he must have abandoned her, the same way her own father abandoned her poor mother. You've heard the story, of course."

"Of course," he said dryly.

"She's so ashamed that she won't even tell anyone who he is—"

"*If* she knows," Agnes interrupted.

"And she should be ashamed," Minny said quietly. "Lydia Harper was one of our dearest friends, and she taught that girl better than that. Why, she would turn in her grave if she knew what had become of her great-niece."

Ethel shook her head sorrowfully. "Now poor Faith has to sit in that church tomorrow, all too aware of her sins, and watch your brother and that sweet little Parker girl get married and know that her own young man didn't want her—"

Agnes interrupted again. "Well, except in bed."

"*Agnes!*" Ethel scolded, and the old woman's face turned red. With a chastening look, she continued. "A person could almost feel sorry for the girl if she showed even the slightest remorse for what she's done, but she just goes on as if nothing's happened. Why, she wouldn't even hear of giving the baby up for adoption to some deserving married couple who could give it a good home. We suggested that she consider it back in the beginning, and she absolutely refused."

"She was *rude*," Agnes said, her expression turning miffed at the memory.

"I can't imagine anyone giving a baby a better home than Faith," Nick said before anyone else could speak. His words, or maybe the harshness that underlaid them, made the women stop for a moment, speechless. He took advantage of the rare event to escape. "Ladies, if you'll excuse me, I'll say goodbye to Faith and then I have an appointment to keep."

They offered their own goodbyes as he made his way around racks and displays to the storeroom. He didn't knock, didn't hesitate at all, but opened the door, stepped inside and shut it firmly behind him. He took a moment to breathe deeply, to clear his mind of the anger the old women had created, then he focused his gaze on Faith.

Two days ago he had carried her into this room, had laid her on the couch, checked her pulse, talked to her doctor. He had been concerned about her fainting spell only in a professional sort of way—was her time near, should he call an ambulance or take her to the hospital, or, in a worst case scenario, would he have to help deliver her baby? He had done it once before, more or less, back when he was in uniform. A frantic man with a flat tire had flagged him down three miles from the nearest hospital. Nick had called for an ambulance, then gone to the guy's car to check on his wife and had gotten there in time to catch the kid. It had been an interesting experience—a little unnerving, a lot different— but no big deal.

Just as carrying Faith in here, checking her and talking to her doctor had been no big deal. But if he had known then what he knew now . . .

She was standing in front of a small window at the back of the room. Its view was nothing special—a parking lot and the back of some business on the next street—but she was staring at it intensely. Then she lowered her head and rubbed her eyes. "I'm sorry to keep running out on you, Beth," she said with a sigh. "I just can't deal with those nosy old women now."

"I don't know how you deal with them at all."

Startled, she turned quickly to face him, then her shoulders seemed to sag a bit. "I can't deal with you, either. Not today. Not here."

"I just came to tell you that I'll see you tomorrow at the wedding." Remembering what the old ladies had said, he asked, "You *are* coming to the wedding, aren't you?"

"Yes," she said with a sigh. "I'll be there."

"Good. Michael and Michelle would be disappointed if you weren't."

"And how do you know that?"

Because he would be disappointed if she wasn't there, and Michael and Michelle knew her much better—if differently—than him. "You're friends," he said with a shrug. "You held their engagement party at your house."

His answer didn't ease her frown, but she accepted it with a nod before leaning back to rest against the windowsill. He watched her a moment longer, then asked, "Why don't you go home and stretch out on that chaise with your teddy bear friend and take a nap?"

Her matter-of-fact tone indicated that she'd heard similar suggestions before. "I can't leave Beth here alone. It's been too busy."

"No offense, Faith, but you've been leaving her to deal with customers anyway. She seems perfectly capable to me." The last part was actually just a guess. Other than noticing that her clerk was young, blond and sported multiple earrings in each ear, he hadn't paid her much attention. But, based on what he knew of Faith, Beth was undoubtedly the single most mature, responsible teenager in New Hope, or she wouldn't be working here. "Go home."

She shook her head in exasperation. "What is it about being pregnant? It's as if I've become public property. Complete strangers tell me horror stories about their own childbirth experiences. Everyone feels entitled to give me advice. Everyone thinks they know what's best for me. People I've never even shaken hands with want to touch my stomach and feel the baby move. I'm pregnant, not stupid. I'm capable of recognizing when I'm tired, when I need to rest, when I should get off my feet. I'm smart enough to know that giving birth isn't a piece of cake, that it can be long, drawn-out and painful. And I no more want people putting their hands on my stomach now than I did before I got pregnant. Heavens!"

Nick lost track somewhere in the middle of her speech, distracted by one sentence. *People I've never even shaken hands with want to touch my stomach and feel the baby move.* He had never felt an unborn baby move before, not even one of his nieces and nephews. He had never thought that he'd have any such desire. But he had never thought that one day there would be *his* unborn child. It was *his* baby moving inside her, and he wondered how it felt to actually feel her stretch, turn and kick. Other people knew. Faith surely knew. But he didn't have a clue.

Silence penetrated his thoughts, making him realize that she was finished, that she was giving him an odd look that he could feel without seeing. He looked away from the swelling of her stomach, cleared his throat and took a step back. "I'd better go now. I'll see you tomorrow."

She sighed before he walked through the door. The last thing he heard was a subdued agreement. "Yeah. Tomorrow."

Saturday was as beautiful a wedding day as any bride could want. The sun was shining, the temperature was hovering in the high sixties, there was a gentle breeze blowing, and the sky was a gorgeous Texas blue. It was a day perfect for walking down the aisle or along a country road, for dancing at a reception or scuffing in fallen leaves around the lake. It was too perfect a day, Faith thought, for putting on a tent-size dress, panty hose and the dressiest flats she owned and spending the next few hours pretending to share the Russo-Parker family joy.

But pretend she would. She had no doubt that, if she weren't in her seat at least fifteen minutes before the one o'clock service, Wendy or one of her other friends would be on the phone or in the car headed this way. They would think something terrible must have happened to keep her from Michelle's wedding—that she'd fallen or gone into labor or something—and they would probably send out the cavalry.

Besides, there would be talk if she didn't show up for any reason other than ongoing labor. The three old biddies would tell everyone who would listen that her reluctance was due to a heart broken by the unfeeling cad who'd rejected her. She'd heard it all before.

Well, today she wasn't giving them anything to use against her. She was going to the wedding, she was going to be happy for Michelle and Michael, and she was going to enjoy herself, even if it killed her.

And putting on those shoes just might do it.

Sitting on the side of the bed, she gazed forlornly at her feet. Once they'd been small, even delicate. She'd worn strappy, slender heels without even a pinch of pain—but only after Lydia's death, of course. Her great-aunt had believed in sensible shoes and sensible clothing. "Stylish" hadn't been in the old lady's vocabulary, but "serviceable" and "durable" had. Today, though, her feet were swollen and refused to even consider the possibility of being crammed into the widest, flattest shoes she had. No pointed toes or graceful shapes for her, she thought, getting to her feet and going to the closet for her reliable, stretched-out, cushioned-sole loafers.

Not expecting much, she stood in front of the full-length mirror mounted on the inside of the closet door. Her dress was pretty, dark green, with little trim. Her hose were serviceable. She hadn't had the energy to try to wiggle her nine-months-pregnant body into the sheer, elegant styles she preferred. The best she could say for the shoes was that they were leather. They had passed "well-worn" months ago. Her only jewelry was a necklace and a pair of hoop earrings. Her watch fit too snugly, and the few rings she owned wouldn't slide past her first knuckle.

The Russo-Parker wedding was the event of the season for the whole town, and *she* looked like Jumbo the elephant—make that Dumbo, she corrected—in a circus tent.

Turning away from the mirror, she picked up her small, flat handbag and started toward the door just as the doorbell rang. For an instant she wondered if it might be Nick,

but the absence of tension in her stomach indicated otherwise. Listening to the echo of the second peal, she made her
way downstairs, holding on to the railing with one hand. At
the bottom she opened the door and faced Priss—and, in
the driveway, behind the wheel of her car, her husband Jake
Spencer—with suspicious surprise.

"Oh, Faith, you look lovely," her friend greeted her.

"I look like Dumbo," she retorted grumpily. With a scowl
at the barely noticeable swelling of Priss's own pregnancy,
she added, "See what you have to look forward to?"

Leaning forward, Priss patted Faith's belly comfortingly. "I know. I can hardly wait. Come on, sweetie, Jake
and I have come to take you to the church."

"Was this Wendy's idea?"

"Why would you think that?" Priss's attempt at innocence failed.

"Because I turned her down when she offered to pick me
up. I'm going to the wedding, believe me. I wouldn't miss it
for anything." She intended to sit through the ceremony, sail
through the reception line while somehow skipping the best
man, avoid all the gossips and almost everyone else, and
sneak home the first chance she got—which Wendy had
probably suspected and so had arranged this ride to prevent an early departure. Well, Miss Wendy was silly if she
thought the mere lack of a ride would keep Faith where she
didn't want to be. Sacred Heart was less than two miles from
her house, she was wearing her most comfortable shoes, and
Dr. Austin said walking was great exercise for a mother-to-
be.

"Let's go, honey. We don't want to keep everyone waiting." Priss tugged her arm, giving Faith only a moment to
grab her keys from the hall table, only another moment to
lock the door behind her.

In the driveway Faith greeted Jake as she maneuvered into
the back seat of the luxury-size car. Her own little sedan was
getting to be a rather snug fit. There was precious little
clearance between Amelia Rose and the steering wheel.
Thank heavens it was almost time.

Almost time. The two words made her heart ache. She was anxious for Amelia Rose to be born, to hold her own sweet little baby in her arms, but at the same time, she was a little scared, too. Despite her talk to Nick yesterday, the prospect of childbirth made her nervous. How long would it last? she wanted to know. How much would it hurt? How would it feel going through it alone?

Dr. Austin had offered her the option of natural childbirth, and Wendy had volunteered to be her coach, but she had rejected the idea. She needed the delivery to be as easy as possible, so her recovery would be as quick as possible. After all, she would have a baby to take care of, a family to support, a business to run—and she would be doing it all on her own.

The "on her own" part was the largest cause of her fears. She could endure the longest labor and untold pain if the right person were there to hold her hand, to offer her encouragement and to celebrate the end result. She could treasure every moment of the first days of Amelia Rose's life if she didn't have to worry about a fast recovery, about going home alone with her new baby, about getting back to the shop in a few weeks. She could forget the fear completely if she just had someone beside her. Priss had Jake. Valerie and Lucas were still together and more in love than ever. And Wendy might not have technically hooked Travis in the great husband hunt, but it was coming—anyone who'd watched them together could see that—and Michelle had Michael. Faith had nobody, and since the only remote possibility in her future wanted only to use her to ease his guilty conscience, it wasn't likely she would ever find somebody.

The trip passed quickly, Priss providing the conversation so that Faith didn't have to speak at all. She simply stared out the window and brooded.

At the church Jake pulled into the east side parking lot, easing into a space near the back door that led to the classrooms. Faith had been raised a good Baptist, but many of her friends were Sacred Heart parishioners. She had attended various services as their guests, mostly weddings and baptisms. If things had turned out differently, Amelia Rose would have been baptized here.

But things weren't different, she admonished herself, cutting off that line of thought before it became too painful.

Jake came around the car, opened the door and offered his hand. Faith stared at it for a moment before realizing that she was supposed to take it. No matter how roomy the car, getting in and out in her condition was always a little difficult.

"Thank you, Jake," she said, smiling up at him as she climbed out, then straightened.

Movement behind him caught her attention and her smile slowly faded. Dressed for the wedding except for his jacket and looking impossibly handsome, Nick was standing on the stoop outside the back door and watching her with a level, less-than-friendly gaze.

Jake glanced over his shoulder. "Friend of yours?"

"No." She moved away so he could open the front door. She knew immediately from the chagrined change in Nick's expression when Priss joined them. Odd. What could it possibly matter to him whether she came to the wedding alone or with friends?

He moved down to the middle step, and Faith abruptly turned away, joining Priss on the sidewalk, walking alongside her with Jake a few feet behind. "That Nick Russo is one fine-looking man, isn't he?" Priss didn't wait for agreement. "Mary Ann over at the salon was a couple years behind him in school. She said he was a heartbreaker even back then. He had a different girlfriend every few months—I guess he was generous that way—until his senior year. He and Dan Wilson were dating Terry and Tammy Harlot—I mean, Harland—and, according to Mary Ann, the twins were planning a double wedding right after graduation. Nick was smart enough not to get trapped, but poor Dan..."

Faith had little sympathy to spare for poor Dan. Instead, she tried to recall everything she knew about Theresa Harland. She was prettier than her twin. She lived in Austin and had never married or had children. Occasionally she swept into New Hope for a visit, generally for some family event, and she almost always stopped in at the Baby Boutique to buy presents for Tammy's kids. She had always been friendly in a strangers-doing-business sort of way, and, as a customer, she was darn near perfect—she didn't shop often, but she bought a lot and paid cash. Faith had always liked her well enough.

Now, she thought with a scowl as they climbed the broad steps, she would never be able to see the woman again without thinking of Nick and the intimacies he'd shared with her.

At the top of the steps, the two oldest Russo grandsons held the door for them, and, inside the church, Michelle's brothers seated them. As she settled on the padded bench, Faith found her attention drawn to the groom's side of the church. There was the occasional friend, but most of the guests were family, many of them strangers from outside the area. They were Amelia Rose's family, but she would never know them. She would never share holidays with all those dark-eyed kids, would never experience what being a Russo meant. She would never see these people. They would miss out on so much by not knowing her, but she would miss more in not knowing them.

She would miss so very much more.

Chapter 5

The reception hall at the back of the church was packed, but the crowd didn't deter Nick as he circled the perimeter. He'd stood in the reception line between his mother and Michelle's maid of honor and shaken hundreds of hands. He'd had a piece of overly sweet cake, made a toast to the happy couple, sampled a little of his father's cooking and talked to just about every soul he'd ever known in New Hope—except one.

Now it was time to find that one. He knew she wouldn't be out there among all the other guests dancing. She wouldn't want to draw attention to herself, would probably think it improper in her condition, and he doubted that there was a man in town besides him stubborn enough to change her mind. Most likely she'd found a little table in a corner where she could pretend to be enjoying herself while escaping the notice of most guests. But so far he'd checked all four corners and all the tables in between and found no sign of her.

Maybe she had escaped and returned to the privacy of her old house. The couple she'd come with was still here, out on the dance floor, but that didn't mean she hadn't found a ride with someone else or maybe even walked home. But going home early wouldn't save her from seeing him. It wouldn't keep her from having to deal with him—at least one more time.

He was about to admit defeat when a movement outside caught his attention. Glass doors opened onto a small courtyard, the scene of smaller weddings in the spring when the roses were in bloom and the weather could be counted on to cooperate. There was a concrete fountain in the center and paths dividing small patches of grass on their way to the outer walls. Four wrought-iron benches faced the four points of the compass and made for cozy sitting when the day was nice.

Today was nice. Faith thought so, too. She was standing next to the fountain, hands clasped over her stomach, sunshine on her face. Her hair was pulled back, part of it caught with a shiny silver clasp, the rest left to fall past her shoulders, over the rich green of the dress that, once more, emphasized the delicate lines of her body rather than the swelling of her pregnancy.

He had known, even when she was nothing more than a vision disturbing his nights, that she was pretty. The simple word didn't do her justice today, but beautiful was too overpowering. She was lovely. Stunning. Breath-stealing.

For a long time he simply stood there at the door and watched her, even though he wanted to join her. He wanted to walk outside, close the door and shut out the rest of the world. He wanted to look at her—which would ensure, he thought without humor, that those damnable, haunting, erotic dreams would never leave him.

Erotic dreams of a very pregnant, shy, innocent woman. How many of the men he knew would think such a thing was even possible? But he was living proof. He'd wanted her even before he'd known she existed, and her pregnancy didn't change that. Right now, right this moment, no matter how crazy it seemed, no matter how wrong it was, he wanted her—wanted to look at her, talk to her, be with her.

He wanted to touch her, to connect physically with her. He wanted her.

At last, oblivious of the celebration going on behind him, he opened the door and stepped outside. His footsteps made little sound on the brick path. She didn't notice him, though, so when he spoke, he kept his voice quiet, his tone even.

"When Mike was about six or seven, he won a bunch of goldfish at a carnival here. He gave them to me for safe-keeping, but I had other things on my mind." He smiled briefly as he remembered what he'd found so distracting that day—namely, Mary Kate Thomas, who had recently returned to New Hope after a year in California. She had left all legs and pigtails, gawky, plain and shy, and had returned developed, with a capital double D. What a difference a year had made. "I put the fish in the fountain here and went off looking for my own amusement. When it was time to go, Mike and I came back for the fish, and . . . Well, the water was untreated, it was only a few inches deep, and it was a hot August day. He cried and put up such a fuss that I finally went to the store and bought him some more. Within a few days, they were dead, too. He hadn't fed them. He forgot about them."

She didn't speak, but she did manage a little smile. She hadn't smiled for him before, not a real smile, just little mocking gestures or ones so cool they could frost glass. He hadn't yet received one of those smiles like she'd given the cowboy before the wedding. But she wasn't with the cowboy, he reminded himself. The heartbreaker on the dance floor clearly belonged to him, and he to her.

He wondered what it felt like to belong to someone.

"You look nice."

"So do you." She returned the compliment, then took it away with her next words. "But what man doesn't look nice in a tuxedo?"

"Oh, come on, you can be honest. It won't go to my head. I look better than any other man here."

The little smile grew a bit. "Can we say 'arrogant'?"

"Not arrogant, darlin'. Confident."

The casual endearment chased away her smile, and wariness, coupled with weariness, darkened her eyes. How could a simple, meaningless little word cause her such discomfort? he wondered, then irritably answered his own question. Because it *was* meaningless. It could have just as easily been an insult or a who-gives-a-damn. People in their circumstances were supposed to use words like that and *mean* them.

"What are you doing out here?" he asked, forcing his voice into a friendly tone, trying to regain the connection they had so quickly lost.

She moved from the fountain to sit on the nearest iron bench. "It was loud inside."

"Yeah, we Russos are a noisy bunch. At least here we have room to spread out. You should see us all at Mom and Pop's house. I've seen the walls vibrate from the noise level. When I was a kid, my grandma Rosa—"

She interrupted. "Your grandmother's name is Rosa?"

Slowly he smiled. He hadn't noticed the coincidence before because he hadn't thought of that particular relative in years. "My great-grandmother. Rosa Marguerita DeGennaro Russo. She died when I was about nine. Hers was the first funeral I'd ever been to, and it put the fear of God into me. For the next year I was the best behaved kid Sacred Heart had ever seen."

"You Russos were always well-behaved kids. Your parents saw to that."

He shrugged. "Within limits. We all managed to get into trouble from time to time." He was *still* managing. But damned if he wasn't going to find a way to make the best of this latest problem.

"You were going to say something about your great-grandmother when you got distracted."

"Yeah, you've been distracting me a lot lately." He circled the fountain and sat down at the opposite end of the bench. Even though she immediately scooted away, it left only about four inches between them. "I'm sure that night last February you distracted me from every common sense lesson my mother, my father and my priest drilled into me."

"I did not!"

"Maybe not deliberately, but the result was the same. You were the first time—the only time—that I trusted in fate."

"That's your fault, not mine," she declared. "You were drunk."

The teasing forgotten, he faced her. "Didn't you know that?"

Color crept into her face as she stared pointedly away. "I knew you'd had a few drinks. I could taste—could smell it. But you didn't act . . ."

Taste. She had kissed him—or more likely, *he* had kissed *her*. He wished he could remember it, wished he could remember what she had tasted like. He wished he could remember how she had felt, how she had looked, whether he had satisfied her. There was no doubt in his mind that he had been satisfied. Hell, dreams from that forgotten night had brought him damned close to satisfaction countless times since.

"Why did you let me touch you?" he asked quietly. "Considering who you were, who I was, why the hell did you let me near? You knew my life was in Houston. You knew there could be consequences. Why didn't you send me away and lock yourself up tight in that house the way you've been doing all your life?"

She turned her head away from him. It was a sad day when she would rather have this conversation facing the glass doors and all the nosy people inside than look at him. "Maybe I did it because that was how I'd lived my whole life. Maybe I wanted to take a chance. Maybe, just once, I wanted to be like everyone else." Finally she glanced back at him. "*Why* doesn't matter. All that matters is that I did it—and, yes, I knew there could be consequences, and I'm dealing with them."

"No, Faith, *we're* dealing with them."

She shook her head. "I was the only one who went into this with both eyes open. You were too drunk to make a rational choice, too drunk to remember, once it was over, what we'd done. That excuses you from responsibility. It allows you to go home and pretend this never happened.''

Go home and pretend that he hadn't royally disrupted her life, that he hadn't left her vulnerable to mean-spirited gossip and narrow minds. Go home and forget that he had seduced a woman who had likely expected—and definitely deserved—much more than she'd gotten. Go home, absolved of responsibility, free of guilt, and never know about his daughter. Never wonder if she had his eyes or her mother's smile. Never question if everything was all right in her life, if people were blaming her for her father's sin, if she missed having a father, a family, like the other kids. Go home and never see either of them again, never think about them, never care about them.

She thought he was capable of doing that, but he didn't believe he was. ''I can't lie to myself like that, Faith. I know you think it would be for the best—''

''It *would* be best. You don't want to be a father. You've never wanted that. I want to be a mother. I had options. I could have told you no. I could have had an abortion. I could have given Amelia Rose up for adoption. But I chose to have her and keep her. You can't be held responsible for the results of *my* decisions.''

Uncomfortable because some part of him wanted to be convinced by her argument, Nick scowled. ''Under the law, I am responsible. You didn't get pregnant on your own. I was there for the fun part, even if I can't remember it. That means I have an obligation for the rest of it.''

She shook her head sadly. ''The rest of it *is* the fun part—raising her, being with her, loving her. But you don't see it that way. You see duties, responsibilities and obligations. I was raised by a woman who never wanted children, who looked at me and saw only duties and responsibilities. It's a tough way to live, Nick. It's a terrible burden to put on a little girl. I meant what I said the first night. No father at all is better than a reluctant father. I can't expose Amelia Rose to that. I won't.''

Feeling frustrated and helpless, he ran his hand over his hair. "So what am I supposed to do, Faith?"

She slid to the edge of the bench, then rose carefully to her feet. For a moment she simply stood there, then she gazed down at him and spoke with conviction. "Go home. Get yourself a new supply of condoms, lay off the booze and don't trust fate again."

She was half a dozen feet away when he stood up. "I'll see you again."

She didn't respond, didn't slow, didn't glance back at him.

"It's not that easy, Faith."

Reaching the wrought-iron gate, she released the latch and swung it open.

"Damn it, Faith." He watched her pass through the gate and out of sight, then shoved his hands into his pockets and swore again.

Maybe she was right. Maybe the lessons his father had taught him were too old-fashioned. Maybe they didn't fit today's world, today's solutions. Maybe it *would* be best if he did exactly what she wanted—went home and never had any contact with them again. It would definitely be the easy way out. He could keep his job and his condo. He could continue to fill his life with the friends who had become his second family. He could make things normal again—could live as if nothing had changed.

But something *had* changed. No matter how much he wished it weren't so, it was. Wednesday morning he had been unattached, accountable only for himself. Now he was a soon-to-be father. Kids made all the difference in the world, his sister Kathryn had once told him. Now he knew how right she was. Planned or unplanned, wanted or regretted, kids made a difference.

Maybe he could buy his way out. He could go back to his life, send a check every payday and try to ease his conscience that way. She insisted that she didn't need the money, and from what he'd seen, he believed it was true, but it would make him feel better. It would make him feel as if he hadn't completely abandoned his daughter, and it would probably satisfy Faith.

But would it satisfy Amelia Rose? How was he supposed to balance his obligations to her with Faith's desire to be left alone? Which was more important: Amelia Rose's right to have a father, reluctant or not, or Faith's right to make the major decisions about her daughter's life herself?

"You look like you could use a drink."

Nick slowly turned to accept the glass of champagne his father was offering. He took a sip, then cradled the chilled flute in his palm. "It was a great wedding, Pop."

"It was, wasn't it?" Antonio sighed with satisfaction. "I don't suppose it stirred up any urges in you."

"Only one—to run back to Houston just as fast as I can."

"What is it you find so appealing about that place—other than that it's not New Hope?"

Nick leaned against the fountain and considered the question. He'd known when he was in college that he wouldn't be returning home after graduation. He'd wanted to live someplace else, and Houston had won because his roommates were both from there. It was a growing city, vital, diverse, and that diversity extended to law enforcement. The city had a whole lot of everything going on, while police work in New Hope consisted mostly of writing traffic tickets and investigating vandalism complaints. In all the years he'd lived here, he couldn't remember a single rape or murder and only occasional assaults.

"I don't know, Pop. It's where I live. It's my home."

Antonio made a disapproving gesture. "No matter how many places you move to, your home will always be here. Your family will always be here."

In more ways than you ever suspected, Nick thought grimly. He wished he could confide in his father, wished he could ask his advice the way he always had as a kid when something troubled him. But until he had some idea of what he wanted, until he and Faith had reached some sort of agreement on his role in Amelia Rose's life, he couldn't tell anyone. It wouldn't be fair to Faith. It certainly wouldn't be fair to Antonio to say, "Hey, Pop, guess what? I'm about to become a father, but you can't see my little girl because her mother and I agreed that there's no place for me in her life."

"Listen, Pop..." He shifted uncomfortably. "I'm going to head back to Houston in just a bit."

"But the family is here," Antonio protested. "Everyone will be at the house. They're looking forward to spending some time with you."

"I know, and I'm sorry. It's just that there are some things I need to take care of."

His father offered another halfhearted protest before giving in. They returned to the reception hall, and Nick made the rounds, telling family and friends goodbye. He kissed his new sister-in-law, hugged his brother and enveloped his mother and father in a bear hug before leaving.

The house was unnaturally quiet when he let himself in. Upstairs in his old room, he changed from the tux into jeans and a T-shirt, left the rental hanging on the door for return to the formal wear shop and quickly packed his bag. After a stop at the living room desk, he left and locked up again, then made one last stop before heading south.

Faith was still wearing the pretty green dress, but the hose and shoes were gone. Barefoot and with her hair down, she looked too young to be pregnant, far too young to be so alone.

She didn't speak when she opened the door. She simply frowned so intensely that it made her eyes look a little damp.

"I'm going back to Houston now," he said bluntly. "If you want to get in touch with me...if you need to—" Breaking off, he held out the paper he'd taken from his father's desk. On it he had scrawled his home and work numbers, followed by his cellular phone and pager numbers, each clearly identified. She looked at it but made no move to accept it, so he leaned forward, claimed her hand, forced the paper into it and folded her fingers over it. "Call me." The words were shaky, more of a plea than a request.

Then he turned and walked away. As he did, he knew he was making a mistake. It was the wrong thing to do... but he did it anyway.

Clutching the banister with one hand, Faith slowly sank onto the third step. She should be pleased. Nick was returning to Houston, as she had asked, as she had insisted—to both him and herself—that she wanted him to. He was—for now, at least—out of her life. She had won the battle.

So why did she feel as if she'd lost the war? Why did she feel the same sense of abandonment that had swept over her that February morning when she'd realized that he'd slipped out of the house during the early morning hours? Why did she feel the same shock that she'd felt when Michael had announced the news of his brother's phony wedding? Why had some foolish part of her believed that he would stay, that he would find it impossible to walk away from his own little girl?

She gave a great sigh that sounded too much like a sob. Then suddenly tears were running down her cheeks. She hated tears, hated all the lonely times she'd given in to them, hated all the bleak memories they conjured up. She had cried often as a child—when the yearning for her mother was too much to bear, when other kids teased her, when their parents snubbed her, when Great-aunt Lydia was being unusually stern. She had taken refuge in her room, back in the darkest, coziest corner of her closet, and she had cried for all the injustices, all the loneliness, all the helplessness. One day when she was seventeen, when her friends were dating, having fun and leading normal teenage lives while she was living by standards as old as this house, she had decided to turn off the tears. Nothing was so bad that it needed crying over. Not the loneliness, not the emptiness, not even Great-aunt Lydia's death.

But this sense of loss—this was worthy of her tears. She had cried Wednesday when she realized that Nick had absolutely no memory of her and the intimacies they'd shared, and she would cry now for the last time. Any future tears, she decided with a damp smile, would be tears of joy.

Raising her hand to wipe her cheeks, she realized that she was still holding tightly to the paper he'd made her take. She smoothed it on her lap, then stared at the four phone numbers. Did he honestly think she would ever want to call him? After she'd spent three days convincing him that she and Amelia Rose didn't need him, did he really believe that a circumstance existed that might change her mind? Not when convincing him had been so stressful. Not when she knew now that she still needed a little convincing herself.

Getting to her feet was something of a struggle. When she made it, she took a deep breath, then padded barefoot down the hall to the parlor. There she dropped the paper atop the ash in the fireplace, struck a match and let it fall in the middle of the page. The center turned black first, then flames licked out to curl the edges. In a few seconds the fire burned out, leaving only a delicate square of ash that disintegrated as soon as she stabbed it with the poker.

"No more Nick," she said out loud, then patted her belly. "It's just you and me, babe."

The way it always had been.

The way it probably always would be.

Twenty-four hours and three hundred miles hadn't improved Nick's disposition any. He sat in a restaurant Sunday afternoon, bowls of tortilla chips and salsa in front of him, a frozen margarita in a tall glass beside them, and scowled at the world. He'd almost gotten lost twice on the way home yesterday—on a route that he'd traveled countless times in the past twelve years—because his mind had been preoccupied not by his destination but by the place he was leaving behind. Or, more precisely, the people he was leaving behind. He'd finally made it home around eleven, tired and badly in need of sleep, but instead he'd spent most of the night dozing fitfully, staring wide-eyed at the ceiling or dreaming—and it wasn't the same sweet, hazy eroticism he'd almost grown accustomed to in recent months. Oh,

Faith was in the dreams, all right, but so was a tiny dark-eyed girl as fragile as her mother and as familiar as his own self. Faith's daughter. *His* daughter. Sweet, little, helpless and innocent, just waiting to be loved.

Or rejected.

Like her mother.

Across the room the people he was meeting came through the doors. Marcy saw him first and touched Dave's shoulder, gesturing in Nick's direction. He watched as his former partner maneuvered his way between tables and up a short ramp that led to an elevated tier of seating. He didn't notice that, behind Dave, Marcy was pushing a stroller until they were only a few feet away, and the realization made his welcoming smile fade. When he'd called this morning to suggest that they meet for lunch, Marcy had said she would let the baby go home with her parents after church so the meal could be just the adults. Apparently her plans had fallen through.

This was just what he needed.

The hostess removed the chair on Nick's left, and Dave expertly wheeled his chair into the space. In the last year, since he'd gotten shot on a case gone south, he'd gotten pretty good at relying on wheels instead of his own unmoving legs. "You're back early," he said in greeting. "You didn't skip out on the wedding, did you?"

"Just part of the reception."

"Too much family?"

"You could say that." Reluctantly he turned his attention to the other arrivals. Marcy was freeing the baby from the stroller and transferring her to the high chair the hostess had brought. Marcy fussed over her, talking in a silly, high-pitched voice, kissing her on the forehead, teasing her, but the kid looked unimpressed and more than a little cranky. "Marcy."

She flashed him a smile. "Hey, Nick. Look, sweetie, it's Uncle Nick. You remember him. He's the one who doesn't like kids, so you'll have to be on your best behavior, okay?" Finally settling into her own chair, she gave a sigh.

"Wouldn't you know, the one Sunday I needed Mom and Dad to baby-sit, and they'd already made other plans. But she'll be all right. She'll eat a little, then probably take a nap."

The one who doesn't like kids. He hadn't realized his feelings on the subject were so well-known—and misunderstood. It wasn't that he didn't *like* kids. He liked them fine. He just liked for them to go home with someone else at the end of the day. He liked for them to be someone else's responsibility. He wouldn't have any problem at all with Amelia Rose if she were someone else's kid.

But she wasn't, and neither she nor Faith—through no actions of their own but by merely existing—were ever going to let him forget it.

"So tell us about the wedding."

Nick shifted his attention back to Dave. "It was a typical wedding."

His friend hooted at that. "Don't forget, I've met your family. Maybe it was a typical Russo wedding, but that's a whole world removed from your average ceremony. How many were there?"

"As many as would fit into the church and then some."

"All the out-of-town relatives?"

"Enough to fill this restaurant *if* they ate Mexican, which they would never do when there are plenty of good Italian places around." Beside Nick, the baby—Emily, too close a reminder to Amelia—made a fussy demand, which her mother stifled by sticking a bottle in her mouth. He watched her a moment before slowly forcing his attention to the question Marcy was asking.

"How does it feel to be the last single person in your family?" she teased. "To know that your kid brother and all six of your younger sisters are married while you still rattle around all alone in your empty little condo?"

"I like my empty little condo," he replied, and it was true. But he had to admit that he could understand the preference so many people felt for houses. Especially big houses, with plenty of room, a nice yard, a great veranda for enjoying good weather and... He frowned.

"Now that you're the only one left, your parents are going to devote themselves to finding you a mate," Marcy mussed.

"I'm perfectly capable of finding my own women. I've been doing it since I was fifteen."

"We've noticed. We thought by now you would've settled on one in particular," Dave said. "Suitable women aren't that hard to find, Nick."

Faith was suitable—too suitable for a man like him. She needed someone more like his brother. Michael prized the same things she did—family and friends, work, small-town life and small-town values, church on Sunday, quiet evenings, building a future.

And which of those things did *he* not value? His family and friends were the most important part of his life. He gave a hundred and ten percent to his job. He believed in—and practiced—honor, loyalty, decency and all those other old-fashioned values. He liked quiet evenings, and he certainly intended to have a future of some sort. It had been years since he'd been in church for anything other than a wedding, a christening or a funeral, but he still believed the teachings he'd learned there.

But none of those things made him a good candidate for the husband in Faith's life—which didn't matter anyway, since he already was the father in Amelia Rose's life.

They ordered dinner and talked about nothing in particular through the meal. After all the serious conversations of the past few days, it felt good to speak of nothing important. But the feeling faded when Marcy slung the diaper bag over one shoulder, balanced Emily on her hip and left for a major cleanup in the ladies' room. That was Dave's cue to ask quietly, "What's the problem?"

Nick avoided meeting his gaze. "Who said I have a problem?"

"Like I need to be told? I worked with you for more than ten years. I know you as well as I know Marcy. What's up?"

Nick looked around the dining room. Ordinarily he could look at a crowded room like this and barely notice anyone under four foot ten. Today every little kid in the place grabbed his attention. They were everywhere, so much a part of everyone's life except his. That was the way he wanted it . . . didn't he?

"Nick?"

Finally he faced Dave. "When Marcy got pregnant, what did you think?"

"That she was an idiot. That *I* was an idiot. I knew she wanted to get pregnant, but I'd said no. I didn't want kids, not like this." He gestured to the wheelchair. "I didn't want to be responsible for anyone else. I couldn't even take care of myself. I wasn't used to the chair yet. I didn't know how to get by. I wasn't even sure at the time that I wanted to live, and she was talking about having a *baby.* I said no. No way. And she got pregnant anyway."

None of that was really news to Nick, although they had never actually discussed it. He remembered Dave's anger over the bullet that had robbed him of the use of his legs and his resentment over the fact that Nick had stopped the man who'd shot him even as the bastard prepared to finish the job. He would have been better off dead, Dave had argued. He was of no use to anyone. He was a burden to Marcy—she deserved a whole man. He had been convinced that their three-year marriage couldn't survive the trauma, and for a time Nick had been convinced that their ten-year friendship wouldn't survive it, either. That was part of what had made him so determined to bring down the Sanchez brothers. Diego Sanchez had shot Dave, but Emilio had ordered it. Nick had spent nearly a year proving it, much of that time undercover with Phoebe masquerading as his wife. In another month or so, he would put in a little more time as the star witness against the Sanchezes, and then it would all be done with. With a little luck, more of the bad guys would be off the street and Dave would have some little bit of justice.

"When she told me she was pregnant," Dave went on, "I demanded that she have an abortion, but—you know Marcy."

He certainly did. Forget that Nick had stopped Diego from delivering the fatal shot or that the finest doctors at Houston's best trauma center had used their considerable skill to bring Dave back from the brink of death. It was Marcy who had saved him. With her love, determination and refusal to consider any other alternative, she had dragged him kicking and screaming back to life.

"We split up over it," Dave admitted. At Nick's startled look, he grinned sheepishly. "I never told anyone about it. She moved in with her folks for a week or so. She said that if I was going to be a part of her life, then I was also going to be a part of the baby's life. I finally gave in and said I wanted the baby, but it was a lie. I didn't. I kept hoping that it would turn out to be a mistake, that the pregnancy test was a false positive."

"When did you change your mind?" Nick asked, certain that he had. It was clear that Dave doted on Emily. He was as devoted to her as any father could be.

"Not until after Emily was born. They came home from the hospital on the second day, and Marcy was exhausted. She went to bed and left me to take care of this baby that I'd never wanted and didn't know what to do with. Well, Emily began to cry, and I didn't want her disturbing Marcy, so I went into her room and picked her up, and she stopped. Just like that." He gave a bemused shake of his head. "She snuggled in my arms, wrapped her hand around my finger and went to sleep, just as if she belonged there. Just as if she knew she would be safe there." He gave an embarrassed laugh. "It sounds corny, I know, but that's when it happened."

It did sound corny, Nick agreed—and believable, scary and reassuring. Maybe he wasn't so different from his father and the rest of his family, after all. Maybe, like Dave, actually holding Amelia Rose would make all the difference. Maybe he had the same paternal instincts as everyone else, but they just hadn't been awakened yet.

Maybe he could come to see her as more than a problem, much more than a duty. Maybe he could be as good a father to her as his own father had been to him. Maybe he could learn to appreciate the changes she would require in his life.

If he could convince Faith to give him a chance.

"What interest does a confirmed bachelor have in babies?"

Nick considered his answer. He could brush off the question with some remark about his sisters and their kids. He could simply say, "I don't want to talk about it," and Dave would accept that. Or he could tell the truth. Some part of him really wanted to, wanted the easing of conscience that came with confession. He wanted his old friend's opinion and advice—even though he knew what it would be. Don't think about it, Dave would say. Don't debate it. Just do what you believe is right, what you feel is right.

It was one circumstance in which what he thought was right and what he believed and felt was right were the same things. Taking responsibility for his actions was right. Being a father to his daughter was right. Giving her his name, protecting her from cruel gossip, being a part of her life—those were all right.

He and Faith might have gone about this all wrong. They might have skipped a few vital steps in the friendship-courtship-marriage-babies process, but it was never too late to make it right. It was never too late to give Amelia Rose the absolute best circumstances to grow up under.

He wasn't sure exactly what those circumstances would be. Ideally, she would be a part of a family, with a mother and father, three happy people, but that seemed a bit much to ask at this late date. Maybe just having both parents around—not married, not living as a family, but friends for the sake of their child—was the best she could hope for. However he and Faith resolved the issue, it meant one definite change for him: he had to move to New Hope. He couldn't be much of a father from three hundred miles away.

"So who's the mother?"

He looked sharply at Dave, who shrugged. "You have this troubled look. You're asking how I felt about becoming a father when I didn't want kids. You've never tried to hide the fact over the last twelve years that you don't want kids. It doesn't take a good cop—though I happen to have been one of the best—to figure it out. Who is she?"

"A woman I met in New Hope when I went home for Michael's engagement party."

"Jeez, Nick, you were only there—what, eight hours? She must be something."

Mentally comparing the women he'd dated here in Houston and Faith, he smiled thinly. She was as different from them as day from night. She was everything he'd always avoided, everything he didn't want in a woman—and he had no doubt that Dave would like her better than all the others rolled up in one.

"I assume you found out this weekend."

"The day I got home."

"Why didn't she tell you sooner?"

"She'd heard from someone in the family that I'd gotten married. No one ever told her that it was just part of the job."

"What's her name?"

"Faith."

Dave repeated the name softly, then chuckled. "I'm having trouble envisioning this. I can see you with someone named Barbi. Andi. Brandi. But I can't imagine you with a woman named Faith. What is she like?"

"She's . . . nice."

"Well, that's something new." He welcomed Marcy and Emily back to the table with a smile. "Honey, would you ever in your wildest dreams describe any of the women Nick's dated as 'nice'?"

She laughed as she settled in her seat, then cradled Emily in her lap. "Yeah, right," she said dryly. "Flashy, maybe.

Fluffy. Brain-dead on occasion. About the best I can say for them is that they're all gorgeous and they all have long legs and big boobs.''

So he liked a certain kind of woman. Blame it on Mary Kate Thomas. He'd been young and impressionable when he'd fallen for her. But Faith didn't fit the type. She was pretty, but not gorgeous. She was of average height with average legs, and the only reason her breasts were heavy now was because of her pregnancy. She was far from flashy and fluffy and was probably smarter than he'd ever hoped to be. And she was nice. Sweet. Innocent.

What had attracted him to her that night? He'd met women like her before without feeling the slightest desire. Had it been the booze? Would any woman have served just as well? He didn't think so. He'd been drunk plenty of times before, but never so drunk that he'd awakened the day after not knowing what he'd done, never so drunk that he'd seduced a total stranger who was the complete opposite of the women he preferred. So what was it? What mystery had compelled them both to do something so out of character?

"Has Nick met a new woman who's actually nice?" Marcy asked as she stroked her hand lightly over Emily's blond curls. The soothing touch made the baby yawn, made her eyes flutter shut.

Dave remained silent, leaving it to Nick to answer as he chose. "I meet lots of women," he said with a casual air.

"It's those dark eyes," she informed him. "They get to women every time."

"And here I thought it was my sparkling personality," he said drily. He didn't believe Faith had been seduced by a pair of dark eyes. It must have taken a hell of a lot more than that to persuade her to forget Lydia's teachings, to discard common sense and years of strict living and fall into bed with him. He would give almost anything to know what it was. What had tempted her? What had convinced her to take such risks with a stranger, especially with a stranger like him?

"Are you serious about this nice woman?" Marcy asked. "When do we get to meet her?"

"She doesn't live here." As for a meeting, well, that depended on Faith. On whatever decision they arrived at regarding their roles in Amelia Rose's life. On whether she was really serious about wanting nothing from him for either of them and, if so, whether he could persuade her otherwise. He was pretty sure he could. Hell, he had seduced her, hadn't he? He had somehow convinced her to give up her status for just one night as New Hope's resident saint and indulge in a few hours of passion. He could convince her to do what was right for the baby.

And if that failed, there were always legal remedies. No matter how much she wished it were so, *she* couldn't decide what, if any, contact he had with his daughter. The law gave him rights that she couldn't take away. He would hate to go that route, would hate like hell to force her into court, to air their disagreements publicly, but even the mere mention of it, he suspected, would convince her to be reasonable.

Marcy looked surprised. "You're going to end up marrying some woman back home in that dreary little town, aren't you?"

"New Hope's not so bad," Dave said. "It's the kind of town, Marce, that's so quiet and peaceful that people die of boredom. You know, somebody gets bored and kills 'em."

Nick gave his ex-partner a sardonic look. "It's not a bad place. Rush hour lasts about fifteen minutes. You can breathe the air without worrying what it's doing to your lungs. The cost of living is manageable. Everyone knows and looks out for everyone else. There isn't any crime of the sort that would make a cop wonder if someone's going to—" With another glance at Dave, he broke off, looking guiltily down at the table.

There was a moment of silence, then Dave broke it. "Shoot him," he finished. His tone was even and normal. "You're right. It's sounding better every minute. So answer the woman, partner. You planning to leave here and go back home?"

For a moment Nick didn't reply. The decision, made sometime over the last few days but recognized only now, was still too new, too strange, too old-fashioned. He didn't have to live in the same town to be a good father to his daughter. And what about his job? Was he really ready to give it up, to throw away all that he'd worked for the past twelve years and start over again? He might not even be able to get another job in law enforcement. He might wind up washing dishes in the kitchen at Antonio's. And the condo. He had a lot of money tied up in it. With the real estate market so unpredictable, it might sell the first day it was listed, or it might not sell for a year or more.

And the biggest obstacle of all: Faith. She wouldn't be pleased to find him back on her doorstep. Even though he had asked her—had damned near begged her—to call him if she needed him, he was willing to bet that hell would freeze over before he'd hear her voice on his phone. What if he gave up everything here and went back only to be shut out by her? Wouldn't it be easier to be a father in Houston without a daughter close by than to be living in the same town and be kept away from her?

Sure, it would be easier. But that didn't change his answer. He gazed at Marcy, looking so content and so motherly with Emily asleep in her arms, then at Dave, his closest friend and best partner for twelve years, and he shrugged. "Yeah, I'm going home. I'm leaving tomorrow."

Faith was sitting at the desk behind the counter when the bell over the door chimed. Swallowing a sigh, she glanced automatically at her watch. It was 5:25, and she had already started working on the bank deposit in preparation for going home. It had been a long day, and she was tired, and no matter how nice she always was to customers, she didn't want to sell one more thing today. Still, she put down the stack of bills she'd been counting and got to her feet, resigning herself to an additional fifteen or twenty minutes' work.

By the time she'd turned, the customer had reached the counter. He was standing there, arms resting on the rose-hued countertop, hair a little windblown, expression more than a little belligerent. He was prepared for the coldest of welcomes, and she wished she was prepared to give it, but she was too surprised. Too *pleasantly* surprised, she realized with dismay.

After a long, still moment passed, she finally spoke. "I didn't expect to see you again." But that wasn't true. She had known that he would come back on the pretext of a family visit but really to check up on Amelia Rose. She'd known that he felt the responsibility too deeply to stay away completely. She just hadn't expected his return so soon. She had figured that he would wait a while—that, in a week or two, he would call some family member and, in the course of the conversation, casually ask if Faith had had her baby yet. Then eventually duty, mixed with curiosity, would draw him back, and eventually she would have been ready to deal with him.

But she wasn't ready today, not after having cried because of him Saturday, not after having spent all day Sunday doing exactly what he had once suggested—curling up on the chaise in Amelia Rose's room with her giant teddy bear, occasionally drifting off and constantly feeling sorry for herself. It had taken a real effort today to pretend that things were normal, to force her life and herself back into some semblance of normalcy. Now here he was again, upsetting the tenuous balance she'd achieved, threatening to topple it completely.

"I'm harder to get rid of than that." Drumming his fingers on the counter, he glanced around the shop, then nodded toward the money spread out behind her. "Go ahead and finish that. We'll take it by the bank on our way to dinner."

She didn't move. "It's customary to *ask* someone to have dinner with you, not just assume that she will."

"Will you have dinner with me?"

She shook her head.

"That's why I didn't ask. That's why I'm not giving you a choice." Once again he gestured toward the desk. "Go on. Finish up there before some customer comes in. I'm hungry."

For a long time she continued to study him warily, then she glanced at the deposit. The work had to be done, whether he was here or not, whether she went out with him or home alone. Sinking into the chair, she reluctantly swiveled around so that her back was to him and picked up the stack of one dollar bills to count them again. It wasn't easy to concentrate, though, with him standing only a few feet away, with her hands trembling just the slightest bit, with her heart beating fast and loud enough to drown out the mental count she was trying to make.

Finally she set the money down and faced him once more. "What are you doing here?"

"Waiting to take you to dinner."

"Two days ago we agreed that you would go home and forget about—"

He began shaking his head, cutting her words off. "I can't think of anything we've agreed on, Faith." Then he deliberately added, "Except that we both want what's best for Amelia Rose."

"And *I* am the best judge of that."

"No, you're not. You're the best judge of what's good for you. I'm the best judge of what's good for me, and together we'll have to compromise on what's good for her." His shrug was expressive—a little arrogance, a little censure and no uncertainty at all. "If you wanted complete, undisputed authority over this child, you should have gone for complete anonymity down at the sperm bank. But that baby didn't come from a test tube. She's a part of me, and that gives me rights, sweetheart."

Turning cold inside, she tried to hide her fear when she asked, "Legal rights?"

His expression filled with annoyance. "*Moral* rights, Faith. She's my daughter."

"But you don't want a daughter. You never wanted children, remember?"

"A man's entitled to change his mind."

"Sure. And what about later, when this attack of conscience becomes so familiar that you don't even notice it anymore, when you get tired of the responsibility, when you discover that being a father is more than you'd bargained for? What will you do then? Change your mind again? Decide once again that you don't want to be a father?"

"No."

She waited for more, but that was all he had to say. *No.* As if he had no doubt. As if sometime in the past forty-eight hours, he had come to terms with the fact of her pregnancy and the changes it could make in his life. As if he'd seen the possibilities instead of merely the responsibilities. As if he really might *want* the child he had helped create.

She wasn't sure how she felt about that. On the one hand, it had broken her heart for Amelia Rose's sake to know that he would prefer that she'd never existed. On the other hand, his earlier rejection had left her the sole person of importance in their daughter's life. With him—and his family— out of the picture, that meant more of Amelia Rose's time, attention and affection for Faith. It meant *all* of Amelia Rose's love for Faith. But now he was telling her that she had to share.

It wasn't fair. He had a family, the biggest and best family in all of Texas, while she had no one. Why couldn't Amelia Rose be hers and hers alone? Why did she have to share when he already had more relatives than she could even imagine? Why did he have to want Amelia Rose, too?

Because she was his daughter, not just a part of him, but of his parents and grandparents, his brother and sisters and all their children. She was a Russo, and, to him—to all of them—that mattered.

Scowling hard, Faith turned back to her work. "I wish I *had* gone to the sperm bank," she muttered.

"It wouldn't have been nearly as much fun," he replied. His next words came from a spot just off to her left. If she let herself, from the corner of her eye she could see his boots, scuffed and damp, and the legs of his faded jeans. "I'm assuming that it *was* fun the way we did it."

Her cheeks turning pink, she made no reply.

"Come on, Faith, tell the truth. You enjoyed it, didn't you?"

She risked a sidelong glance. "It's none of your business."

"Darlin', I was there. That makes it my business."

"Then you should have stayed sober enough to remember."

He crouched beside the desk, more on her level. "I wish I had been sober. I wish I did remember." He looked and sounded achingly serious, causing her a moment's sympathy. What was it like to know you'd done something—something that affected not only your life but other people's lives, too—yet have absolutely no memory of it? How frustrating would that be?

Up front a rap on the window startled Faith, drawing her attention from Nick. It was Mr. Chambers, who owned the bookstore down the block. She returned his wave with a feeble smile and a wave of her own, then looked back at Nick. "Why are you here?" she asked quietly.

He rose to his feet and backed off as far as the counter before answering. "I wanted to tell you the news before the family grapevine spread it around town. I quit my job and put my condo up for sale." He stopped, took a breath and shrugged as if what he was about to say meant nothing at all. Then he said the words that threatened to change her entire life. "Welcome me home, Faith. I'm moving back to New Hope."

Chapter 6

"Welcome me home," he'd said, but that was a joke. Judging by her expression, Faith was the last person in the world who would want him back in town. She had actually turned so pale at the news that her eyes were the only bit of color in her face—beautiful blue eyes that were growing colder by the moment. She opened her mouth to speak, but couldn't find her voice. She started to rise from the chair, but couldn't find the strength.

"It wasn't an impulsive decision," he said, his voice calm and steady though no other part of him was. "I haven't been able to think of anything but Amelia Rose since last Wednesday. I knew even when I left Saturday that it was wrong. I think some part of me knew then that I'd be back."

"We don't need you," she whispered.

"Maybe you don't—" although he had a few doubts about that "—but you can't speak for her. She's my daughter. Kids need their fathers."

"But they adapt beautifully to not having them."

"Did *you* adapt beautifully? Can you honestly tell me that there was never a time in your entire life when you

didn't wish you had a father? That you didn't see your
friends with their dads and want one of your own? That you
never wondered what you had done, what was wrong with
you, that you didn't deserve a father?''

She didn't answer his question, not with words, at least.
But her eyes... She was a grown woman, independent,
about to give birth any day, and even now in her eyes was
just a little bit of longing, just a little bit of the lonely, unwanted girl she still protected inside. Undoubtedly, she had
needed a father when she was little. Some part of her still
wanted one now.

After a long heavy silence, he approached her, and she
pulled back, making the muscles in his jaw tighten. He
didn't back off, though. Reaching past her, he picked up the
stack of bills and started counting. ''Thirty-one,'' he said,
but she didn't move. ''Faith.'' He nudged her chair, turning her an inch or two until the desk stopped her. ''Let's get
this finished and go to dinner.''

Another moment passed before she picked up the pen and
made a note next to the listing for ones. It took only a few
more minutes to count out the rest of the money and balance the drawer, then another minute for her to fill out the
deposit slip. While she went into the storeroom for her coat
and purse, Nick shut off all the lights except the ones at the
front. They were shining on Christmas displays—toys and
holiday-themed clothes spread around a miniature tree dec-
orated with tiny foil-wrapped gifts. Right in the center was
a pair of footed sleepers, one in red with a matching Santa
cap, the other in candy cane red-and-white stripes. He'd seen
photos of assorted nieces and nephews in similar outfits,
usually posed on Grandpa Santa's knee. He wondered if
Faith would dress Amelia Rose in such an outfit. Maybe,
though he would bet his final paycheck from the Houston
P.D. that she would prefer something along the lines of the
velvet or satin and lace dresses. No doubt she realized that
infancy was just about the only time she would have much
control over her daughter's clothes, and she would choose
the fussy and frilly every time.

But that was all right. Eventually Amelia Rose would get the jeans and T-shirts, the scuffed sneakers and skinned knees. Her Russo cousins would see to that.

Faith joined him from the back, glanced outside at the rain and sighed. On his drive up here from Houston, he'd been happy that the temperature slide had stopped in the low forties so he wouldn't have to contend with sleet or ice. She looked disappointed that it hadn't gotten another fifteen degrees colder so she could have snow.

"I have to go by the bank," she announced unnecessarily.

"We'll drive."

"I'd rather walk."

He started to point out that forty-two degrees was chilly enough on its own, that forty-two degrees and wet from a three-block round-trip in the rain was downright uncomfortable, but he stopped himself. She was a bright woman— and a stubborn one. She knew the downside of a cold walk in the rain, and if he protested, she would no doubt remind him that he could go away and leave her to do it on her own, which she would prefer anyway. Instead he stepped outside and, while she locked the door, zipped his leather jacket and turned the collar up against the wind.

"Where do you want to eat?" he asked, prepared for a reminder that she hadn't accepted his invitation or an announcement that she much preferred to go home and eat alone. It came as a bit of a surprise when she actually replied.

"There's a barbecue place a few miles north of town."

"Johnny's." He knew the place, a cinder-block building painted red and set in the middle of a gravel parking lot. It was small, shabby and looked disreputable, but the always-full parking lot attested to its popularity. He usually managed a couple of meals there on every trip home, but on the last two, he hadn't even come close.

They walked a half block in silence, until they caught a red light at the intersection. There she glanced up at him. "Do your parents know you're back?"

"Not yet. I'll tell them tonight."

"Everything?" She sounded and looked more than a little anxious.

He brought her attention to the green light, then started across the street with her at his side. Going public would be one way to gain the upper hand, he mused. If everyone in town knew that he was the father of her baby, she would find it harder to push him away and impossible to avoid his family. From his grandparents on down through Lucia—and, when he returned from his honeymoon, Michael—all the Russos would be dividing their time between welcoming her to the family and pressuring her to make it official. He regretted the possibility of unleashing them on someone so innocent, but if Faith didn't come around to his way of thinking soon, he just might have to do it. In a situation like this, a man had to use whatever weapons he had available, and his family would be a formidable weapon.

"No," he replied in answer to her question. "Not everything." Then, just when she started to relax, he added, "Not yet. Mom will think it was the wedding—being home, seeing the family—that brought me back. Pop will think it was something he said, about Houston just being the place I lived while New Hope was always my home." He looked at the shops along the street as they walked. "I hate to admit it, but I think the old man was right. I liked Houston—I liked it a lot—but there's just something about being here, about seeing places I used to go when I was a kid, about remembering things I'd forgotten." It was a familiarity, a sense of belonging, but he didn't know if it came entirely from the town or, at least in part, from Amelia Rose. Fathers were supposed to share things with their kids. He knew almost as much about Antonio's growing-up years in New Hope as he did about his own. Someday, maybe Amelia Rose could say the same.

"I wouldn't know about that," Faith said stiffly. "I've always lived here."

"Have you ever wanted to live elsewhere?"

She paused in front of the heavy glass bank door, standing there even after he'd opened it and warm air rushed out to meet them. "No," she said at last. "I belong here. I can't say that about any other place." Turning, she walked into the brightly lit lobby, dropped the bag in the night deposit, then came out again. "So you're serious about moving back."

"I told you, I quit my job and put the condo up for sale."

"You quit just like that? No notice? No warning?"

"I had vacation time on the books. I'm using two weeks of it as notice, and I'll get paid for the rest." He shoved his hands into his pockets to warm them. "Under the circumstances, I didn't think I should delay by working out the notice."

"You don't need to be here. I have a telephone. I can call you when she's born."

He didn't respond. He knew as well as she did that any notification would come well after the fact and very, very grudgingly. He also knew—or, at least, suspected—that if he gave her time alone with Amelia Rose, his chances of making a place for himself in their lives would drastically lessen. Once she held their daughter in her arms, once she had the baby all to herself for hours of very private, very intimate one-to-one bonding, she would be more convinced than ever that neither she nor the baby needed him around. She would want Amelia Rose all to herself.

With a sigh of resignation, she changed the subject. "What will you do? What about a job and a place to live?"

"I'll put my application in with the New Hope P.D. and the Frisco County Sheriff's Department tomorrow. If they're not hiring, I can try the departments in the Dallas area. If worse comes to worst, there's always Antonio's. You pointed out yourself that Pop had always hoped one of us would follow him into the business."

"And you said yourself that you couldn't face doing it for a living."

"I could do it short-term. I can do *anything* short-term," he said with a shrug. "As for a place to live, I'll be staying at Mike's apartment while he and Michelle are gone. Then…" He shrugged again. Maybe by the time they came back, he would have moved into a nice old Victorian on Sycamore Street.

As they approached his truck, Nick pulled the keys from his pocket. Unlocking the passenger door, he pulled it open and waited for Faith to climb in. She looked at it suspiciously. "I'd really rather go home."

"And miss Johnny's ribs?"

"I prefer the brisket," she said absently. After a moment she met his gaze. "You know, there will probably be people there that we know."

He acknowledged that with a nod. "Are you ashamed to be seen with me?"

"Not ashamed."

"Just afraid people will remember that I was home for the party you gave Mike and Michelle, that they'll start counting the months?" He wiped away a drop of rain that splatted on the upholstery. "Darlin', you aren't going to be able to hide it too much longer. When was the last time you saw a Russo baby that didn't look damn near identical to all the other Russos?" He waited, but she didn't reply. It wasn't necessary. "People have already seen us together. They're going to take one look at Amelia Rose and they won't have to bother with counting. It'll be obvious who she belongs to."

Panic surged in her eyes. "She belongs to *me*," she insisted.

"I just meant—" He ran his fingers through his hair, and they came out wet. "Quit being so damned argumentative. You know what I meant. Now, are we going to dinner or not?"

The only thing that stopped Faith from saying *not* was the fact that Nick so obviously expected it from her. He thought that she would try once more to back out, that he would have to once more insist, so instead she said nothing. She stared at him for a moment, then slowly turned and raised one foot for the high step into the cab. His help was unexpected—and, she insisted silently to herself, unwanted. It wasn't anything intimate—a hand on her arm, another on her back—but any touch at all was unwelcome. Even if it did warm her in a way her coat couldn't possibly manage.

She settled into the seat, pulled the long folds of her coat around her and, with a scowl through the rain-streaked window, slammed the door. He was scowling, too, as he moved around the front of the truck, then climbed behind the wheel.

After he made a U-turn on the unusually quiet street, they drove the few miles to the restaurant in silence. There wasn't a big crowd at Johnny's, she noticed, blaming the weather. Who wouldn't rather be snug and dry at home, eating a big bowl of steaming homemade beef stew, on a night like this? *She* certainly would...wouldn't she?

There was no hostess awaiting them inside, just Johnny's wife at the cash register. She greeted them with a Texas-size smile and a cheeriness that Faith couldn't come near matching on her best day. "Sit wherever you want," she said with a wave around the dining room. "If you want the buffet, you can help yourself, and if you want to order off the menu, the waitress will be around in a bit."

Faith slipped out of her coat and hung it on a rack near the door, then wandered past the buffet table. She had voiced a preference for brisket earlier, but now that she was faced with a wider selection, she had to admit that the ribs did look good. So did the chicken, the sliced pork, the Polish sausage and everything else in the stainless-steel pans. She did love good barbecue, she thought with a sigh.

"Do you want to go someplace else?"

She went to join Nick, who was waiting near the closest booth. "No, this will be fine."

"You just looked a little..."

"Dazed? I see all this food, and my eyes glaze over." She carefully maneuvered onto the bench, pushing the table a few inches away to accommodate her stomach. As lean as he was, Nick could do without the extra space. "Dr. Austin told me at my last checkup to watch my weight. I'm sure he didn't mean eat here and watch it go up even higher."

"How often do you see him?"

"Monthly at first, weekly now. Every Tuesday until I pop."

His look was just short of teasing and it almost made her smile. "Until you 'pop'?"

"That's the proper medical term for giving birth—at least, in Dr. Austin's office." Rubbing the spot on her stomach where Amelia Rose most frequently aimed her kicks, she blew out her breath. "Sometimes I feel as if I *will* pop, literally. I don't think my skin could possibly stretch enough to gain one more pound. I can barely squeeze behind the steering wheel of my car, and all those maternity clothes that were way too big four months ago are now stretched to the limits. I'm ready for this to happen."

"Are you doing natural childbirth?"

"No." Her tone was even, her manner deliberate. "I don't need the pain or the partner."

"I'd like to be there anyway."

For a long time she simply looked at him. She understood his request. Wasn't that desire to be there from the very beginning a small part of what had caused the medical community to do away with the practice of sedating mothers in favor of allowing them to be awake and alert during birth? Hadn't that same desire led to a policy of admitting fathers to the delivery room? Millions of fathers had done it; millions more would in the future. But Nick? In the room with her when Amelia Rose was born? The idea made her squeamish. "What with the nursing staff," she said flatly, "there will be enough strangers in the room as it is. I don't need one more."

"But I'm not a stranger," he politely observed.

"For all practical purposes, you are."

"Then we'll have to spend the next few days remedying that."

She started to protest, but the arrival of the waitress forestalled her. She ordered the buffet and a pop, went to the steam tables to fill her plate, then came back to wait. Nick had also ordered the buffet and joined her with his own dinner only a minute later.

"I thought you preferred the brisket."

She looked down at her plate. The thick slices of brisket were there, somewhere underneath the Polish sausage, the chicken legs and the beef ribs—and all that was in addition to baked beans, cole slaw and a mound of potato salad. "This is why the doctor told me to watch my weight," she said, indulging in a moment's contemplation before reaching for the first sauce-dripping rib.

"Has it been hard?"

"Watching my weight?"

"Being pregnant alone. Having no one to help out."

She chewed a bite of tender rib meat, then wiped her fingers on a napkin. "What kind of help do you think a pregnant woman needs?"

"Someone to lift things for you. To help around the house and the shop when you're tired. Someone to rub your feet when they swell or your back when it hurts." He shrugged. "Someone to just hold your hand once in a while."

His words made her uncomfortable, because she had spent those few days between finding out that she was pregnant and hearing that he was married imagining just that sort of togetherness. She'd built an elaborate fantasy in which she told him about the baby and he, with a perfectly good excuse for not contacting her, was thrilled, in which they were immediately married and he did all those things often, especially the back rubbing and the hand holding. The dream had brought such pleasure while it lasted, and it had died a hard death. The mere mention of a back rub— the mere thought of *his* hands on *her* skin—was enough to bring it back in all its bittersweet futility.

"There are plenty of people I can ask if I need help moving heavy things," she said, being deliberately obtuse. "I have part-time help at the shop. I don't like having my feet rubbed, and holding hands is juvenile."

"My folks have been married nearly forty years, and they still hold hands."

Forty years. She used to dream about such stability, about living literally happily-ever-after with her own Prince Charming. It was those damned fairy tales that had gotten her into trouble in the first place. They had made her believe in magic. *Nick* had made her believe in magic... and then he had destroyed that belief.

Now she dreamed about having a good mother/daughter relationship. She dreamed of finding satisfaction with her status as an unwed mother, with her house too big for only two people to fill, with her bed too empty ever to provide a baby brother or sister for Amelia Rose. She dreamed of finding happiness with her tiny family of two until Amelia Rose was grown and married and having babies of her own. She dreamed of not minding the long wait, twenty years or more, until she had a real family. Twenty years.

"That's a long time," she murmured.

Nick misunderstood, thinking she was referring to his parents' marriage. "Not for a Russo. You know there's never been a divorce in the Russo family?"

"Then there must be some very unhappy marriages." She made her tone a little scornful, but she didn't feel it. Like any intelligent adult, she had a good idea of what went into making a marriage work, and she respected anyone willing to try. Divorce was so much easier than commitment. Leaving was so much less trouble than working out the rough spots, compromising, giving and taking, giving in without giving up.

"Probably a few," he admitted, "but none that I know of personally. I think they go into it with a different attitude. A lot of people get married thinking, 'If it doesn't work out, I'll get a divorce and try again.' My family gets married with the intention of staying married, forever and ever. They've got more invested in it. They need to make it work."

Faith polished off another rib, wiped her hands, then sprinkled a few grains of salt on the potato salad before scooping up a forkful. "I can't tell you much about the Harper philosophy on marriage," she said with a touch of sarcasm. "I assume my mother's parents were married at least sixteen years. I don't know if my mother ever married at all. Great-aunt Lydia never did. She thought men were evil and sex was an abomination to be endured only for the purpose of procreation."

"And what do you think?"

"Some men *are* evil."

He grinned. "About sex."

As she studied him, his grin widened. He was too appealing, too handsome, too wickedly sexy, for a woman to resist. Even if magic did exist only in fairy tales, it was no surprise that she had willingly thrown away a lifetime of teachings for a little of his attention. Those few brief hours had made her feel things she'd only dreamed about. They had given her pleasure, passion and hope for a future, for love, for a family. They had given her the first truly intimate connection she'd ever made with another human being and had made her feel alive, desired, special, normal.

And they had given her the second intimate connection she'd made with another person: Amelia Rose.

"It was okay," she said grudgingly.

"Okay?" He feigned a crestfallen expression. "That's all? It was *okay?*"

"It was very nice."

"You do wonders for my ego, lady." Abruptly, he sobered. "Tell me about that night."

She thought about telling him everything, all the details, all the intimacies. How tired she had been after the party, how surprised she had been to walk into the kitchen and find him there, looking even more done-in than she'd felt. How she had sat down across from him at the table and they had talked a little. Her usual shyness in dealing with a man had been compounded by who the man was. Nick Russo had a reputation in New Hope as a charmer, a ladies' man, a threat to any woman who might cross his path. She had watched him earlier in the evening, making lashes flutter and hearts skip beats. Every woman there except her, it seemed, had flirted with him, and he had responded to them all.

But, alone in her kitchen, he had seemed like just a nice guy—handsome and sexy, yes, but genuinely nice. She hadn't hesitated more than a heartbeat in offering him one of her guest rooms. She hadn't thought more than twice about the wisdom of such an offer, about safety or propriety. He was a Russo, for heaven's sake. He was Antonio's son, Michael's brother, a dedicated cop.

She could tell him how she had shown him upstairs to the front bedroom, how she had been folding down the covers when he'd bumped her, knocking her against the iron headboard, catching hold of her arms to steady her, then moving his hands to the rail to trap her. She could tell him about the absolute shock that had passed through her at the contact and how he must have felt something, too, because a purely impersonal touch had instantly become very personal, a caress, a gentle stroking, and it had led to a kiss that left them both dazed.

She could tell him everything, and when she was finished, he would know, but he still wouldn't remember. He wouldn't feel any of the feelings he had felt that night. He wouldn't recall his desire or the gentle coaxing or the incredible sensation of *oneness* when he'd finally taken her. He would know in the same dry, secondhand way he knew about history or about crimes that took place before he arrived on the scene. He would know, but he wouldn't *know*.

When moment after moment passed without her answer, he spoke again. "You can't blame me for being curious, Faith. For questioning how in the hell I managed to forget a night with you. For wondering what made a woman like you do what we did with a man like me."

"I think we've had this conversation before," she began slowly. "But tell me again, what do you mean, a woman like me?"

He looked uncomfortable. "A nice woman. A woman who doesn't engage in casual affairs. The kind of woman that men marry. *Not* the kind of woman who goes to bed with strangers."

Having eaten as much spicy food as either she or Amelia Rose could bear, Faith pushed her plate away, then eyed the homemade banana pudding at the near end of the buffet table. Pudding couldn't be bad for her. After all, it had milk and fresh fruit, two items that Dr. Austin had encouraged her to eat plenty of. Then, with a sigh because she knew better and she really was too full, she turned her attention back to Nick. "I'm not the kind of woman who normally attracts a man like you," she said flatly. "That's what you're saying, isn't it?"

Discomfort made him shift uneasily. Embarrassment brought a flush to his cheeks. "No, it's not—" Breaking off, he muttered what sounded like a curse, then confessed. "All right. You're right. You're not my usual type. You're too smart. You're too *real*. But that's not what I was saying. It's for damned sure that I'm not your type, either, but you weren't drunk that night, so you can't blame it on that. So why in the hell did you let me stay? Why did you let me…" Impatiently, he gestured toward her stomach.

Not her type, she thought with just a little wistfulness. How could it be so obvious to him that handsome, charming, sexy, nice and passionate wasn't her type, when she thought it was? Exactly what did he think she deserved? Some little geek who favored bow ties and double-knit slacks, who greased his hair better than his car and fixed his broken eyeglass frames with masking tape? Some shy loner who couldn't speak to any woman but his mother to save his life? Or maybe no one was her type. Maybe he thought she'd followed in the footsteps of the wrong female relative. Instead of being easy and loose like her mother, maybe he thought she should have emulated Lydia and lived out her life a bitter, dried-up, untouched old prune.

"Maybe I let you—" she mimicked his gesture "—because I wanted to. Because I wanted *you*. Maybe you've got all it wrong, Nick. You've been blaming yourself for seducing me, but maybe I seduced *you*. You were drunk." She smiled coolly. "You were easy. When would I ever again have had such an opportunity? This weekend at the wedding? You wouldn't have even looked at me if I hadn't been pregnant, if I hadn't fainted in front of you, if I hadn't—"

"That's not true," he interrupted. "I would have looked . . . but I wouldn't have touched. I learned the difference a long time ago between the having-fun-with kind and the marrying kind, and, darlin', you are definitely the marrying kind."

And that was *definitely* not his type. "What does it matter?" she asked irritably. "You keep asking all these questions, but what the hell does any of it matter? We did what we did. It's over and done with. End of story." She dropped her napkin on the tabletop and scooted to the end of the bench in preparation for standing up. His next words stopped her in place.

"It's not the end, Faith. Not as long as our daughter lives, or our granddaughter, or *her* granddaughter. This story will never have an ending. *We'll* never have an ending."

"What are you going to do now that you're home?"

Before answering his father's question, Nick folded his hands over his stomach and leaned back in his chair. It was lunchtime Tuesday, and so far the morning had gone well. His earlier business had been successfully taken care of, and his parents had been thrilled to hear that he was back home to stay. It was a pleasant change from Monday evening and Faith's reception. "Go to work for the New Hope Police Department."

"You put in an application?"

"This morning. Got hired before I left the building. I'll be starting in two weeks in patrol, since that was the only opening they had, but eventually I'll work my way back up to detective."

"You know, you could come to work here and make your father happy," his mother suggested. "It would mean a lot to him to have at least one of you kids working in the business."

Antonio snorted. "She means you could come to work here and make *her* happy. She worries about you being a police officer. She says it's too dangerous." To his wife, he said, "At least it'll be safer for him here. We don't have much crime, and there's never been an assault on an officer in the whole history of the town. So what changed your mind, son? Three days ago you're telling me that Houston is your home, then you call this morning and tell us that you've moved back to New Hope to stay. What happened?"

"It was the wedding, wasn't it?" his mother asked. "Seeing your brother and Michelle get married, visiting with all the relatives, seeing how your nieces and nephews have grown up hardly even knowing who you are. It made you realize what you were missing, didn't it? It made you realize that New Hope will always be your home."

"It was a combination of things," he said noncommittally. The reason, of course, was one he couldn't yet share with her or his father, but the time was coming—and quickly. Amelia Rose's due date was only five days away. Then they would know—then he would tell—regardless of whether things were settled with Faith.

Faith, damn her blue eyes. She kept trying to pretend that he was going to go away and leave her alone. Last night, when he'd taken her back to the shop after dinner, she had primly thanked him for the meal, told him goodbye again and pretended not to hear when he'd told her that he would see her the next day. Well, it was the next day, nearly noon, and he hadn't made good on his promise yet, but he intended to. As soon as he finished visiting with his parents, he planned to go to the Baby Boutique if for no other reason than to remind Faith that he was still around. Sooner or later she would accept the fact. She would get used to the idea of him being there. She might even start to miss him when he wasn't.

Yeah, he thought with a scowl, and she would die before admitting it.

"It's a good thing all the family's gone," his mother said, starting to rise from her chair. "I'll go home, change the sheets, give your old room a quick cleaning and—"

He extended his hand to stop her. "Mom, it's not necessary. I'm going to be staying at Mike's place until he and Michelle get back. By then, I'll have found a place of my own."

"Don't be silly. If you don't start your job for two more weeks, then you won't have a paycheck for nearly a month. There's no need for you to be spending your money—"

Antonio laid his hand on his wife's arm and tugged her back into her seat. "He's a grown man, Luisa," he gently reminded her. "He's too old to be living at home. He's used to being on his own. And he's perfectly capable of budgeting his money so that he doesn't get into a bind."

She gave both of them dismayed looks. "No child of mine will *ever* be too old to live in my home."

"I'll be around, Mom," Nick said with a chuckle. "You'll see so much of me that you'll get tired of the sight of me."

"That'll never happen," she insisted. "From the moment you were born, when the nurse laid you in my arms, I've always found such pleasure just looking at you. You're my first, my oldest. You've always been special because of that."

He wondered if *he* would feel that way, if Amelia Rose would always be special because she was the first. When she had brothers and sisters—something he fully intended, even if Faith did seem resigned to having only the one—would he always feel a little differently about her?

"Even as a baby, you would do that—go from smiling to serious in the space of a heartbeat," Luisa said, reaching out to pat his hand. "What were you thinking just now?"

Before he could come up with some answer other than the truth, one of the waitresses showed a party of young women to a table on the opposite side of the dining room. He wouldn't even have noticed them if it hadn't been for a flash of long light brown hair and the unnatural—but somehow still graceful—gait of the woman in the middle. Faith and friends. He was surprised that she would set foot in the Russo family restaurant knowing that he was back in town. It must have been someone else's idea, and she hadn't found a way to politely decline.

Following his gaze, Luisa twisted in her seat to look. Amused, she made a chastising sound. "New Hope has its share of unattached women, but those girls aren't among them. They're all either married or about to be married. In fact, they're here celebrating Wendy's birthday and her engagement to Travis Donovan." She gave him a sly look. "See, some sons don't mind making their parents happy by settling down."

"I *am* settled," he said absently before pointing out, "Faith isn't married. She's about as unattached as a woman can get."

The odd silence at the table finally drew his attention back to his folks. They were looking at him, his father's expression blank, his mother's puzzled and just a little worried. "Unattached?" his father repeated. "She's *pregnant.*"

He glanced back at the half-round booth as the women pushed and pulled the table to one side to make room for Faith on the other, and he grinned. "Yeah, it's kind of hard to miss."

"Nick, Faith isn't that sort of girl," his mother said quietly, seriously, making him look at her once more.

Normally, from his mother "that sort of girl" meant exactly what some people in town thought Faith was: easy. Shameless. Immoral. In her kitchen Thanksgiving afternoon, Luisa had implied that Faith *was* that. She should be ashamed of herself, Luisa had declared—and so should the man responsible for her condition. If she'd known she was talking about her own son... He cowardly backed away from the thought and asked, "What sort, Mom?"

"The sort that you like. She's sweet and kind and generous. Everyone loves her. You couldn't ask for a better friend. She'd do anything for anyone."

Interesting. He'd never known that his mother described the women he dated with the same judgmental phrase that

she used for the local shameless hussies. Keeping his voice
carefully steady, he commented, "You make her sound like
a saint."

"She practically was," Antonio answered. "At least, until
she got pregnant."

And that had changed her in his father's eyes, and his
mother's, as well. How many other people had changed
their opinions of Faith because of what he had done? Exactly how much had those few forgotten hours cost her?

"So are you warning me away from her because you like
her so much or because she was so foolish as to get pregnant without getting married first?"

Both parents looked more than a little embarrassed as his
mother answered, "Faith is a good woman, but she's different. That old woman who raised her had such strict rules.
She was cold, rigid, unforgiving. She was so obsessed with
keeping Faith from repeating her mother's mistake that she
never allowed her a chance to be a normal child. She's never
had much experience. She never dated much and never had
a serious boyfriend."

"She's old-fashioned, Nick." His father took over. "Naive. If you paid her attention, she would likely think it
meant something when everyone else would know you were
just having fun."

Was that what had happened nine months ago? he wondered. Had she believed their time together was something
special, something real? Had she thought he would call her,
come back to her, build a serious, maybe even permanent,
relationship with her?

"She's vulnerable," Antonio continued. "She's not
someone you amuse yourself with. It would be too easy to
hurt her. Besides . . . there's the baby."

"No one knows who the father is, not even her friends."
His mother gestured toward the table of women, and Nick
glanced that way. If Faith had noticed him yet, she hadn't
let it show. The blond woman beside her, though, was
looking his way. She had introduced herself as Wendy that
first day in the shop, and she had stayed with Faith when

she'd fainted, watching her, fussing over her and, he would bet from her expression, accepting her confidences. Maybe none of the rest of them knew he was the father of Faith's baby, but Wendy did.

Turning back to his parents once more, he forced a laugh. "What is it with you guys? I make a simple statement that Faith isn't married and you automatically assume that I'm going to use her for a little fun, then break her heart. I promise you, I'm not the least bit interested in that." God's honest truth. He was interested in marrying her, in making a home with her for their daughter, in making a future for all three of them.

It hurt just a little, though, that the possibility that he could be serious about Faith had obviously never crossed his parents' minds. That they automatically believed his only interest in a sweet, kind, generous woman was in using her for his own entertainment, then discarding her. That, in spite of their disapproval of the choices she'd made, they felt the need to protect her from him. That they had so little respect for him.

It hurt even more to know that, when he told them the truth, he would be proving them right. He had used Faith, had taken advantage of her, had seduced her, and then literally forgotten her. It hadn't been a conscious decision—he hadn't voluntarily decided to wipe an entire evening from his memory—but he had to wonder, if he hadn't been so drunk, if he would have done the same thing. If he'd been sober—or reasonably so—would he have made love with her? He would like to think the answer was no, that he would have a little better sense than that. But he had been alone a long time back in February, and she was an incredibly pretty woman, so fragile and feminine. If she had shown the slightest interest, if, as she had claimed last night, she had felt the same desire he obviously had...

He would have made love to her, and he would have returned to Houston the next morning, assuming that it was over, that it had been nothing more than what it appeared to be: two mature adults choosing to indulge themselves in one night of good sex. He probably wouldn't have called her—probably, he was ashamed to admit, wouldn't even have given her another thought. At least, until time for the wedding came, bringing with it the possibility of another damned near anonymous night of sex.

He was no better than everyone thought the stranger who had abandoned their sweet, innocent Faith was.

Rising from the table, he gave his mother a kiss and his father a hug. "I have to take care of a few things," he said, keeping his gaze focused tightly on them and away from the booth across the room. "Thanks for the lunch, Pop. It was great, as usual. Mom, I'll call you."

It was nearly five o'clock when Beth pulled a stack of hangers from Faith's hands and gave her a little push toward the storeroom. "Do yourself and the baby a favor. Go home early. Build a fire, curl up in that big old rocker and dream away the evening. No one else is going to be out in weather like this. I can close up and do the deposit."

Faith glanced out at the street. It had been dreary all day, either raining or threatening to do so, and it was just cold enough to make Beth's suggestion tempting. She didn't know why the weather today had made her so blue. She liked cloudy, rainy days as much as she liked bright sun, snow, thunderstorms and spring breezes. She never got depressed over the weather.

Which meant it probably wasn't the weather. It was probably the fact that she was only days from Amelia Rose's scheduled appearance. The closer she got to her due date, the heavier and clumsier her body seemed to get. This morning she hadn't even wanted to get out of bed. Even though she'd slept a solid eight hours, every part of her being had ached for another hour of rest—or two or four. Getting dressed had exhausted her. Walking down the stairs had been a chore. She had opened the shop, gone into the storeroom to put up her coat and purse, and had wound up resting on the couch until her first customer had sounded the bell over the door forty-five minutes later.

But it probably wasn't that, either. Amelia Rose's due date being so close meant that she could arrive at any time now, Dr. Austin had announced at this morning's checkup. The date, he'd needlessly reminded her, was merely an estimate. The baby could be several days early or several days late. She could even be born tonight, and that was an event to anticipate. It was cause to be happy, not down.

She was probably blue, she admitted grudgingly, because here it was nearly five o'clock and, except for a glimpse at lunch, she hadn't seen Nick all day. She hadn't acknowledged him last night when he'd said he would see her today, but somewhere deep inside, she had been waiting for him all day. Every time the bell had sounded, she had expectantly looked up, only to be disappointed.

It wasn't that she *wanted* to see him, she quickly insisted. Hadn't she tried her best to talk her friends out of going to Antonio's on the off chance that he might be there? Her days were much more peaceful without his intrusions. It was just that she had *expected* him to come, and that was why she was reluctant to follow Beth's suggestion. Two of his three visits to the shop had been right at closing time. What if that was when he intended to come today?

He knew where she lived, she thought with a frown, and even if he didn't, Beth would be happy to give him directions. If he really wanted to see her, he could come to the house. That was where she would prefer such a meeting to take place, anyway, away from curious eyes.

"Earth to Faith," Beth teased in a singsong voice. "Go and get your coat, go out the back door, and go home."

"All right," she said, smiling when she saw the surprise in her assistant's eyes. "You thought I would say no, didn't you? That'll teach you to make such an offer again."

Squeezing around the cardboard carton of sleepers that she'd been unpacking, she made her way into the back. There had been a time, she thought with a sigh, when pulling on her coat had been a simple task—one arm here, the other there, voilà. Not so anymore. One arm went here quite easily, but getting the other there required effort, and voilà was definitely out. The coat, once roomy enough to make her look like an underfed waif, just barely fit across her stomach. Fortunately for Amelia Rose, the portion of Faith's anatomy that received exposure was well-insulated by nature.

"Thanks a lot, Beth," she called as she lifted her hair free of the collar, then slung the strap of her handbag over her shoulder. "I'll see you tomorrow."

Beth popped into the open doorway. "Take care. And if anything happens tonight, let me know."

With a wave, Faith let herself out the back door, locked it securely behind her, then crossed the small parking lot to her car. She was looking forward to a nice, quiet evening. She would put on her favorite flannel nightgown and fuzzy slippers, heat a bowl of homemade stew in the microwave, build a fire, tuck herself into Amelia Rose's rocker and catch a comedy or two on TV. At nine o'clock, when the not-for-family dramas came on, she would drag herself up the stairs, go to bed and sleep the night away.

Unless, as Beth had put it, anything happened.

The thought made her stomach a little queasy. She was excited, sure, but underneath all those quivers of anticipation and all that incredible longing to hold her baby in her arms, there was fear, too. Would Amelia Rose take her time, allowing Faith to get herself to the hospital with a little dignity, or would she be impatient to see the world? Would Faith be able to manage on her own or—after all her insistence that she didn't need anyone else—would she have to ask for help? Wendy had told her to call her the moment labor began and she would drop whatever she was doing and rush over. But Faith wasn't one to ask for help, not unless it was absolutely unavoidable. And if she *was* going to ask for help, didn't she sort of owe it to Nick to ask him?

Wriggling into the front seat, she started the engine and switched on the windshield wipers, then waited for the heater to send welcomed warmth into the small car. She hated to admit it because she loved her friend dearly, because she'd spent so much time trying to convince Nick that there was no place in their lives for him, and because it just seemed such a weak *female* thing, but she suspected she would feel more comfortable calling Nick than any one else, even Wendy. He was a cop, trained to handle the unexpected, calm in a crisis. He was Amelia Rose's father, and he wanted to be there when she was born.

And, no matter how badly things had turned out, no matter how deep her disillusionment, he was still the man who had once, for a very short time, made her believe in magic.

He was also, she pointed out to herself in a no-nonsense manner, the man who had promised to come by and see her today—the same man who hadn't shown.

The drive home was short and easy, but long enough to get her mind on the comforts that awaited her there. She was anticipating them so much that she almost didn't notice the pickup parked on the curving brick drive. She couldn't miss the sudden butterflies in her stomach, though, or the perceptible lightening of her mood. Damn him, he shouldn't affect her like this. After the past nine months, he shouldn't have this sort of power over her. He shouldn't be able to leave her hanging all day long, then brighten her entire day by showing up at his convenience at her house.

But he could. God help her, he could.

She parked at the end of the veranda in her usual place and tried to ignore the rain as she climbed the steps to the roof's protection. He was sitting in the wicker rocker, apparently oblivious to the chill, her evening paper open but unread in his lap.

"You're home early," he needlessly announced.

She approached him, clutching her keys tightly in one hand, brushing the rain from her hair with the other. "Beth thought it would be a good idea if I came home early and let her close up."

"Funny. I made the same suggestion a few days ago and you acted offended."

"I didn't act offended."

"Yes, you did. You launched into a tirade about how complete strangers think they know what's best for you."

She almost smiled at the image his words conjured. "I might have been frustrated or exasperated or even a little moody, but I do not indulge in tirades. I'm too polite."

He did smile, a flash of white in the quickly darkening evening. "You are, huh?"

"Isn't that what they say about me? 'Sweet Faith. She's such a nice girl, so well mannered, so polite.' I don't raise my voice, I don't lose my temper, and I'm never rude—except on occasion with you, but that's your fault."

"Why, you're just about perfect, aren't you?" He rose from the rocker, took the keys from her before she realized he was coming close and unlocked the front door. After opening it, he waited for her to pass through, and when she did, he politely contradicted her. "The old crones said you were rude to them."

The old... She smiled in the dimly lit hall as she shrugged out of her coat. Misses Agnes, Ethel and Minny. But as soon as she recalled the incident when she was, indeed, rude to them, her smile faded. "They suggested that it was my Christian duty to give Amelia Rose up for adoption. They said I couldn't possibly give her the kind of home she deserved, that there were so many suitable couples out there who would raise her in the proper environment. They said it was the least I could do for her after the shameful way I'd brought her into the world."

Nick took her coat and hung it on the wooden tree, then added his own jacket. "And what did you say?"

"That they would burn in hell before I would ever give up my baby. They said that poor Lydia was shuddering in her grave at the proof of how grievously I'd failed her, but, after all, blood will tell. My mother had been shameless, and apparently so was I. I showed them to the door and told them not to come back."

"But they were there Friday."

She shrugged. "They stayed away maybe a week, and then it was business as usual. They love to shop for their grandchildren and great-grandchildren, and I don't turn away regular customers." Laying her purse on the hall table, she went into the parlor and straight to the fireplace. Before she'd moved even one log to the grate, Nick was there, brushing her aside, kneeling to lay the fire. "They're really nice old ladies," she said with a sigh, watching him work. "They just love to talk and pass judgment. Some people listen to them, but most are amused by them. I guess I just discovered that it's not so easy to be amused when *you're* the one they're passing judgment on."

He arranged half a dozen small logs over kindling from the brass bucket on the hearth, then held a match to it. The well-seasoned chips flared to life, immediately sending a whiff of wood smoke into the air. Instead of moving away, he remained there, gazing into the flames. "Did you ever consider their suggestion?"

"No."

"Not at all?" His tone suggested that he didn't entirely believe her, and why should he? He had already shared with her his opinion that she was too traditional, too old-fashioned, to *choose* to be an unwed mother in a town where people still talked about her own unwed mother. He had already pointed out that her own illegitimacy made Amelia Rose's illegitimacy so much more interesting a topic for gossip.

Crossing the room, she sat down in the big wood rocker, eased her shoes off with a little sigh, then propped her feet on a crewel-topped footstool. "I thought about it," she admitted. "But never with any intention of actually doing it. I knew that it would have been better for me if my mother had put me up for adoption, but from the moment I suspected that I was pregnant, I *wanted* this baby. I knew it wouldn't be easy. I knew there would be comments about following in my mother's footsteps, jokes about virgin births and unending speculation about who the father was, but I didn't care. I thought about adoption because it was there— it was an option. But it was no more viable an option than abortion. Call me selfish, but I couldn't do it."

He turned and sat on the hearth, facing her. "I don't consider wanting your baby selfish."

"Some people do." Leaning forward, she pulled out the quilt draped over the back of the chair, gave it a shake and spread it across her lap and over her legs. Early winter weather was so unpredictable. Tonight she was chilly. Tomorrow it might be seventy-five degrees, and the day after that it just might snow.

"So," Nick started casually, "tell me the jokes about virgin births."

She stared at him a long time, her hands knotting into fists underneath the quilt. She shouldn't have mentioned the jokes. She should have known that he would ask about them. But, heavens, this was New Hope, where little in her life remained a secret. Once he announced that Amelia Rose was his daughter, her life would be a totally open book. All it took was asking the right questions of the right people, and a person could find out anything and everything about her.

"You think you're such a hotshot cop," she said softly. "You figure it out." She watched him, recognizing the very instant he arrived at the right answer. It was the moment his eyes widened and his face paled, the moment a look of unmistakable horror flashed across then disappeared from his face.

"I wasn't allowed to date while I was in school," she said quietly, "but that didn't stop the guys from making jokes about it. When I did start, they always seemed to see me as a challenge—you know, who could succeed where the others had failed. The last man I dated sent me a bouquet of jewelweed when he broke up with me." She smiled thinly. "They're little yellow flowers, more commonly known as touch-me-nots."

The few minutes she'd spoken had allowed him to regain control. Now he looked only slightly repulsed. "You were a *virgin?*"

"Didn't you suspect it?" she asked dryly.

"*No...yes...not—*" He blew out his breath. "I thought you probably didn't have much experience. I thought you were probably pretty damned innocent, but—" Abruptly he got to his feet and shoved his hands into his jeans pockets. He looked edgy, ready to burst. "Why didn't I know?"

She simply shrugged.

"You're supposed to bleed. It's supposed to hurt."

"It did hurt. But you were drunk for that part, remember?"

Squeezing his eyes shut, he muttered a string of curses before looking at her again. "It's supposed to be obvious. It's supposed to be messy."

"Well, it wasn't. I don't know why, although logic says it's going to be different for every woman." She waited a moment, then matter-of-factly went on. "So that's why it was such a surprise to everyone. I was the woman considered least likely to ever 'do it.' I was prim, proper and prudish. I was untouched by male hands. And I was pregnant. Can you blame everyone for being shocked?"

Chapter 7

A *virgin.* The mere idea appalled Nick. He had never been anyone's first, not even back when he was sixteen and a virgin himself, and he didn't want to be Faith's. She deserved more. After waiting all those years, she deserved someone who appreciated and cared, not some sloppy drunk who couldn't remember a thing afterward. She deserved better than a few hours with a stranger who would hurt her, impregnate her, then disappear from her life.

She hadn't deserved him.

After a moment he released his breath in a heavy sigh. "You keep finding ways to confuse me."

She almost smiled. "It was strange enough that sweet, innocent Faith chose to have a one-night stand with a stranger. Now you want to know why sweet, innocent, *virginal* Faith would do it."

"Do you have any suggestions?"

"Nope." Her eyes got a little bit misty. "It was just something I wanted to do."

He supposed that could be true. She must have been curious, must have heard her friends talk about the things she was missing out on, must have wondered just how much fun it could be. So for him she had been—hell, he wasn't sure exactly what—a few hours' easy pleasure? And for her he had been curiosity. Experimentation. Simply the means necessary to achieve the ends.

As he'd told her last night, she worked wonders on his ego.

"So how was it?" he asked, offering a hesitant smile to cover his need to know.

"Male pride," she scoffed. "If you wanted to know, you should have stayed sober."

"Come on, Faith." He teased her gently. "Have mercy on a poor fool and at least tell me whether it was worth waiting for."

Tossing the quilt aside, she got to her feet and started toward the kitchen. At the doorway, she turned back. "All right. It was the best I've ever had."

He stood there for a moment, staring as she disappeared from sight, then burst out laughing. "Gee, thanks, sweetheart. Mom and Pop were right. You *are* generous."

The soft, alien sound of her own laughter drew him in her direction. He stopped just inside the door, leaned against an old pine cabinet and watched as she padded around in socks, fixing dinner for two. Last night she had wanted an invitation to dinner that she could turn down. He was pleased that she didn't bother with an invitation but simply assumed that he would stay. In fact, if he considered it too closely, he might discover that he was *too* pleased, too eager to spend time with her—and not for Amelia Rose's sake. For his own.

So he didn't consider it too closely. "I like your kitchen."

She glanced around. "It's just a kitchen."

"No, 'just a kitchen' is what I have in my condo. It's about four feet wide and six feet long. It has a little refrigerator, a little stove and no cabinet or counter space to speak of." This kitchen was easily three times that size, big enough for an island, an old pine icebox, a pie safe, a scarred table that showed prime evidence of its years of use and a half-dozen mismatched chairs. This was the sort of kitchen his mother and sisters could cook in, the sort that became the heart of a house. "The first time Mom and Pop saw my kitchen, they just about dropped dead. Neither of them could imagine living with a place like that."

"I spent a lot of time in here growing up. I learned to cook at an ancient old stove. I made cookies at the island, kneaded bread at that counter. I did my sewing and my homework at the table that used to be in here, and I washed a ton of dishes in that sink." Her shrug underscored the faint sarcasm that laced her voice on the next words. "This was where Great-aunt Lydia taught me everything a proper young woman should know."

Everything except how to live in the real world. How to choose her men wisely. How to prepare herself for the unexpected. Other than the everyday skills like cooking and cleaning, he doubted that Lydia had taught her much at all of value.

When the microwave dinged, she used a hot pad to remove a steaming bowl of stew and placed it on a large wooden tray with smaller bowls, spoons and napkins. She added napkins, salt and pepper and fixed drinks for them, then faced him, one brow raised.

He carried the heavy tray into the living room and set it on a table between her favored rocker and an armchair with lace doilies on the arms and the back. After his first bite of stew, he complimented her, but she brushed him off. "Who can't make stew? It's idiot-proof."

Most of the women he'd dated couldn't make it. Cooking skills for the majority of them went no further than opening a can or turning on the microwave.

They ate in silence, but it wasn't of the strained variety. It was comfortable enough, in fact, that it could worry a man. A week ago it would have worried *him,* but a week ago he hadn't known that he was about to become a father. Even in his wildest imaginings, he hadn't known that he was going to become a husband as soon as he could persuade Faith—which might be a very long time, since he hadn't yet found the courage to broach the subject with her. By the time he convinced her that it was not just the right thing but the *only* thing to do, he figured Amelia Rose would be contemplating marriage herself.

It wasn't until they were finished with dinner that he brought up something Faith had mentioned before, something that had caught his attention and wouldn't let go. "When we were talking about adoption, you said that it would have been better for you if your mother had let someone adopt you. Was growing up with Lydia really so bad?" She had implied so last week, when the best thing she'd been able to say was that the old woman had never hit her. He wanted to know more, though. He wanted to know everything.

"It could have been worse," she admitted in a feeble attempt at teasing. Sobering, she went on. "She did exactly what she had promised to do. She fulfilled her familial duty. She took me in, fed me, clothed me, gave me a place to sleep. She saw to it that I received an education and she filled in the gaps in that education with her own training. She was never cruel, but she was very strict. She never understood that there was more to raising a child than feeding, clothing and teaching."

Like affection. Love. Fun.

"From the time I was little, she always reminded me what a terrible person my mother was, but she was family, and one has a duty to family. I knew I was here because of that duty long before I understood exactly what the word meant."

So she had lived twenty-one years with a hateful old woman who had denied her love, made her feel unwanted and little more than a burden, and tried from the beginning to warp her view of life, of people, of her mother in particular and of men in general. Maybe all that, Nick admitted grimly, had something to do with why a sweet, innocent, virginal woman went to bed with an absolute stranger.

She shifted in the rocker, tucking the quilt once more around her legs. "I saw you at lunch today."

From somewhere among all those grim thoughts, he summoned up a grin. "I was surprised to see you come walking in there. I figured you would avoid the place like the plague for fear of running into me."

"It wasn't my choice," she said dryly. "I voted for the diner or Little Joe's, but it was a special occasion. Wendy—she was in the shop last week when you came in—turned thirty today, and last night she got engaged." She rubbed her hand over the pattern quilted into the pastel fabrics. It was a light touch, gentle, the kind that could soothe a cranky baby—or arouse some lucky man. He wondered if she had touched him like that, wondered if she might ever do it again. "I was surprised when you left without coming by our table."

"I wouldn't have, if my parents hadn't just spent ten minutes telling me all the reasons I should stay away from you." That brought her attention back to him—a startled look, an embarrassed flush, an aching vulnerability. "Not because of you, sweetheart, because of *me*. They think you need to be protected from me. They think you deserve better than me, and they're probably right, but you're already stuck. Of course, when we tell them that they're about to become grandparents—for the twenty-fifth time—they'll change their tune. They'll think we're a perfect match, that no one could settle me down better than sweet, old-fashioned Faith, that no one could take care of you better than their eldest son, the cop."

His words made her uncomfortable, made her gaze skitter away like some frightened creature, made her fingers nervously work the edges of the baby quilt. If she reacted like this to the mere mention of settling down, how was she going to respond to the *M* word? How frightened would she be by a proposal of marriage?

Rather than venture into territory that obviously scared her, Faith focused on the least important thing he'd said. "Don't you mean ex-cop? Didn't you tell them that you'd quit your job?"

"I got a new one this morning with the New Hope P.D. I start in a couple of weeks. I figure that'll give me a little time with Amelia Rose."

Unable to sit still any longer, she slid to her feet and wandered over to the fireplace, standing with her back to him. "You're serious about moving back here, aren't you?" she asked, her voice low and shaking a little.

He left his chair, too, crossing the richly patterned area rug, not stopping until he was right next to her. She turned a little, keeping him behind her, and he let her. He didn't try to make her face him, didn't try to get a glimpse of her face so he could see the emotion there. Instead, he touched her. He laid his hand on her shoulder and felt tension ripple through her. Laying his other hand on her other shoulder, he gave her taut muscles a squeeze or two, then deliberately pulled her back against him. She squirmed, trying to force his hands away, trying to wriggle free, but he wrapped his arms around her and held her tighter.

"Would you stop it?" he demanded, his mouth only millimeters above her ear. "I just want to hold you. I've done it before. I did a hell of a lot more than this before. Just let me hold you."

She took a deep breath that pressed her breasts against his arms, then went still, but the tension didn't leave her body. She practically hummed with it from head to toe.

Closing his eyes, he gave free rein to his other senses. She smelled of flowers he couldn't identify, something exotic and just a little bit sweet. Her skin—what little was exposed by her sweater—was soft and smooth, warmer on the side nearest the fire. Her breasts were soft, too, and full, flattened underneath the weight of his arms. They weren't normally so large, he knew—and then wondered exactly how he knew. Was it a guess, based on his experience with six sisters who shared twenty-four pregnancies between them? Or a memory, buried somewhere in the mystery of that long-ago night?

He slid his hands around her stomach, then back to her waist. The appearance of delicacy was an illusion. Her body was strong, lean in spite of the extra thirty pounds she carried. The muscles that were tensed against him were well developed.

And familiar. It was all somehow familiar. He couldn't remember details, couldn't recall anything that could be clearly identified as a memory, but somewhere deep inside he knew he'd done this before. His arms, his body—his desire—recognized her. He'd held her before. He had kissed her, undressed her, stroked her. He had found pleasure of such intensity inside her that it haunted him even now.

"Faith?"

A moment of silence, then, suspiciously, warily, "What?"

"It was unusual, wasn't it—the sex. Making love."

She didn't speak.

"It was different from what you'd thought it would be."

After another moment of silence she sighed heavily and much of the tension left her body. "It was everything I'd thought it would be, and then some." She sighed again and injected sarcasm into her voice. "How many virgins can say that about their first time?"

Beside them, the fire popped and crackled, its heat intensifying. Reluctant as he was to let her go, he did, and took a few steps back to the opposite side of the fireplace. Slowly, reluctantly, she turned to face him.

"Ever since that night I've had dreams," he admitted. "There was nothing of substance—sweet blue eyes. Long brown hair. Arousal intense enough to make a man beg. I thought they were just dreams. I didn't believe you existed. I knew I had certainly never met you. Then you fainted last Wednesday and I carried you to the sofa in back. That was when I got a good look at your face. That was why I went back that evening."

She folded her hands across her stomach. "That was why you didn't need proof about Amelia Rose."

He nodded.

"You still should have waited before you made any major changes like quitting your job and moving home."

"Waited for what? For Amelia Rose to be born? For blood tests to confirm what I already know?"

"Most men would want proof."

"Most men aren't dealing with you. You can't lie worth a damn. Besides, I know what I feel. And if it's proof you want, you'll have it when you see her." He risked a grin. "She's going to look just like my entire family. Although, to be honest—" reaching out, he brushed his hand over her hair, and the grin disappeared "—I wouldn't mind one bit if she has her mother's eyes."

Faith was as conscious of her appearance as any other young woman, but until that very moment she'd never thought there was anything of particular interest about her. Her hair was long and wavy and behaved best in a no-nonsense braid. Her complexion was fair. Her nose was too uncomfortably close to earning a description of "pert," but was no more remarkable than her mouth, chin or forehead. As for her eyes, what could she say? They were blue. Not dark blue or pale blue, certainly not the vivid blue of tinted contacts. Just plain blue.

But Nick had called them sweet blue.

He remembered them, more or less. Of all the details of that February night, he remembered her eyes, her hair and... How had he put it? *Arousal intense enough to make a man beg.*

It wasn't much, but it was a whole lot more than she'd had ten minutes ago.

She cleared her throat, then did it again, and still her voice came out sounding choked. "Blue eyes would look odd with your coloring."

"They'd make her stand out in the crowd."

"She'll stand out anyway because she'll be so special."

"You really believe that, don't you?" His smile this time was serious, intense, touching. "She's a lucky kid."

His compliment sent warmth through her, a freeing sensation that melted away the tension and made her feel about fifty pounds lighter. He was right. In spite of what anyone else might think, Amelia Rose *was* one lucky little girl. She had a mother who already loved her more than life itself and a father who seemed determined to do his best for her. What more could she ask for?

Maybe a real *family,* answered the old-fashioned, traditional voice inside Faith. Parents who'd done things in the right order, who had met and dated and fallen in love, who had married before giving thought to children, who lived together and provided a loving, stable environment, who could one day give her brothers and sisters to love, tease and protect.

But it was much too late for that, so Amelia Rose would have to settle for what fate had given her—a mother right here in her home and a father nearby. That was a lot more than anyone in town believed she would have. It would be enough.

"Your parents must be glad to have you back."

Finally he left the fireplace, but he didn't sit down. Instead he prowled around the room, looking, touching, bending once to sniff the flowers on a Christmas cactus. "I'm sure they are," he absently agreed. "Pop's lived here all his life and Mom's been here since they got married. They both love the place, so it was hard for them to understand why I didn't want to stay. They think I've finally come to my senses."

"If they knew the truth, they wouldn't be so pleased."

He glanced at her over his shoulder. "Are you kidding? They're going to be thrilled."

"Excuse me," she said dryly, "but I've gotten to know your parents reasonably well over the last few years. They're not going to be thrilled to find out that they have an illegitimate granddaughter."

He stopped at the library table in front of the big back window. For Christmas she always cleared everything off and used the oak surface for a display of nativity scenes, but for now, in addition to its usual potted ivies and brass candlesticks, it also held assorted baby items that hadn't yet made the trip upstairs to the nursery. There was a lovely book of sweet poetry, illustrated all in pastels, a pair of soft, fuzzy booties, a hooded terry-cloth towel for after-bath snuggling, and a dress. *The* dress. The green-velvet-and-white-lace, destined-to-become-a-Harper-heirloom dress.

Nick lifted it from its box and tissue paper and held it up for inspection. It looked so fragile in his hands, a doll's dress, delicate and beautiful. The hunter green was striking against the darkness of his fingers, giving her a hint of how it would flatter a baby who shared his coloring. He studied it a moment, tested the softness of the fabric. Then, with more care than she would have expected from a man, he folded it back into its box and resumed his tour of the room. He also, finally, responded to her last remark. "She's not going to be illegitimate."

He said it so casually, so naturally, as if he were stating an obvious fact. He said it as if it were unimportant, but, of course, it wasn't, not to him and certainly not to her.

"I'm sorry," she said, striving for the same casual tone, "but I don't see any way around it. She's due in a few more days. I'm not married. That makes her illegitimate."

"You can be married." Now he was in front of the bookcase, looking over the volumes there. She doubted, though, that he was as interested in them as he appeared. She honestly didn't think he could care less about the row of baby books, the romances and mysteries above them or the biographies underneath them. "It's a relatively simple procedure. You get a blood test, a license, a priest, and it's done."

The chill that swept over Faith made her blood cold. She had realized as early as last Thursday that he might suggest getting married. It had been clear that his sense of duty was strong, and, for someone in his circumstances who was determined to do the right thing, marriage was the next logical step after accepting responsibility. But she had hoped—had prayed—that his sense of duty wasn't *that* strong, that he would be satisfied with the responsibility. She had prayed that he wouldn't offer her everything she'd dreamed of—except, of course, love—in such a manner that guaranteed she couldn't accept any of it. She had hoped he wouldn't

make her feel so unwanted, so burdensome, so unwel-
comed.

Thankful that she was talking to his back, she clasped her
hands tightly together and tried to control the quaver in her
voice. "A priest?" she echoed. "You seem to forget that I'm
not Catholic."

"But I am."

"But we're talking about me, not you."

Then he turned. Somehow, in the last few minutes, his
jaw had taken on a new and decidedly stubborn set. "Don't
play dumb, Faith. If you marry anybody while you're carrying my child, it will damn well be me."

"*Your* child? Just last week, you didn't want a baby.
You'd never wanted a baby."

"Well, I've got one, and I'll be damned if anyone else is
going to play father to her."

She found his possessiveness both frightening and, in a
strange way, comforting. On the one hand, she was much
happier thinking of Amelia Rose as solely hers, believing
that no one else could ever have a claim on her daughter as
strong as her own, and it was bothersome to admit that Nick
not only had such a claim, but also had some quite forceful
feelings about it. On the other hand, it was reassuring that
he did have those feelings. *Her* father certainly hadn't. He
had abandoned her mother without hesitation, had abandoned *her* without even a qualm. In twenty-five years, she
doubted that he'd given her a moment's thought, doubted
that he had ever wondered whether he had a son or a
daughter, what had become of her or whether she missed or
needed her father. Amelia Rose was luckier. She would
know her father from the beginning. He would always be a
part of her life.

But not a part of Faith's. He deserved better than that.
Damn it, *she* deserved better. "This conversation is point-
less," she said. "I'm not getting married, not this week, not
next week, probably not ever."

His hard gaze didn't waver. "Before the middle of the
month. Preferably before Sunday."

"No."

"You owe it to Amelia Rose."

"Excuse me? I *owe* it to her to let her be born into a family that will break up before her first birthday rolls around?"

The stubbornness intensified. "And how do you figure that?"

"We don't even know each other!"

"We know each other well enough to bring a baby into the world," he reminded her needlessly. Making an obvious effort to remain calm, he sighed heavily and softly, almost regretfully, continued. "I know this isn't the marriage proposal you imagined receiving someday. I understand that the circumstances are less than ideal. I know you would prefer hearts and flowers over necessities and responsibilities. But, Faith, this is right. We'll make it right, and we'll make it last."

Not the marriage proposal she had imagined herself receiving someday. That was an understatement and a half, she thought sadly. Even when she was a little girl, she had dreamed of being wanted only for herself, for the quirks, qualities and flaws that made her Faith Harper. She had dreamed of being loved, of fairy-tale romances and happily-ever-after. What Nick was offering was a nightmare. He wanted her only for the baby she was carrying. He didn't know her, didn't appreciate who and what she was. He certainly didn't love her, and it was highly doubtful, under these circumstances, that he ever would.

"You're crazy. I don't want to marry you. I don't want to marry anybody."

"You know it's right, Faith. You know it's best for Amelia Rose."

"Best for her to be raised by two miserable people who share a house and a name and nothing else?"

A glint came into his dark eyes. "Sweetheart, when I say married, I mean *married*. Living together, raising a family together, making a future together. Growing old and gray and hosting Sunday dinners for the kids and the grandkids." He came toward her, his pace slow, his movements deliberate and, to Faith, so very threatening. "Besides, I don't get miserable."

"You will," she warned in a low tone that merely made him shake his head with a faint smile.

Then he grew serious again. "Give me one good reason why we shouldn't get married."

"We don't know each other," she said sarcastically.

"We know each other well enough, and we'll learn all the other stuff in time."

"Oh, really? Tell me one important thing you know about me."

"I know you love this baby more than life itself."

"Everyone knows that."

He ignored her scorn. "I know you would give anything to give her the security of a traditional family, the love-marriage-and-*then*-the-baby-carriage type. I know you wanted that for her almost as much as you needed it for yourself. I know—" For just an instant, he glanced away, then looked back with new resolve. "I know that you need Amelia Rose to love you because none of the other people who were supposed to ever did, not your mother or your father, not your grandparents or your aunt."

And now not the man proposing that he become her husband. By sheer force of will, she kept back the tears that were trying so hard to fill her eyes and instead increased the chilly sarcasm in her voice. "Four tries, and you failed. None of that is secret. Everyone in town knows it."

"Does everyone in town know what it's like to hold you? To make love with you? To have a baby with you?"

She stared at him. "You don't even remember touching me."

"I remembered your eyes. I remembered wanting you."

"You remembered wanting someone you didn't believe even existed. That *memory*—" she gave the word scathing emphasis "—has nothing to do with me." Even though she wanted it to have *everything* to do with her. She wanted to inspire the sort of intense emotion he'd mentioned. She wanted to be special enough, desirable enough, memorable enough, to dominate a man's dreams.

"Damn it, Faith—"

"Please go home," she said curtly. "I'm tired. I'd like to go to bed."

He spared a glance at his watch, giving her a blessed moment's relief from his sharp-edged gaze. "It's barely eight o'clock."

"I go to bed early these days."

After another long, hard stare, he turned away and headed down the hall. At the coat tree, he retrieved his jacket, then shoved his arms into the sleeves with enough force to strain the leather. She followed as far as the parlor door, hoping he would leave without another word and hoping that he wouldn't. He did walk as far as the front door, then he faced her once more. The light overhead cast shadows on his face, making his expression appear even grimmer.

"We'll discuss this again tomorrow."

"There's nothing left to discuss. I'm not marrying you or anyone else. That's final."

"It's not final. You're not that selfish."

Selfish? She was willing to share her daughter with him, willing to let his family dazzle her with their tremendous capacity for love and joy, willing to let the Russos make what little Faith could give her look pitiful indeed. She was willing to acknowledge his equal claim to the baby she'd waited all her life for, the baby he hadn't even known existed until a week ago, and he was calling *her* selfish because she wouldn't agree to an ill-advised marriage that would be doomed from the start?

"Amelia Rose needs a traditional family," he insisted.

"No. She needs parents who are happy. That doesn't mean married."

He gave her a speculative, narrow-eyed look. "I could make you happy."

"Sure," she replied, even though she didn't doubt him for a minute. He'd swept her off her feet once before. She had little doubt that he could do it again, if he so chose. "And when you leave?" If he set out to seduce her again, into marriage this time, what would happen when he got bored or the resentment became too great or he met someone else, someone he liked for herself, someone he wanted to spend the rest of his life with, someone he could love?

"It's not going to happen."

"Right," she agreed skeptically.

He fished his keys from his pocket, then opened the door. A chill seeped into the hallway, ominously underscoring his words. "This isn't finished, Faith." A moment later the door closed behind him, but his quiet promise lingered long after he was gone.

So did Faith's chill.

Michael's apartment was on the other side of town, about as far from Faith's house as a person could go and still stay in the city limits. Nick was halfway there when, abruptly, he made a U-turn and headed back to Main Street. His father didn't always work the dinner shift, but chances were as good as not that he'd be at the restaurant. As he drove through the back lot where employees parked, he spotted Antonio's car, pulled into the vacant space beside it and went into the restaurant by the back door.

His father was seated at a desk in a distant corner of the kitchen. He had an office up front, done up to match the dining room decor, with a gleaming desk and a big leather chair, but he preferred to do his work at a scarred oak table in the kitchen. He liked being accessible when problems arose in the kitchen, he insisted, but the family agreed privately that he was just too nosy to remain shut up in the front office while everything was going on back here.

"Hey, Pop."

Antonio's thoughtful expression immediately turned to pleasure. "Nick, I wasn't expecting you. Pull up a seat. You want some dinner?"

"No, thanks, Pop, I already ate. What are you doing?"

"Working on the banquet room reservations. December's a busy month for us. How about a little dish of fettuccine? Gerard's Alfredo sauce is especially good tonight."

Nick glanced across the kitchen to where Gerard was ladling sauce over plates of pasta, then shook his head. "Nah. Some other time."

Antonio put his pencil down, leaned back comfortably in his chair and studied him. "What brings you to my kitchen?"

"I was on my way back to Mike's place. I just thought I'd stop in."

"Back from where?"

Nick picked up a pencil holder, then sat down on the corner of the desk. The holder was an old coffee can covered with construction paper that had once been bright purple, now faded to a bluish hue. It was probably the handiwork of one grandchild or another. All the kids in the family made things for their grandfather, and he displayed them proudly. "From dinner," he replied, at last putting the can down, but not yet meeting his father's gaze. He had never lied to Antonio, not once in his entire life, and even this wasn't a lie. But it *was* evasive. It wasn't quite the truth, which made it feel like a lie.

"Good food?" his father asked, ever the restaurateur.

"Yeah, it was."

"Good company?"

Nick avoided answering the question by asking one of his own. "What do you do, Pop, when you make a big mistake?"

His father instantly looked worried. "You aren't talking about your decision to move back here?"

"No. I'm sure about that."

"You make a mistake, big or small, and you make it right. You take whatever steps are necessary to fix it."

"What if it involves someone else, and that person won't let you fix it?"

Antonio's smile was apologetic. "I can't talk in riddles, son. If you need advice, you have to tell me what's wrong.

What mistake did you make, and who is this person who won't let you take care of it?''

The urge to confide was strong. All his life, Nick had taken his problems to his father, and he'd come away with advice, guidance, or at the very least, the comfort that came from sharing troubles with a sympathetic listener. Tonight, he needed guidance. Was he wrong in wanting to marry Faith not because he loved her, not because she felt anything at all for him, but solely for the sake of their daughter? Was marriage too drastic and too important a step to take for anything less than love and commitment? Or was having a baby too momentous an occasion for anything less than marriage?

Sighing, he got up to restlessly pace. "I really can't tell you, Pop. It wouldn't be fair to—" He caught her name just in time and flushed uneasily. "To the other person involved."

"Then all I can tell you is to do what you know in your heart is right. And if this other person stands in your way, well, then you give it your best effort. No one could ask more of you."

Nick scowled at the wide array of dishes he found himself facing. Plenty of people could and would ask more. When he announced the birth of the newest Russo grandchild in a few days' time, everyone would ask more. They would want to know why the youngest Russo was illegitimate, why her father had disgraced the family by not marrying her mother. They would demand to know why he had treated Faith so callously nine months ago, how he could have seduced, then abandoned her. They would say it was no wonder that she wanted nothing to do with him now, and they would blame him for her decision and for Amelia Rose's illegitimacy.

They would ask him all their questions and make all their judgments, but they wouldn't care—in the beginning, at least—about his answers, explanations or excuses. All they would see would be their newest granddaughter, great-granddaughter, niece and cousin, too young and helpless to be saddled with the stigma of illegitimacy, and her mother, sweet, innocent and—at least until *he* had come around— saintly, virginal Faith. They wouldn't believe that he'd given his best effort. They would find plenty lacking in everything he'd done.

"Son?"

He turned toward his father.

"Does this have anything to do with your decision to move back? You didn't get into trouble down there in Houston, did you? You aren't running away from something?"

"No, Pop. It's nothing to do with Houston." With a sigh, he changed the subject. "What time is Mom expecting you home?"

"In another fifteen minutes. Why don't I call and tell her that I'm going to be late? We can go someplace quiet and talk."

Talk. Ordinarily Nick would welcome the chance to go someplace quiet and talk with his father. Between Antonio's obligations to the business, the community, his parents, his wife and each of his eight children, private time with Antonio had always been hard to come by. But Nick didn't anticipate it tonight, the way he always had in the past. Tonight the best he could do was talk circles around what was really bothering him, taking care to give not even the slightest hint that Antonio could make a guess from. It would worry his father and frustrate *him,* and he would go home feeling no better than he did right now.

He summoned his best smile. "Nah, I'm kind of tired. I'm going to head home."

"If you change your mind, you know where to find me."

"I've always known that, Pop. You've always been there for me." The way *he* wanted to always be there for Amelia Rose. He wanted to follow his father's example. He wanted to make him proud, and someday twenty or thirty years down the line, he wanted Amelia Rose to be proud.

And one of the big steps toward reaching that goal was giving her a home and a loving family, which included persuading her mother to marry him.

He gave his father a hug, then left the restaurant the same way he had entered. This time he managed the drive to Michael's apartment without changing his mind.

The place was quiet, dimly lit by one lamp and about as welcoming as an anonymous motel room. As apartments went, it was typical—white walls, gold carpet, sliding doors opening onto a narrow balcony, compact spaces and the same floor plan as about a million other apartments in the state of Texas. It was similar to the place where he'd lived in college, nearly identical to the apartment he'd rented in Houston before buying the condo. It was perfectly suitable housing, but it had a temporary feel about it. People came and went, staying six months, a year, maybe even two. He could probably come back in five years and not a single one of the current residents would still be there.

Faith's house would always be there.

So would Faith.

And—with help from God, the family and anyone else he could call on—*he* would be there, too.

He'd known she wouldn't react kindly to any proposal of marriage right now, and he could even understand why she had found his particularly unwelcome. Except for the last few years, she'd lived her entire life made to feel as if she were a burden. Her parents had abandoned her, her grandparents had rejected her, and her great-aunt had taken her in only out of a sense of duty. None of them had ever seen her as the unique, special person that she was. To them, she had been something to be passed on or a responsibility that couldn't be ignored.

Now she believed that he was proposing marriage solely because of his responsibility to Amelia Rose, that she was the burden he was willing to accept in exchange for getting to be with his daughter.

And she was right . . . wasn't she?

If the baby was the only reason he'd come back here, the only reason he'd committed himself to the idea of marriage, why did it bother him so much that he couldn't remember that night with Faith? Why did he feel queasy inside when those blue eyes of hers turned distrusting, wary or hurt?

He had to admit that there was *something* between them—some connection, some sharing—that had little to do with Amelia Rose. There was the desire he'd felt for her, the dreams in which she'd haunted him, that aching sense of familiarity when he'd held her in his arms tonight. There was the pleasure he found in her company, talking and listening, just being with her or waiting for one of those rare smiles. There was the protectiveness he'd felt every time someone had gossiped about her. And there was his absolute certainty that getting married was the right thing to do—not just for Amelia Rose, but for them, too. He felt it down in his soul.

She could deny it until she was blue in the face, but there was more than their daughter between them. They had the foundation to turn their relationship into something stronger, more solid, lasting till the end of time. Or they could deny it, ignore it, concentrate solely on the baby and let whatever potential they shared wither and die.

There was no doubt in his mind what *he* wanted.

Now he simply had to convince Faith.

Faith awakened Wednesday morning to the insistent ringing of her alarm. Holding a pillow over her head with one hand, she flung out the other to connect with the snooze button on top of the small clock. It didn't stop the noise, though. Rising groggily from the pillow, she looked around the room, then realized that it was the doorbell. Nick, she thought with a scowl. Who else would come by her house at seven in the morning?

She swung her legs over the side of the bed, then pulled her robe on as she slid to her feet. Just as she made it to the top of the stairs, her alarm clock started beeping, a shrill, insistent sound guaranteed to rouse even the soundest of sleepers. Hesitating, she considered expending the effort to go back and shut it off, then shrugged and started a slow descent down the stairs to the front door.

She was right. It was Nick, holding in one hand a brown paper bag from which wafted all kinds of wonderful scents and, in the other, two large cups. "Did I wake you?"

Shoving her hair straight back from her face, she glowered at him. "Of course not. Why, it's seven o'clock. What kind of slug stays in bed that late?"

He gave her a perfectly innocent, straight-faced look. "No wonder I left so early last February. You're cranky in the morning."

"I am not." Steam rising from the vent in the lid of one of the two cups distracted her. "Is that coffee?"

"Uh-huh."

"You can come in, but don't talk to me." Leaving him to close the door, she shuffled down the hall into the parlor. She had banked the fire before going to bed last night, so there was nothing but cold ash beneath the grate. She should have turned the heat on when she passed the thermostat, she realized, but instead of going back, she sat down on the sofa and pulled a heavy quilt over her. With her flannel nightgown and cotton robe, it helped some, but her feet were bare and slowly turning to icicles.

Nick disappeared into the kitchen, then returned a moment later with two plates of food and the foam cups. He set them on the table in front of her, then left again. The rumble of the heater coming on preceded his return. "You always sleep with it cold?" he asked as he settled onto the floor in front of her. She watched him, envying his easy grace. Once she had moved like that, so easily, so fluidly. On mornings like this, stiff and feeling every single ounce of the extra bulk she carried, she doubted that she would ever move like that again.

With a sigh, she pushed aside the jealousy and turned to his question. She did normally keep the house cold at night—heating bills on a house this size were substantial, and she always slept under warm covers—but she wasn't in the mood to admit so. "Just because I let it get cold last night doesn't mean I always do."

"It was cold that night in February. I remember the iron rails on that old bed. They were like ice."

Hoping the heat seeping into her throat and face came from the afghan and not intimate memories, she answered grumpily. "The house had been full of people that night, so of course I hadn't turned the heat on high. When I went upstairs with you, I had every intention of going straight back down."

"Do you regret that?" he asked softly.

"Going upstairs with you?"

"Not going straight back down."

She wanted to say yes, just to see what effect it had on him, but she was a lousy liar, as he'd pointed out before. Besides, even if she managed to appear halfway convincing, he still wouldn't believe her. He knew too well how she felt about Amelia Rose to ever believe that she regretted the night that had brought her daughter into being. "No," she admitted. "What I regret is ever letting you know your role that night."

"Letting me know?" he echoed. "Sweetheart, I figured it out on my own. You certainly weren't forthcoming with the details, and what you did tell me in the beginning was mostly lies."

Ignoring the truth of what he said, she leaned forward to pick up the nearest foam cup. Anticipating the first sip of richly brewed coffee in—well, she couldn't remember how long, she pulled the lid off...and stared into a cup of pulpy, fresh-squeezed orange juice. She raised her gaze to him. "I want coffee."

"You don't need coffee. All that caffeine isn't good for the baby."

"If I'm going to face you first thing in the morning, I want coffee."

"Orange juice is good for you." He pulled the lid from his own cup, dumped a couple packets of sugar in along with two little containers of cream and stirred it with a fork. She watched greedily as he lifted it, preparing to drink, then almost smiled when he reluctantly offered it to her. "A drink, that's all."

She took the cup, her fingers brushing his before wrapping around the warm foam. For a moment she simply closed her eyes and savored the aroma. Then she took a tentative sip. "This is Sue Ellen's coffee, isn't it?" No one in New Hope made coffee the way the proprietor of the diner did. No matter how miserable the day, a cup of Sue Ellen's coffee made it better.

"Yeah. She said to tell you good morning."

She opened one eye, then the other, giving him a narrow, suspicious look. "You're lying," she decided.

"She said you would complain about the orange juice but to tell you that it's good for you. She also said that you come in occasionally for breakfast and that your favorite is scrambled eggs, crispy bacon, hash browns with cheese and buttery biscuits."

Her scowl returned, proportional to his grin. "Now I *know* you're lying, because my favorite breakfast is pancakes with peanut butter and maple syrup." But eggs, bacon, hash browns and biscuits *were* a close second.

He handed her a plate, napkin and fork, then started on his own food. "I really didn't mean to wake you," he remarked as he spread jelly on the biscuit. "Sometimes I forget that not everyone in the world wakes up early just because I do."

"I'm usually up by six." She made the admission with her mouth full, then swallowed. "Lately I'm just so tired."

"You're carrying an entire person inside you. Gee, maybe that's why." Adding bacon, he made a sandwich of the biscuit, then leaned back on one hand while he ate. "Isn't it normal to take a few days off just before giving birth and rest?"

"And who would run the shop?"

"Who's going to run it after the baby's born?"

"Beth's mother, but only for two weeks. That was all the time she could spare."

"There must be someone else in town who can read price tags, run the cash register and restock displays."

She shook her head, although she knew he must be right. All she would have to do was run an ad in the New Hope *Journal*. Temporary help at this time of year would be easy to find. But she didn't want to ask for help, and she didn't want to pay out any more of the shop's profits than necessary. She made a comfortable living—and was coming into her most profitable month of the year—but she still felt a little anxiety deep inside. After all, she would be supporting two soon, and it was important that her daughter's life be secure in every way.

"Then why don't you just close the store for a few days?"

"It's December," she protested. "People are starting their Christmas shopping. I can't afford to close up for a few days."

This time he was the one scowling. "Oh, pardon me for thinking that your health might be a little more important than the Christmas rush."

Some part of her was touched by his concern. Some smaller part wondered if it was genuine. "My health is fine. I'm just a little tired. Someone insisted on coming over last night and arguing with me for two hours. It made it kind of hard to fall asleep."

Whatever response she expected from him, it wasn't the grin that brightened his eyes. "Payback, sweetheart. You've cost me a hell of a lot more than one night's sleep in the past nine months. Sometimes I could see you. Sometimes I could feel you. Sometimes I could smell that perfume you wear." His eyes turned shadowy and his voice grew huskier. "I can't even begin to count the number of nights I woke up hard and hot and *this* close to. . ."

Her mouth went dry as she stared at him. Just last night she had insisted that those dreams had nothing to do with her. This morning she *wanted* to believe that he'd dreamed about her. She wanted to believe that, in some way, he had been as affected by their few hours together as she had been. She especially wanted to believe that she could make him *hard and hot and* this *close to*...

He finished his breakfast, pushed his plate away and rested both arms on the table. "So you won't take time off and you won't close the shop," he said. "How about some temporary help?"

How did he do that? she wondered. How could he talk about sex in that throaty, husky voice and then, in the next moment, return to their earlier conversation as if it had never been interrupted? "What kind of temporary help?" she asked, partly suspicious and still partly unbalanced.

"The cheap, charming kind. I'll probably be hanging around down there anyway, so why not let me work?"

The suspicion was well deserved. "No."

"Why not? I'm not an idiot, Faith. I can learn to run a cash register. I can deal with people. You can stretch out on the sofa in the storeroom, prop up your feet and supervise. You won't have to close the shop, you'll get some rest, and it won't cost you a thing. I'll work for free."

"You'll annoy me for free. How generous of you," she said sarcastically. "No. It's a lousy idea."

"Why?"

"What would people say?"

He got to his feet as easily and smoothly as she'd known he would, came around the table and sat down on the edge of the cushion right beside her. "Who gives a damn what people say? They're all going to know the truth in a few days anyway."

"You don't have to tell anyone right away," she mumbled, fumbling with the belt knotted over her stomach. "You could wait until they figure it out on their own."

Reaching out, he lifted her chin so that the only way to avoid his gaze was to close her eyes. She didn't. "Right, Faith. I'll just let Mom and Pop and my sisters and grandparents and everyone else find out about my daughter when they figure it out on their own. They would disown me, and they wouldn't be too happy with you. That's not the best way to begin a relationship with them.''

"It wouldn't take them long to guess," she said, managing to lower her gaze to the ribbed neck of his T-shirt. "Why else would you be hanging around me?"

He moved his fingers along her jaw, a gentle caress that made her clench the muscles there tighter. "Maybe because you're a lovely woman," he said softly. "Maybe because you're smart, capable and independent, but you still manage to rouse every protective instinct I've got. Maybe because you're the most stubborn woman I've ever met. Hell, Faith, who knows what draws people to each other?''

She knew—in this instance, at least. It was Amelia Rose he wanted, not her.

And that knowledge damned near broke her heart.

Chapter 8

Nick sat on the couch, propped his feet on the coffee table and tilted his head back to stare at the ceiling. Faith was upstairs, the sound of running water indicating that she was taking the shower she'd been mumbling about as she disappeared down the hall. She had thanked him for the breakfast and invited him to leave, but he had no intention of doing so, not unless she left with him.

A clock chimed somewhere, drawing his attention to his watch. Eight o'clock in the morning, and it already promised to be a long day. He didn't mind long hours—didn't mind hard work, either, which was good. Judging from her earlier question—*Why else would you be hanging around me?*—winning Faith over was going to take a lot of both.

A better question in most people's minds, he thought scornfully, would be why she was *letting* him hang around. Even his own parents didn't want her involved with him. Even they had suspected that he might use her, then walk away.

How could he blame her for not trusting him, either?

And how in the world could he change her mind?

Feeling restless, he left the couch and walked around the room, but he'd seen all there was to see last night. He'd already taken a few minutes to wash their breakfast dishes, so there was nothing requiring his attention in the kitchen. The formal living room at the front of the house was too dreary a room for so bright a day, and the study across the hall didn't interest him.

What did interest him was upstairs. The nursery. The guest room where he'd slept—where they'd made love. And Faith.

He rested his hand lightly on the balustrade and stepped onto the first tread. After a moment's hesitation—a brief moment's guilt at giving himself free run of someone else's house—he climbed to the top and stopped. If he turned left in the hallway, then right into one of the back bedrooms, he would be in Amelia Rose's room. The room on the left was Faith's. Sandwiched between the nursery and the front bedroom was a bathroom, its closed door muffling the splash of water. That left the two front rooms.

It was the one that shared a wall with the bathroom. His footsteps muted by the faded runner that ran the length of the hall, he stopped in front of the closed door, wrapped his fingers around the cut-glass knob and slowly twisted it open.

The door squeaked, and the floor creaked just inside. He kept his gaze deliberately to the right as he entered, making note of heavy furniture, faded wallpaper and lace curtains fluttering just a bit as he passed. He didn't look at the rest of the room until he reached the foot of the bed and could see it all at once.

It was exactly as he'd remembered and yet different, too. His memory had been hazy at best, thanks to poor lighting and too much booze the night before. What he remembered in soft tones and softer focus was sharper, more vivid, this morning. The bed was iron, once painted white, now only a few flakes remaining. There were small tables on either side, dark wood topped with green marble. The table nearest the door held a lamp. What looked like a delicate piece was cut glass, heavy and substantial. He'd knocked it over that morning, had cringed when it landed on the marble, had checked it for chips or cracks and, to his relief, found nothing.

The bedspread was lace, not the fragile stuff at the windows but heavier, old-fashioned lace. Underneath it a crimson sheet showed through, and underneath that... Moving to the side of the bed, he lifted the top corner of the covers and turned them back, pulling the pillow free from its neatly tucked niche. Then he moved once more to the foot of the bed and simply looked.

The fitted sheet underneath was white and new. Brandnew. Still had the creases from the cardboard folded in with its package. Why a new sheet? Had it simply been time? Or had the old one been too soiled to use again—and if that was the case, how could he have missed noticing?

It had been dark. He had relied on streetlight rather than lamplight to get dressed and leave. It had been cold. He had slid out from underneath the covers, gotten dressed and left without ever looking back at the bed. After the six-hour drive back to Houston, he'd taken a shower, then fallen into bed for a good long nap. He had never noticed that he'd bedded a virgin, had never suspected that there was anything to notice.

A virgin. Last night he had been shocked and dismayed. This morning there was still a little of the shock—after all, in his experience, there weren't too many mid-twentysomething virgins running around Texas—but the dismay had given way to something else, to regret that he couldn't recall the event and to satisfaction—blame it on pure male vanity—that no other man had done what he'd done. No other man had touched her the way *he* had touched her. No other man had experienced the pleasure of her body. No other man would ever know her the way he would know her.

"Hoping a visit to the scene of the crime will jog your memory?"

He glanced at Faith, standing in the doorway, hands deep in the pockets of her robe, long brown hair falling damply over her shoulders. For breakfast she'd worn the same robe, belted over a flannel gown of the sort designed to discourage any red-blooded man from taking liberties. Now she was naked underneath it. The fabric clung to the slope of her breasts, revealing her nipples, then swooped out to drape over her rounded belly. For a woman scheduled to give birth any day now, she looked damned sexy.

Sexy. As in desirable. As in easy to lust for. As in he was about to get hard right here and now for a woman who, by rights, should be about as desirable as a blow to the head.

He rested his arms on the footboard and felt the metal's chill on his bare arms. "So this is where we did the deed."

She came further into the room and busied herself for a moment with smoothing the sheets, retucking the pillow and respreading the lace coverlet. "This is the place," she said as she took a step back, folding her arms underneath her breasts and above her stomach.

She didn't have a clue, he thought with mild amusement, how enticing she was. How lovely, how incredibly *womanly*. And if he told her, she would think he was crazy. Hell, *he* thought he was crazy, and he was the one with the arousal.

Warning himself that he must be a sucker for punishment, he moved toward her and, as casually as if he did it every day, he pulled her into his arms. As uneasy as if she never engaged in such casual intimacies—and he knew well how little physical intimacy of any kind there had been in her life—she immediately stiffened, but she didn't push away. She didn't fight him.

"Didn't you ever stop to think that I might be a threat to your virtue?" he asked, drawing his palms lightly up and down her arms, making her shiver.

She tossed her hair back, then met his gaze unflinchingly. "Why in the world would I think that?"

"You must have had some hint that something was going to happen. You must have thought—"

She shook her head.

"You didn't simply say, 'Tonight's a good night to lose my virginity. I'll do it with the man who's last to leave.'"

Another shake of her head made her hair brush tantalizingly over his forearms.

"When did you know?"

For a moment she remained silent. She was so protective of herself, so afraid of sharing anything personal even with the man who had already shared it. Did she think that she could keep herself intact that way, that when he left—as she seemed convinced he eventually would—she wouldn't lose anything if she'd kept it all to herself?

Then, when he was about to give up hope, she replied in a quavery, hoarse voice. "When you touched me."

Pleased that she had answered, he smiled just a bit. "I guess I must have lost the magic. I'm touching you now, and you look as if it's all you can do to keep from running away."

Another jolt of tension shot through her, intensified almost immediately by the surprise that widened her eyes. "You're— You've got—*Nick*."

Chuckling, he leaned forward until his mouth was only inches above her ear. "An erection, sweetheart. Don't act so shocked. I would worry if I could hold you like this and *not* get one."

She pushed against him. "That's not normal. I'm pregnant."

"And that has what to do with this?"

"Pregnant women aren't—"

"Sexy?" he supplied. "You're right. I can honestly admit that I've never gotten turned on by a pregnant woman before, but—" he brushed his mouth across her ear and made her shiver "—I've never known you before."

Her eyes were so wide, so innocent, so blue. "Don't be silly. I'm not—"

Changing his hold but never letting her go, he pulled her over to the dresser. It was old, probably verifiably antique, and consisted of drawers on two sides stacked high, a low center shelf connecting them, green marble tops and a tall, three-piece mirror that offered a slightly distorted image. He turned her to face their reflection, but she demurely lowered her gaze. So very pregnant and so damned innocent.

"Look at yourself, Faith," he commanded, standing close behind her, holding her snug against him. "Look at your face, your body. All those guys you used to date—yes, they saw you as a challenge, but not because they wanted to succeed where other men had failed. They wanted you because of who you are, because you're so damned lovely."

She raised her gaze at last, but it was obvious she didn't see the same image he did. "I'm heavy and clumsy," she said flatly. Then, curiously, she leaned forward, unintentionally pressing her bottom against his groin, making him bite down hard on a groan. "This is the first time I've seen my feet in weeks. I'm awkward and slow. Everything I do is a chore." She made eye contact with him in the mirror. "And if you find any of that attractive, then you've been alone too long."

"Maybe I have," he agreed with a sigh, but he didn't believe it for a moment. It wasn't conceit to say that when he was alone, it was by choice. He knew enough women, and he knew all the lines for picking up new ones, if he was in the mood. But he hadn't been in the mood for a long time. For... oh, a few days short of nine months.

The realization made him wonder just how good that night had been. What kind of magic had passed between them in that bed that had caused him to remain celibate—faithful to a memory that he hadn't believed existed—for nearly nine months? It must have been incredible, heartstopping, amazing—like Faith herself. He would sell his soul to remember.

He would give it away free to do it again.

Forcing himself to release her, he moved back as far as the bed. "Why don't you give me the key to the shop? You get some rest, and I'll take care of things for you."

She shook her head.

"I'm perfectly capable."

"I know you are."

He hesitated, studying her. "I'm going down there with you anyway."

"I know that, too. I'm going to get dressed."

He waited until she was at the door before he spoke again. "I don't suppose you need help."

She looked back. "No. But I think you do."

With a grin, he watched her leave. After a moment he went across the hall to the fourth bedroom. Great-aunt Lydia's, he was sure, although Faith had never said so. It was hard enough to imagine her throwing away a lifetime of rigid teachings to jump into bed with him, but it was impossible to imagine her jumping into Lydia's bed with him.

Besides, the aura of the room fit his image of the old woman perfectly. It was dark, oppressive. Deep mahogany furniture. Dusty drapes of a fabric so heavy that not even the most powerful beam of light could pierce them. Plain wood floors stained dark walnut and unsoftened by even one small rug. Ugly portraits on the wall, no knickknacks, nothing personal or even remotely feminine anywhere in the room. How difficult it must have been for Faith, being raised by a woman who could live comfortably in these quarters. How damned unfair it had been.

Closing the door once more, he turned toward the stairs and the back of the house. Toward Faith's room. It was the one room in the house he hadn't yet seen, and he was willing to bet that it was as airy and light as Lydia's was suffocating. One quick glance inside the open door was enough to confirm his hunch, but it wasn't enough to satisfy his curiosity.

He stood in the doorway, hands in his hip pockets, and made a leisurely study of the room. The first thing he noticed was Faith's absence and the open closet door. A light was on, and from inside came the rustle of clothing. The next thing to catch his attention was her bed. It was a double, the headboard finished in a rich light oak stain, the sheets a rose and pale green print, the comforter striped with wide slashes of rose and pale ivory. This was where he would make love to her next time, on this bed, surrounded by soft, light colors. He would lay her down amid all those pillows, and he would satisfy every curiosity she'd ever had—and some she'd never had—about the mysteries and the magic of making love. He would make up to her for the first time, would make her forget the first time, and he would remember every single detail about it for the rest of his life.

The mere thought made his recently settled arousal stir again. Swallowing hard, he forced his attention away from the bed and to the rest of the room. The walls were papered in patterns that coordinated with the bedding, part floral print, part striped, and the rugs scattered around the room were ivory or green. The furniture—bed, night tables, dresser, makeup table and chair—was mismatched but all oak, all lightly colored. There was a collection of little glass bottles on one table, a half-dozen miniature oil lamps on another and paintings and a few postcards framed on the walls.

All in all, it was a welcoming room. It was definitely a place where he could live.

And Faith, he acknowledged as she walked out of the closet, was definitely the woman he could live with.

She was wearing disreputable loafers and a cotton slip that was about as simple as a garment could get—white, wide straps, a little bit of lace at the rounded neck and again along the hem—and managing once again to look incredibly, improbably sexy. For reasons totally beyond his understanding, she had put on hose and was about to pull on the same pretty green dress she'd worn to Michael's wedding. If he were a woman in her condition, he would wear the most comfortable clothes available. A floor-length muumuu sounded just about right.

If she objected to him invading her personal space, she didn't show it. She simply glanced at him as she made her way to the unmade bed, where she laid the dress down, then opened the zipper that ran down the back. "I have an entire closet full of clothes that don't fit. If Amelia Rose waits much beyond Sunday, I'll have to take your advice and close the shop, because all I'll be able to squeeze into will be that awful flannel nightgown.'' She pulled the dress over her head, tugged it down over her belly, adjusted the sleeves and the shoulders, then turned her back to him. "Do you mind?"

He crossed the room, brushed her hair out of the way, then slid the zipper to the top. "What kind of idiot makes a maternity dress with a zipper in back?"

"What kind of idiot buys a maternity dress with a zipper in back?" she retorted, then sighed deeply. "I'm sorry. I *am* really cranky this morning."

"I think you're entitled," he said quietly. "It's been a tough week."

"Yeah." Her agreement was soft and just a little forlorn. It made him want to pick her up, carry her to bed, crawl in and hold her there until she went to sleep—and continue holding her until she woke up again. But before he could do more than think the idea, she moved away, seating herself at the makeup table. Her hair was still a little damp, but she didn't bother drying it. Instead she quickly fashioned it into a braid, securing it with a band the same shade of green as her dress. She applied her makeup with the same quick, confident movements, then added a pair of earrings and, sliding it over her head as she stood up, a pendant.

It was the same necklace he'd caught occasional glimpses of, normally tucked inside her clothing. This time, before she had a chance to hide it away, he reached for it, dangling the chain from his fingers. The pendant was oval, a cameo set in sterling, and the carving was as delicate as the woman who wore it. Black onyx encircled a relief in mother-of-pearl of a serenely smiling mother cradling an equally serene baby. It was exactly the sort of gift he would have chosen to give her, had he seen it first. Had he known her first.

"Nice," he murmured before replacing it—not letting it fall, but gently laying the pendant at the end of its chain between her breasts.

For a long moment they simply stood there, only inches apart, her hands hanging loosely at her sides, his hand still resting lightly on the cameo. His fingers ached to move one way or the other—to her breasts, heavy and sure to be sensitive to his caresses, or lower to her stomach. He felt an incredible urge to spread both hands wide across her belly, to gain that sort of intimacy with her, to make whatever contact he could with his daughter. He had never felt an unborn baby's movements, and he had discovered that he wanted to. He wanted very much to feel his daughter moving within her mother's womb.

But the moment passed. Faith broke the spell by taking a step back, clearing her throat and looking around uncomfortably as if she might have forgotten something. "We'd better be going," she said, striving to sound normal but coming out shaky instead. "If I'm late opening the shop, my friends worry."

His own voice was a far cry from normal, too. "Tell them they don't have to worry anymore. I'll take care of you."

Her laughter was unexpected and as warm as a summer breeze. "Oh, darlin'," she said in her rich Texas drawl. "That'll make them worry even more."

Magic.

Nick had said the magic word—*magic*—and nearly four hours later, Faith's heart rate hadn't quite returned to normal yet. Do you believe in magic? an old song asked. For years she had, but last spring's disappointment had stolen her faith. Now...maybe it existed, after all. Maybe Nick believed in it, too, and between the two of them, maybe they could conjure some up for Amelia Rose and for themselves. Especially for themselves.

She was sitting on the couch in the storeroom, feet propped on a box of winter coats, size two toddler. The Closed sign was on the door, with the hands on the little clock pointing to one o'clock, and Nick had gone to pick up lunch.

True to his word, he had insisted on helping in the shop. He hadn't waited on any customers, but he'd run the vacuum and had done all the necessary restocking. She had caught him more than once standing next to a display and studying some toy or fingering some incredibly soft garment. If she didn't know better, she would swear that he was anticipating Amelia Rose's birth almost as much as she was.

But she did know better, she thought, her mouth drooping in dejection. He was simply making the best of their bad situation. He had no choice in becoming a father—the deed was done, the inevitable approaching—and so, by God, he was going to be a good one. Once he held his daughter in his arms and saw her angel's face, her sweet little smile and her trusting soft eyes, Faith believed he would surpass "good" for "loving and devoted." But those qualities would always be overshadowed by the fact that he'd been a reluctant father, trapped by bad luck and careless behavior.

And there wasn't enough magic in the entire world, she suspected, to change that.

Or was there? There was enough to make a man like Nick Russo look at her, as big and clumsy as a whale on dry land, and find something arousing. There was enough to make him propose marriage to her. Even though he'd done it solely for the sake of their child, it was still quite a feat. Maybe there was enough to make him forget his reluctance and bad luck. Maybe there was enough to make him love Amelia Rose unreservedly, with all the enthusiasm and commitment he would feel for a child he had willingly chosen to create.

Maybe there was even enough magic in the world to make him want *her*, not because she was the mother of his child but because he loved her, because he needed her and couldn't live without her.

If she was going to dream, she thought with a sad smile, why not dream the impossible?

A key scraped in the lock, then the back door swung open. She smelled the hamburgers first, then the faint hint of after-shave. It was spicy, masculine. Of course, her own floral scent would smell masculine on *him*. It was something about him, something so essentially male. Even the rose-colored T-shirt he wore today looked as macho on him as black leather and studs would on other men.

He set the food out and, indulging only in the smallest of talk, they ate. When she finished, Faith kicked her shoes off, pulled her feet onto the couch and yawned. "You know, you don't have to stay here all afternoon. I'm sure you have things to do."

He shook his head. "Can't think of a one."

"How about finding a place to live? Michael and Michelle will be back from their honeymoon in a week and a half, and I doubt they'll appreciate his big brother bunking in their living room."

"I've got a place in mind." His grin was as charming and self-assured as any she'd ever seen, but she wasn't charmed. Maybe it was because of that self-assurance, or maybe it was the glint in his eye, but she had a sneaking suspicion she knew exactly which place he had in mind: *hers.*

And there was a part of her that liked the idea so very much.

"I'm not marrying you," she said adamantly.

"Did I ask you again?"

"No. I'm just making it clear that if you think you can move out of Michael's apartment into my house, you're wrong. I'm letting you be a part of Amelia Rose's life, but that's all. So if that's why you're delaying house-hunting, don't bother."

He sat at the opposite end of the sofa, studying her with clear amusement. "You know the one word I've heard others apply to you most often? Sweet. 'Sweet Faith. She's so sweet, such a sweetheart.' You know, I don't believe you've been sweet to me yet."

She tried not to share his amusement, but the corners of her mouth twitched anyway until she managed a firm scowl. "I was sweet to you last February, and look where it got me."

"About to get married and give birth. The two biggest days in a woman's life, and you won't even have to wait. They'll come one right after the other."

"Why won't you take no for an answer?" she asked a little wearily, and his expression turned as sober as she'd ever seen it.

"I can't. Why won't you say yes for an answer?"

She could. She could take the blood test, get the license and let the priest at Sacred Heart perform the ceremony. She could deal with his family's shock and welcome the pleasure he was convinced they would also feel. She could listen to the gossip as everyone else repeated what, by rights, only she and Nick should know: that they'd had to get married, that he'd married her only because of the baby, that she couldn't hold on to a man like him.

And knowing that it was true, knowing that he didn't want her but was willing to settle for her, knowing that he would never love her, that inevitably he would leave her, every day she would die a little inside.

"I can't, either." Forcing back the emotion that clogged her throat, she went on. "It doesn't matter, Nick. Kids are raised in one-parent homes all the time, and they're perfectly happy."

"But why should Amelia Rose have to settle for one parent at a time when she can have both? Why should she have to deal with the same stigma of illegitimacy that you grew up with when it's within your power to change it?"

Guilt made her shift uneasily even as she tried to defend her position. "It wasn't so bad. Besides, that was a long time ago. Things have changed. People have changed. There are so many unwed mothers these days that no one gives them a second thought."

"'No one gives them a second thought,'" he repeated sarcastically. "So why have you been the prime topic of gossip here in town for the past nine months?" When she made no effort to reply, he went on. "Maybe no one notices elsewhere, but New Hope hasn't changed. My family hasn't changed, and I haven't changed. Every single woman of childbearing age in the whole damned state of Texas can give birth without husbands for all I care, but not to *my* children."

Her temper flaring at the possessive *my*, Faith folded her arms across her chest. "Fine. If it's so important to you, we'll get married. Amelia Rose and I will live in my house, and you can live wherever the hell you want, as long as it's not with us."

"That's not a marriage."

"You're not looking for a marriage. You're looking for a suitable way out for your daughter. This is it. You want her to have your name and she'll have it, but we won't be stuck in a miserable marriage that *we* can't get out of."

Annoyance, underlaid by bewilderment, flashed across his face. "What makes you so sure that being married to me would make you miserable? I'm not a bad person, Faith. I'll be the best father Antonio Russo's son could be. I'd never hurt you. I wouldn't run around. I would never run out on you."

And he would never love her. He might like her. He might want her—in the physical sense, at least. He would give her the respect the mother of his child deserved. But he wouldn't love her. He wouldn't be committed to her. He wouldn't have a place in his heart or in his life where she was anything more than Amelia Rose's mother.

Well, she'd been there before. She'd been taken in by her great-aunt because she was Sally's daughter. She'd been accepted here in New Hope because she was Lydia's greatniece. It was a lonely feeling, one that she'd lived with every day of her life for twenty-one years. It had made her feel lost and utterly alone, and she wouldn't go through that again for anything, not even her precious Amelia Rose.

"I don't want to argue with you, Nick," she said wearily and realized that she truly meant it. Under the best of circumstances, arguing was a waste of time. In this case, it was impossibly futile. All he could do was accept her decision, because he wasn't about to change her mind.

He stared at her for a long time, then made a conscious decision to lighten the mood. "Darlin', you've argued with me from the time I walked through the door last Wednesday. Personally, I think you enjoy it."

She wadded the trash from her lunch into a tight ball, then started to scoot to the edge of the couch. Standing, he offered his hand, and she took it, letting him pull her to her feet and uncomfortably close.

No, she amended as he slid his arm around her waist, too *comfortably* close. She shouldn't let him hold her like this, shouldn't let herself enjoy it, but she did. She knew it was risky, knew she was vulnerable to him, knew that he could sweep her off her feet as easily now as he had nine months ago. Still, she liked the closeness. She liked feeling the heat from his body, liked hearing the slow, steady cadence of his breathing. She felt sheltered in his arms. Protected. *Safe.* Even though that was the place where she was really most at risk.

He bent over, his mouth brushing her ear, and she reflexively—naturally—raised her hands to his chest. "You're right," he murmured. "We won't argue anymore. You'll let me have my way, and I'll make damned sure you never regret it."

"We've already done that. You've had your way, and I'll never regret it."

"Yeah, but this time I'll be sober. This time we'll make it legal." His mouth moved closer, his tongue stroking the shape of her ear. "This time we'll make it last."

Sweet promises. Sweet lies.

For just a moment her fingers curled, wrapping around the soft folds of his shirt. Then she forced herself to let go, to push against him, to free herself from him. "Look, Nick, I appreciate all this, but I really need some time alone. Please."

His silence was palpable as one moment slid past, then another. Finally, though, he nodded. "I do have some things to take care of, after all," he said evenly. "I'll be back to take you home."

She nodded, too, then hesitantly offered, "You can stay for dinner...if you want."

His smile came slowly—not a grin, not the charming, confident smile that captured all female hearts, but a simple, sweet, genuinely pleased smile that made her breath catch and her knees go weak. "I do," he said quietly. "I surely do."

The afternoon sun had warmed the air considerably, almost to the short-sleeves comfort zone, but the breeze blowing out of the west dropped the temperature another few degrees. Still, Nick held rather than wore his jacket, clasped between his hands, dangling between his legs, as he sat on one of the concrete benches in the center of the park.

He hadn't been to the park in longer than he could remember, not since the last time he'd made it home for the annual Russo Fourth of July picnic. This was the table they always claimed, loading it down with more food than they could even think of eating. They brought lawn chairs for the adults and spread quilts around for the kids. The women talked and took care of the babies, and the men talked and played games with the older kids. When it came time for the fireworks display, everyone gathered together on the blankets, one great mass of bodies.

In the past sixteen years he'd missed far more celebrations than he'd attended, but as of this month, he had missed his last. He would be present for every Christmas and New Year's, every Easter and Memorial Day, every Fourth of July and Labor Day and, *absolutely,* for every Thanksgiving. He would make it to every birthday celebration, too, and every anniversary—he and Amelia Rose and somehow, some way, Faith.

He knew she missed having a family of her own, knew in his heart that it was something she had always longed for. She would positively blossom in his own family. They were already fond of her, already protective of her. They would welcome her as one of their own.

If only he could change her mind about his proposal. If only he could make her believe he wanted more than their baby. And if only he could convince her that, for the first time in her life, somebody wanted *her,* that *he* wanted her.

The sound of a car door behind him made him turn toward the parking lot. His father was striding across the grass, wearing an overcoat with his usual black trousers and white shirt. Nick couldn't remember the last time he'd seen Antonio in something different—if he ever had. Even at weddings, baptisms and funerals, it was the same, with the simple addition of a coat and tie. It was familiar. Comforting.

"You picked a beautiful day for a visit to the park," Antonio said as a greeting.

It *was* a nice day, in spite of the chill. The sun was shining, the sky was intensely blue, and it was easy to believe that winter was leaving and not arriving. "Thanks for coming, Pop."

His father shrugged. "Gerard can handle the kitchen without me. So...I take it you're ready to talk about whatever was bothering you last night."

As Antonio sat down, Nick stood up. He tossed his jacket on the bench, paced a few feet away, then faced his father. "I need to know that—for right now, at least—this will stay between you and me."

"All right."

It was that simple, Nick thought with relief and more than a little respect. His father had no idea what kind of secret he was about to be entrusted with, yet he could swear silence that easily—and he would keep his promise. In all his life, Nick had never known his father to break a promise, no matter how important or how insignificant.

Now that Nick had the promise, though, confiding his problems wasn't so simple. He didn't want his father to be disappointed with him. He didn't want to see regret or shame in Antonio's eyes when he looked at him.

Dismayed, Nick shook his head. "I don't even know how to say this."

"Start from the beginning."

The beginning. That night he knew so little about. The night that had changed so many lives. Taking a deep breath, he followed his father's advice. "Remember when I came home last February for Mike's engagement party?"

Antonio nodded.

"Everyone thought I'd gone back to Houston before the party was over, but I didn't. I spent most of the night here in town. With a woman." He swallowed hard. "With Faith Harper."

His father stared at him, his expression totally blank. He must know what was coming, Nick thought regretfully. He had to recognize the significance of what little he'd already heard, but he probably didn't want to acknowledge it. He wouldn't want to believe that the self-centered, cold-hearted bastard who had seduced—then abandoned—sweet, innocent Faith was his own son.

He forced himself to go on. "I was drunk, Pop. I woke up in the early dawn, alone in a strange house with one hell of a hangover, and I had to get back to Houston. I didn't know—didn't remember anything. Faith found out she was pregnant about the same time she heard that I'd gotten married. No one ever told her that I hadn't, so she never told me about the baby."

Antonio slowly got to his feet and looked Nick in the eye. The disappointment was there. The regret and, yeah, the shame. "You're the father of Faith's baby."

"She never told me," he repeated. "I didn't find out until last week."

"You seduced that girl, then went home and *forgot* about her?" There was anger in his voice, a cold, cutting anger that Nick had never received from anyone in his entire family. It made him feel cold and raw inside.

"No, Pop," he said, his tone too sarcastic, too shaky. "I forgot about her before I even left her house."

"You left her to go through this alone? Left her open to ridicule and gossip because of *your* actions?" Antonio shook his head in disgust. "How could you, Nick? Your mother and I raised you better than that. We *taught* you better than that."

Nick paced a few yards away, breathing deeply to stay in control, then turned back. "Pop, I'm not proud of what I did. I shouldn't have gotten drunk, but I did. I damn well shouldn't have touched her, but I did that, too. I'm sorry about it, but I can't change any of it."

"You're sorry," his father repeated. "Sorry you seduced her? Sorry you got her pregnant? Or just sorry you got caught?"

Nick stared at him for a moment, then shook his head. "I'm sorry I don't remember it. I'm sorry I wasn't here for what happened afterward, and I'm sorry I didn't find out sooner. But I'm *not* sorry that it happened."

Antonio turned away, walked to the opposite side of the table and stared across the park. There was a parking lot back there, along with one of the two playgrounds in the park. Nick knew his father often brought the grandkids here to play, one at a time, so they could all have a little special time with Grandpa. Was he thinking about bringing Amelia Rose here?

After a long, uncomfortable time, Antonio turned back around and faced Nick, his expression hard and disapproving. "Now that you know, what do you intend to do about it?"

"I moved back."

"That's not enough."

"No," Nick agreed with a sigh. "It's not. I asked Faith to marry me."

"And she said?"

"Something along the line of 'when hell freezes over.'"

Antonio's mouth twitched, but he bit back the smile. "Maybe we underestimated young Faith. So what are you going to do?"

"I don't know. Wear her down. Keep at her until she finds it easier to say yes than no." He shrugged. "I know it's hard for her. She's disappointed. She's never had anybody, but she had a lot of dreams." The words he was about to say hurt—he was surprised by how much they hurt—but he forced them out anyway. "I don't measure up. This whole damned situation doesn't measure up."

Finally his father's attitude turned sympathetic, though whether to him or Faith, Nick couldn't say. "She had higher hopes for marriage than what you're offering."

He nodded.

"Any chance that you can offer more?"

Define "more," he wanted to say, just to avoid answering, but he knew exactly what his father meant. Was there any chance that he might change a marriage that was—in her mind—for all the wrong reasons into the sort of marriage she wanted? Was there any chance that a marriage for the sake of their child could become a marriage for their own sakes?

Was there any chance he could come to love her?

It was a hard question to answer, even harder than it had been to admit that *he* was the dishonorable bastard who had abandoned her. It was hard to look that closely at what he already felt, even harder to consider what he might feel in another week, another month, another year—especially knowing that she might never feel the same. It was damned near impossible to admit, after years of promising himself that he would never fall in love, that he was well on the way to doing exactly that.

And it hurt to admit that she wouldn't believe him, that she couldn't believe she was worthy of anyone's love beside Amelia Rose's.

"I see," his father said with a quiet sigh.

"No, Pop, you don't. Faith is—" He echoed the sigh. "Different."

"As your mother and I tried to tell you yesterday." Antonio gave a bemused shake of his head. "Obviously, we were more than a little too late."

"What I feel for her doesn't matter—" *Like hell it doesn't.* "Because she's never going to believe it. She's convinced that I only want to marry her because of Amelia Rose."

Just as Nick had done only a week ago, his father focused on one particular point. "It's a girl? My new grandbaby is a girl?"

"She believes so."

"A girl." Antonio's smile was filled with pride. "We have seventeen boys and only seven girls. A new baby girl. Rose after your great-grandmother?"

With faint regret Nick shook his head. "She chose the name herself, probably the very instant she suspected she was pregnant."

Antonio waved away the regret. "Go on. She's convinced that you want to marry her only for the sake of my granddaughter. What? She doesn't believe that's a good enough reason to marry?"

"You know her background better than I do, Pop. Her father took off before she was born. Her mother gave her away before she was a month old. She was raised by an old woman who knew everything about discipline and nothing about love. She knew from the time she was a baby that her aunt had taken her in only because she had—" how had Faith put it? "—a family duty to do so. Lydia made her feel like a burden, unwanted and unloved."

"I remember the old woman. She wasn't fit to raise such a small, needy child." Antonio sat down on the bench again. "You probably don't remember because she's so much younger than you—she's Michael's age, you know—but Faith used to play at our house sometimes. On a hot summer day all the kids would be in shorts and T-shirts, dirty, barefoot, playing in the sprinklers, and Lucia would be sitting on the porch with Faith in her little dress, shoes and socks, absolutely spotless, her hair fixed just so. She never got to get dirty, never got to have fun. She was the most frighteningly polite child I'd ever seen."

After a moment's silence his father asked yet again, "So, son, what are you going to do?"

Nick sat down beside him. "Actually, I was hoping you could tell me."

"When is my grandbaby due?"

"In a few days."

"Not much chance you'll get her married before then, is there?"

Nick looked up at the sky. "I doubt it. It's a little cool today, but I think we're a long way from hell freezing over."

They sat in silence for a time, then his father glanced at him. "Are you happy about the baby?"

"I wasn't." His grin was shaky. "But the more I get used to the idea . . . I don't know. It just seems so—"

"Miraculous?"

After considering it a moment, Nick nodded. "Yeah. *Miraculous.* A week ago, all I could think was, 'Oh, God, please don't let this be true.' Now—"

His father laid his hand on Nick's shoulder. "Now you're ready to be a father."

Again, Nick considered it for a moment, then once more nodded. "Yeah." He was ready to be a father—*and* a husband. He just had to convince Faith.

"You know, I can't keep this from your mother for long, and once I tell her, the whole town will know. She'll be too excited to keep it to herself. She'll have to brag to everyone about her new granddaughter."

Nick knew that, of course. He'd told Faith, even though she hadn't believed him, that his parents would be thrilled. Regardless of whether Amelia Rose's parents were married, Antonio and Luisa would welcome the baby into their family with the same excitement, love and joy that had accompanied the births of their other two dozen grandkids.

They would welcome Faith into the family with the same enthusiasm. They would make up for the family she'd never had. They would welcome her, love her and protect her. If they had a chance. If she gave them that chance.

"Pop . . . could Mom have everybody over for dinner Friday evening?"

Immediately catching on, his father grinned. "She would be happy to. You know she never misses a chance to get all the kids together. Does this mean I can tell her?"

Nick drew a deep breath. Some part of him—the part that wanted to take care of Faith and shelter her—disliked his plan. She was one shy, delicate little woman. There was no way she could stand up to any Russo—with the obvious exception of him. It wasn't fair to unleash the whole bunch of them on her at once.

But wasn't all fair in love and war? Wasn't anything he did for the sake of their child, anything done for Faith herself, all right? If he didn't honestly believe they could have a good marriage—a strong, happy, *loving* marriage—he would never push her like this. But he did believe. He believed enough for the both of them.

"Not until Friday, Pop," he answered at last as he stood and tugged his jacket on. Offering his father a tight, uneasy smile, he finished, "You can tell everyone Friday."

Chapter 9

Faith was with a customer when Nick came strolling into the shop that afternoon. She hadn't expected him back so soon—it was only a little after three-thirty—but she was happy to see him—so happy that it made her scowl.

"Are you all right, dear?" Mrs. Willingham, her old high school English teacher, set the educational toy they'd been discussing aside and worriedly patted Faith's arm. "Should I have that young man with Beth get you a chair?"

"No," Faith blurted, then flushed. If Mrs. Willingham called Nick over, he would probably insist on carrying her into the back room to rest, or, more likely, he would make her go home and to bed.

Which wouldn't be a bad place to be.

Especially with him.

"I'm all right," she hastily reassured the elderly woman. "It's just a little indigestion."

Immediately the worry faded and was replaced by a knowing smile. "Oh, yes, I remember that well. I never suffered from morning sickness, but by the last few weeks of each pregnancy, I couldn't eat anything without suffering an incredible case of heartburn. When is the baby due?''

"Four more days."

"Oh, honey, you should be home resting, not in here on your feet all day."

"Exactly what I've been trying to tell her."

Faith cringed as Nick joined them. What was he doing? Mrs. Willingham might be old as the hills, but she was as quick and sharp as ever. She was more likely to recognize even the most subtle of hints than probably anyone else in town.

"Nick Russo. I'd heard you were back for your brother's wedding."

He contradicted her with a shake of his head. "Back to stay, Mrs. Willingham. I've moved home."

The old lady smiled. "How nice. However, I'm not surprised that you've returned. Family ties are powerful, and your family ties seem unusually so. Your parents must be overjoyed."

"They are," he agreed with a grin that Faith found both smug and endearing. "In fact, I just came from a visit with my father. He was thrilled." He said the last with a quick glance at Faith.

Was that a little extra emphasis he'd put on his last word? As in his reply when she had warned that his parents wouldn't be pleased to find out he was about to have an illegitimate daughter. *Are you kidding? They're going to be thrilled.*

No. She was being overly suspicious. He wouldn't have told his father about them. He wouldn't tell them until Amelia Rose was here. He would want to try to resolve their disagreements before bringing his family into the situation... wouldn't he?

Mrs. Willingham directed her next words to Faith. "I taught Nick English, also—or rather, I tried. He wasn't very enthusiastic about learning. All he wanted was a C so he wouldn't jeopardize his place on the football and baseball teams."

"Yes, but I earned a B," he reminded her.

"Faith earned straight A's, and I taught her for three years," the old lady said with a smile. "She was such a good student—such a good girl. She was a teacher's dream."

He gave Faith a long, measuring look before agreeing. "I imagine she could be anyone's dream."

Even his? she wondered, the conversation continuing without her attention. Her head said no, but her heart...her heart wanted to believe *maybe*. Of course, in her heart, she wanted to believe all sorts of things. That people were basically good. That parents didn't give away their children by choice. That children weren't responsible for the actions of those parents. That no one meant to hurt those children with thoughtless words and insensitive labels. That everyone deserved a family and someone to love them. That *she* deserved a family and someone special to love her.

But did she deserve the Russo family? Did she deserve Nick Russo? And could he ever find it in his heart to love her? Longing coupled with fear made her eyes grow damp. Quickly, before anyone could notice, she closed them, lowered her head and pinched the bridge of her nose as if she had a headache, as if she could somehow push the tears back inside where they belonged.

Immediately Nick laid his hand on her shoulder, a stronger, more solid, more reassuring touch than Mrs. Willingham's. "Are you okay?"

Hoping he wouldn't see any evidence of weepiness, she lowered her hand from her face, opened her eyes and forced a smile. "I'm fine."

"She's tired," Mrs. Willingham stated flatly. "She needs to go home and rest."

"I agree," Nick said, stalling Faith's protest. "Why don't you ask Beth to close up this evening, and I'll take you home."

Upon hearing the conversation, Beth joined them. "Sure, I'd be happy to close."

"I'm fine," Faith repeated, but no one seemed to be listening.

Beth slid her arm around her shoulders. "Look, you're going to be having this baby any day now. Mom will be working during the day, but I'll be closing every day until you come back. I've done it before, and I'm perfectly capable of doing it now. Go on. Go home. Go to bed."

She hesitated, but knew it would be easier to agree than to argue. Besides, she did want to go home. She wanted to nest, to curl up in her warm, safe, welcoming home and not come out again until her daughter was born. Letting her breath out heavily, she said, "All right. I'll go home."

Satisfied that they'd won the battle, Beth returned to the counter where she'd been studying and Nick went to the storeroom to get Faith's purse and coat. They left her alone with Mrs. Willingham, who was studying her intently. Faith tried to smile, but such scrutiny, especially now, especially when she felt so vulnerable, was hard to take.

"He's a nice young man," the old lady said at last, an odd, knowing tone to her voice. "Solid, responsible, comes from a good family. You could have done worse."

Faith stared at her for a moment, then suddenly tears welled again and her lower lip trembled. "Please," she whispered.

Mrs. Willingham reached out once more and patted her arm. "Dear, I've kept secrets longer than you've been alive. I won't tell anyone. Though I don't know how much longer it can stay a secret. I've taught more Russos than you could shake a stick at, and I've yet to see one who doesn't look just like all the others. Besides, Nick was never one to hide things. He's not going to be a proud papa in secret."

That was one of the problems, Faith wanted to sob. She wasn't sure he was going to be a *proud* father at all.

As he came out of the storeroom, Faith wiped desperately at her eyes. Mrs. Willingham pressed a lavender-scented handkerchief into her hands, then patted her once more. "It's your hormones, dear," she said with a chuckle, for Nick's benefit, Faith suspected, rather than her own. "Your entire system is out of whack, you're exhausted, and every little thing you do is a major undertaking. When I was pregnant, I cried at the drop of a hat. Take her home, Nick. Make her lie down, prop her feet up and do nothing for a change."

"I intend to." Sliding her purse under his arm, he lifted her left arm and slid it into the coat sleeve. She cooperated by raising her right arm, but he took care of the rest. When he was finished, he gave Mrs. Willingham one of those charming smiles. "It was nice seeing you."

She implied the same with a regal nod. "I hope to see you again soon."

"I'm sure you will. Come on, Faith."

She let him usher her out of the store and a few yards down the street to where his truck was parked. There he practically lifted her into the seat, then leaned across and fastened the seat belt around her before closing the door. The instant he climbed into the driver's seat, she asked, "Did you tell your father?"

He became very still for a moment, not moving, not breathing, not looking at her. Then, his voice even and almost normal, he replied, "Yes, I did."

"Why?"

He started the engine and turned the heater on low. It wasn't really cold, Faith realized, but she was. The warm air on her feet felt almost as good as sliding into a tubful of fragrant, steamy water—a pleasure she hadn't indulged in since the sixth month of her pregnancy when her body had changed enough to start making simple things more difficult.

Finally he looked at her. "When I need advice or someone to talk to, I go to my father. A lot of people do. You would know that if you'd ever had one of your own."

She should be angry that he'd told her secret to someone else, but she didn't have the energy. Besides, it was his secret, too. She had told Wendy and had just confirmed it for Mrs. Willingham, so he was entitled to tell whomever he wanted. More than angry, she should feel threatened. If any one bunch of people in the world could make her accept his marriage proposal, it was his family. Hadn't she wanted to be part of a family like that all her life? Hadn't she marveled over them every time she'd gone to their house to play with Lucia—over the love, the affection, the respect, the strength? Weren't they exactly the sort of family she'd dreamed about bringing Amelia Rose into?

"He's the only one who knows so far. But, Faith, trying to keep it secret is just delaying the inevitable."

She knew that. Eight days ago only she had known. Then Wendy had found out, and Nick. He'd told his father, and Mrs. Willingham had guessed. His father would tell his mother, who would tell all the other Russos. Wendy might slip and confide in Travis. Faith herself would eventually admit it to Valerie, and in a few more days she was going to have to come forward with the information for Amelia Rose's birth certificate. Common knowledge was inevitable...but the secret had been kind of nice while it lasted. Amelia Rose had been hers and hers alone. There had been no father in the picture and no pressure from him, his family or anyone else.

But wasn't a family worth the secret becoming common knowledge? Wasn't a father for Amelia Rose worth giving up that selfish claim to her daughter?

"Are you angry?" Nick sounded hesitant, unsure—something totally new for him, she was certain.

She stared out the window and sighed. "No."

He pulled away from the curb, turned at the next corner and took the side streets to her house. There he hustled her inside, took her coat from her, hung it with his, then guided her toward the parlor where he left her standing next to the old rocker. Disregarding the chill that had filled the house, he took the quilt from the sofa, wrapped it around her, then lifted her into his arms.

"Nick," she protested, but he shushed her as he sat down in the rocker and settled her across his lap. "You're going to hurt yourself," she said in halfhearted complaint even as she let him pull her head to his shoulder. He was solid, just as Mrs. Willingham had said, only in a totally different way.

He felt comfortable and warm and smelled of after-shave and fabric softener and of just plain, pure Nick.

"Darlin', I've picked up people who weigh twice what you do and never gotten hurt. Granted, I usually wind up throwing them to the ground, though, and putting the cuffs on them."

She smiled sleepily. "Sometimes I forget you're a cop."

"In a few more weeks that'll be hard, since I'll be in uniform again. It'll be the first time in seven years."

"Moving up here and taking this job is a big step back for you, isn't it?" She hadn't thought about it before, but his work wasn't just a job. It was a career, one he had studied for and had worked hard to advance in. According to his brother, he'd been a real hotshot detective in Houston. Here he would never handle the sort of cases he'd had down there. If he was going to be in uniform, that meant he would be patrolling the streets, investigating accidents, writing tickets—a far cry from the work he was used to.

"Depends on how you look at it. I worked some long hours in Houston. They weren't exactly conducive to relationships, you know. Neither was the risk. A lot of the people I worked with had never married, but a lot were divorced. Their wives got tired of spending so much time alone, of competing with the job for their attention, of always worrying." He tucked the quilt closer around her, then brushed her hair back. Simple little touches, but they spread such heat through her. "There are some advantages to big-city police work if you like excitement, variety, experience. But if you want a safer environment, if you want to go home at a reasonable hour every day, if you want both a job *and* a family, a small-town department has a lot to offer."

She just hoped he didn't find himself resenting the trade-offs he'd had to make for Amelia Rose. She prayed he didn't someday blame his daughter for forcing him to give up the career he'd chosen and become instead just another small-town cop.

As he set the chair in motion, Faith yawned. She could go to sleep right here. He would wind up squished and aching, but she would be more comfortable than she'd ever been. Fighting another yawn, she asked, "What did your father say?"

"He was angry." He must have felt her tense, because he quickly went on. "With me. Not about the baby. I already knew what my folks thought about the horrible person who seduced you, then took off, so I was prepared. About the baby—just as I told you he would be, he was thrilled. Pop loves kids. He loves little girls. I guarantee you, he's already making plans to spoil her rotten."

"Not *my* daughter," she protested, and he laughed.

"That's what grandparents do. If your grandparents had been deserving of the title, you would know that. Parents teach, train and discipline, and grandparents spoil, pamper and indulge."

She liked the sound of that—liked that Amelia Rose would have that sort of typical, normal relationship that she had missed out on. She liked that there would be grandparents—especially people she was fond of, people she respected—willing to pamper and indulge her little girl. She very much liked that Amelia Rose's life would be full, rich and loving from the very beginning, instead of sterile and lonely as her own had been.

Of course, Nick could be wrong. Just because Antonio was willing to accept Amelia Rose didn't mean Luisa or any of the others would be. Luisa could have easily chosen any number of young women right here in New Hope with whom she would prefer that Nick had a child. After all, Faith wasn't Catholic, and Luisa very much was. Faith wasn't outgoing. She didn't know how to be friendly in the way they were. She didn't know how to be part of a family. She'd become just the slightest bit notorious in the past nine months. She'd been the subject of whispers and the target of finger-pointing. Her refusal to identify the father of her baby and her decision to go through the pregnancy and raise the baby alone damned her in some eyes. And that was in addition to all the baggage of her past.

No, as much as she liked Luisa Russo, she found it hard to imagine the woman being happy that her eldest son was having an illegitimate daughter with Lydia Harper's illegitimate great-niece.

Maybe she would mind less if he was having a *legitimate* daughter with Lydia's illegitimate niece, if Nick and Faith were married before the baby came. It wouldn't stifle all the gossip, but wasn't late better than never? Wasn't Amelia Rose's legitimacy more important than her own pride? Nick obviously thought so, or he never would have proposed. Her mother's heart thought so, too—thought there was no sacrifice too great for the good of her child.

Her woman's heart, though, threatened to break in two at the thought.

"What are you thinking about?"

Tilting her head back, Faith gazed up at Nick. She could see only one side of his face, but it was a perfect side. He was a handsome man. He was the sort of man who dated beautiful women, the sort who never looked at women like her, the sort that women like her had crushes on that never developed into anything real. That long-ago night in her kitchen, she had looked at him and had felt exactly like a schoolgirl with a crush. She had been nervous, clumsy, at a loss for words.

But he *had* looked at her. He had touched her, kissed her, made love to her, and her little crush had mushroomed into dreams, hopes and fantasies of happily-ever-after. She had thought those dreams were dead, the hopes snuffed out by the reality of never hearing from him again, the fantasies destroyed by the news of his make-believe marriage. But somewhere deep inside her, they still existed. There was still a small part of her that wanted not just love, romance and marriage—she had always wanted that with her entire soul—but love, romance and marriage with him. With Nick, who was offering only the marriage part.

Nick, who was looking down at her now, waiting for an answer to his question. "What are you thinking about?" he had asked, and she could answer truthfully. She could tell him that she wanted to marry him and raise a family with him more than almost anything in the world. More than that, though, she wanted him to love her. She *needed* him to love her, because she was very afraid that she just might be falling in love with him.

Grasping for any topic that would keep her from being truthful, she thought back to their earlier conversation. They'd been talking about grandparents, about his father in particular. "Why do you call your father Pop? None of the others do."

He shifted her weight just a little, leaving her lying a little more snugly against him. "We all did when we were kids. We started with Papa—that's what he still calls his father— then we shortened it to Pop. The others eventually started calling him Dad. It was less old-fashioned, I guess. Less Old World."

"What do you want—" She had to stop, clear her throat, then start again. "What do you want Amelia Rose to call you?"

His expression turned serious and thoughtful. "I don't know. What would you prefer?" Then he grinned. "Mr. Russo? That man?"

She smiled. Then, hearing a similar phrase in a similar tone, she let the smile slip away. "My mother's name was Sally. I didn't know it until I was about six years old. Lydia always called her *that girl*. She always made it sound so contemptible."

"Lydia was a hateful old woman," he said flatly. "You deserved better than her."

Faith closed her eyes and concentrated on breathing deeply, on letting all the tension of the day—of the past week, of the past nine months—slip away. She had never experienced moments like this—quiet moments, peaceful moments, with a man's arms around her—but she could grow used to them. She could learn to love the end of the day if it meant sharing such simple intimacies as her head on his shoulder, his arms holding her close.

Marriage—most marriages, at least, and all happy ones—were full of moments like this. Snuggling like this could be commonplace instead of a rare experience. Sharing a bed, waking up in the morning to another face instead of alone, considering someone else's likes and dislikes as well as her own, coming in each evening to a warm, welcoming home instead of a big, empty house—all of those things were a part of marriage. All of those were things she wanted very much in her life—things she wanted very much with Nick. If only he could love her.

"That night last February—" His voice was soft, curious. Contented. "Did I hold you?"

"Yes." Her voice was softer. "Afterward. You fell asleep." Then, regretfully, she added, "Or passed out."

He let another moment or two pass, the only sound between them the creak of the rockers as the chair moved lazily back and forth. Then his direct gaze connected with hers as he asked, "Why did you leave me alone in bed?"

How many times had he asked her about that night, and how many times had she avoided telling him much at all? She treated her memories of the night as something to be ashamed of, or something that belonged solely to her, and neither was the truth. "I felt guilty," she admitted.

"Because you let Lydia down?"

"She didn't want me to be like my mother, and neither did I, but having sex with a stranger was exactly the sort of thing my mother would do. I'd broken the promises I'd made to Lydia and to myself, and I hadn't even had the decency to not enjoy doing it. After you fell asleep, I felt guilty, so I removed myself from temptation and went to my room."

With one hand he tugged out the band that secured her hair, then worked his fingers through, loosening the braid, combing lightly, soothingly, through her hair. "So this whole thing is Lydia's fault—your not being able to tell me about the baby, my not finding out until last week. If she hadn't raised you to be such a prim and rigidly proper young woman, you would have stayed in bed with me where you belonged, and when I woke up the next morning and found you there, I would have stayed, too. I would have made love to you again and again. I would have guaranteed that you got pregnant, and when you found out, I would have been the next to know.''

Laying the blame on her great-aunt amused her, but even as she smiled, she wondered about his assertions. If he had awakened beside her, would he have stayed? Would he have wanted her again? Would he have been there to find out about the baby right at the beginning? Would he have cared from the very beginning?

Her head said no. He still would have been hung over. He still wouldn't have remembered. Instead of waking up alone in a strange room, not knowing how he'd gotten there, he would have awakened in a strange room with a strange woman naked at his side, not knowing how either of them had gotten there.

But her heart disagreed. So he would have been hung over and would have forgotten the night before. They could have recreated the magic. They could have created new memories. They could have changed everything.

Maybe...maybe they still could.

Using one foot Nick slowed the rocker to a gentle stop. The house was quiet and cool, the silence disturbed only by Faith's slow, steady breathing. *He* couldn't seem to breathe at all as he studied her. There was an incredible tightness in his chest that squeezed his lungs flat, that made him feel warm and cold, eager and reluctant, nervous and more than a little afraid, all at the same time.

She looked so damned sweet, her eyes closed, her lips slightly parted. She looked like someone who needed his protection, someone who needed *him*. With or without his baby, she looked like his future.

He had never wanted to fall in love, had never wanted to get married and have kids. Those were decisions he'd made half a lifetime ago, decisions he had lived by for more than sixteen years. Not once in all those years had he been tempted, not as his friends and sisters had gotten married, not as they'd started their own families, certainly not as some of his friends' marriages had ended. Not one of the beautiful, sexy, sophisticated women he'd dated and made love to had ever made him think even briefly about changing his mind, about marriage or love or forever. How had Faith—sweet, innocent, shy, frightened, insecure Faith— ever managed?

It was fate, his father would tell him. Everything happened for a purpose, his mother would insist, and he suspected that they would both be right. So much that had brought him and Faith together had been uncharacteristic, like his getting drunk at the engagement party. He had long ago outgrown the practice of drinking too much, and yet he had done exactly that at the party. Or seducing a stranger. He'd given up that practice, too, for his health, his safety and his self-respect—and Faith had never taken it up. For years she had kept the men in her life at arm's length, had worked at not becoming like her mother, had insisted on— the old-fashioned phrase made the corners of his mouth lift in a smile, albeit a grateful one—saving herself for marriage. Yet she had invited a man she didn't know to spend the night, had willingly let him seduce her and, as she'd admitted earlier, hadn't even had the decency to not enjoy it.

It must have been fate that had led him into her shop to ask for directions last week. Why else would he—affirmed non-husband, non-father material—choose a boutique for babies, of all places, to ask for directions that he could have easily gotten from the office supply store, the bookstore, the newspaper or any of the other places on that block?

And Faith fainting—that had been a guaranteed attention-getter, causing him to carry her into the back room, leading him to recognize her from his dreams. "Do you often faint like that?" he had asked later, and she had replied more than a little sarcastically. *No, but I'm pregnant. I do all sorts of things that I don't ordinarily do.* He would bet that she hadn't fainted before that day, and he was pretty damned sure she hadn't since.

Fate. Purpose. Luck. Whatever he called it, it came down to one thing: he and Faith belonged together. They were meant to be together. It would have been nice for her sake if they could have managed it differently, if they could have met under different circumstances, if they could have fallen in love and gotten married before bringing Amelia Rose into the family, but he was damned if he was going to turn his back on their destiny simply because the circumstances were less than ideal. Damned if he was going to let her push him away because they'd done things in the wrong order.

She shifted restlessly in his arms, turning, settling, drawing closer. Cradling her carefully, he got to his feet and carried her down the hall before stopping for a breather at the foot of the stairs. "It's a good thing you're so slender," he murmured. "Otherwise, I couldn't even think about carrying you all the way to the top of these stairs."

For a moment, all he did *was* think about it. Even though she was a delicate little thing—who happened to be carrying an extra thirty pounds or so—she was still an armful, and those stairs were long. Still, he was strong, and her bed—soon to be *their* bed—was waiting at the top. Hadn't he wanted this morning to crawl under the covers with her and hold her while she slept? Didn't he want it enough now that he could manage all these stairs and then some?

Taking a deep breath, he started up, and he did manage, though he was winded, his muscles achy. In her bedroom, he made his way through the dim light, laid her on the bed and removed her shoes, all without disturbing her rest. He kicked off his own shoes, tossed his jacket on the chair and joined her in bed, where her only response was to turn toward him, to move easily into his arms again, exactly where he wanted her.

He untucked the quilt from around her so that it lay underneath them, then pulled the covers over them. It wasn't exactly the intimacy he desired. She was sleeping soundly, and he was tired himself. They were both fully dressed, and even if they were naked, the way he would like to be, there was nothing they could do about it. No matter how she aroused him, he had a long, long wait until he could make love to her again.

Still… He yawned, brushed her hair from his face, tucked her more snugly against him, then let his eyes close. Even fully dressed, unable to make love and with little to do but sleep, this was *exactly* where he wanted to be.

The vague sensation of being watched penetrated Nick's sleep and brought him fully awake but not fully alert. It was the middle of the night, the room was dimly lit by moonlight from outside, he was in bed, still wearing his clothes, and someone was lying only inches… *Faith.* He smiled lazily and opened his eyes. He was in bed with Faith, who was lying on her side, one arm tucked under head, watching him.

"Hey," he greeted her, rolling onto his side to face her.

"Good morning. Or good night, whichever it is."

He checked the luminous numbers on his watch. It was 3:00 a.m. "You okay?"

"I'm fine." She was silent a moment before curiously asking, "How did I get here?"

"You don't remember?"

"No. Did you carry me?"

He grinned. "You wake up in the middle of the night in bed with a man, and you don't remember how you got there or what you did once you were there?" He chuckled. "And you thought *I* was bad."

"At least I know what I *didn't* do," she said, trying to scowl but not succeeding. "And at least I'm waking up fully clothed."

He ran his fingertip along the lace collar of her dress, then let it slide down to the beginning swell of her breast. "More's the pity. I would like to see you naked."

Catching his hand, she pulled it away, but didn't let go. Instead she twined her fingers around his. "Oh, right," she said scornfully. "I'm such an appealing sight."

"I've seen you naked before," he reminded her.

"Yes, but you don't remember."

And *that* was really a pity. "I wish I did," he murmured, lifting her hand to his mouth, pressing a kiss to her palm that made her shiver. "We'll just have to make new memories."

"Memories of Amelia Rose." Her voice was soft, her tone uncertain, asking for agreement. He didn't give it.

"That, too. But, darlin', there are going to be certain aspects of our lives that won't involve our daughter. There are going to be times when it's just you and me, and they're going to be sweet."

"Right," she whispered again, but this time the scorn was missing, replaced by longing so pure he could feel it deep inside himself. She wanted to believe him, wanted to believe *in* him, but she was afraid. Someday she would get over that fear. Someday she *would* believe in him. More importantly, she would believe in herself. He could wait. He had the rest of their lives to wait.

"The Russos are all optimists—cockeyed, some might say. I can't believe I'm marrying a cynic like you."

"I never agreed to marry you," she reminded him, still in that soft, wistful voice.

"You're right," he teased, stroking her hair. "You told me no. No way. Never. Not in this lifetime. When hell freezes over—"

"I did not."

"Well, that was what you implied. But you're wrong, Faith. You *will* marry me, and soon. Before Christmas. And you'll live with me in this house and sleep beside me in this room, and when the doctor says it's okay, you'll make love with me in this bed. You'll make me damned glad Michelle's demon-seed nephews spiked the punch last February. You'll make up for all those months I dreamed of you, and I'll make up for all those months you were alone."

Her fingers tightened around his until her grip was painful. "Don't do this, Nick," she pleaded. "Don't tempt me."

He liked the sound of Faith tempted by him. He liked it a lot. "Remember last week when I asked you to dinner? You asked if that was how I caught crooks, if I badgered them until they said what I wanted."

"Just to get rid of you," she added, helpfully supplying what he had left out.

"I'm good at badgering, and I'm hard to get rid of." Pulling his hand free of hers, he touched her again, her face this time, drawing his fingertips along her jaw, brushing her cheek, her soft lips. "And, darlin', you don't yet know the meaning of temptation."

Then he kissed her.

Surely he'd done it before, that night, that infamous February night, but how he possibly could have forgotten was beyond him. Her kiss was so sweet, so innocent, so tantalizing and tormenting. Inexperienced, maybe. Enticing, definitely. Erotic, absolutely. Full of promise, passion and pleasure. It was a kiss that outranked all the first kisses and best kisses a person could ever experience rolled into one. It was the sort of kiss a man remembered forever in his soul . . . or his dreams.

He pulled back, drew a deep breath and wished like hell for a light so he could see her face to see if she was similarly affected. He suspected she was. In the dimness he could see that she was unmoving, unbreathing, still and awed. Then, her breath catching audibly, she raised her hand, her fingers trembling as they touched his mouth.

He kissed the tip of her index finger before she pulled it back. "That was—" At a loss for the right word, he simply shook his head.

"That's what it was like that night," she said simply. "Everything. When you touched me, when you kissed me, I knew what we were doing couldn't be wrong. Even though we were strangers, even though you were going back to Houston the next day, even though I'd always been taught that it was such a sin, I knew. I *knew* it was meant to be."

Rolling onto his back, he stared up at the pale shape that was the ceiling. "I'm so sorry, Faith." He'd never told her that, not once, and he owed it to her. He owed her big-time.

"For what?"

"Sorry I got drunk. Sorry I left the house that morning without seeing you. Sorry I never came back. I'm so damned sorry that I can't remember. No matter how many times we make love the rest of our lives..." His sigh was full of sorrow. "I'll always regret not remembering that first time."

Chapter 10

Seated at the desk behind the counter, Faith plucked a flower from the bouquet the florist delivered weekly and twirled it between her palms. It was straight-up twelve noon, and it had been a quiet Thursday so far. Nick had gone to pick up lunch, the shop was empty, and she was alone. With a sigh, she pulled one petal from the flower, letting it fall to the floor. A moment later another petal followed it down, followed by a third.

She thinks she loves him. He loves her not.

She thinks she loves him. He loves her not . . . but he does have this weird desire for her.

Here she was, nine months pregnant, her belly swollen along with just about everything else, and he *liked* touching her. He'd gotten aroused while holding her yesterday and had certainly been passionate with his kisses this morning.

Two more petals dropped, one catching on her slacks, bright and creamy white against the black fabric, before it drifted on down. *She thinks she loves him. He lusts after her, but he loves her not.* He'd talked a lot about getting

married, about creating new memories, being a family and
making a commitment, but the only time the word *love*
came out of his mouth was in reference to making it. Not
feeling it, not creating and nurturing it. Just sex. Obviously, he didn't love her and didn't ever intend to. Maybe he
couldn't. Maybe she was so different from the women he
preferred that he could never in a million years feel anything other than lust for her.

Another two petals. *She thinks—she* knows *she loves him
and wants to marry him whether he loves her not.* Not that
she would. She still had her pride, which absolutely refused
to be a burden or obligation to anyone ever again. Even if—
unlike Great-aunt Lydia—Nick was willing to accept the
obligation and make the best of it. Even if he was willing to
work at turning burdens and obligations into a family for
Amelia Rose.

Heaving a great sigh, she pulled off the last petal, tossed
the stem into the wastebasket, then dropped the petal. It
floated down, airy and light, gradually landing at an angle
across another petal.

"Well? What's the verdict?"

Glancing up, she saw Nick leaning on the counter,
watching her. He must have come in through the back door,
or she surely would have heard the bell. Front or back,
though, she couldn't believe she'd been so lost in thought
that she hadn't sensed the very moment he'd walked through
the door. "What verdict?"

"Does she love him or love him not?"

Feeling a twinge of pain deep inside, she coolly replied,
"You know, there are other options."

"All right. Does he love her or love her not?"

"There are others. Like, will I have this baby soon or have
her not?"

His eyes widened just a bit and he took a step around the
counter. "Are you okay?"

"I'm fine." She sniffed the air and recognized only baby
things and baby smells—and Nick, of course. That sexy,

tantalizing scent of his would stay with her for the rest of her life. "Where's lunch?"

"In my truck."

"Why would we want to eat in your truck?"

"We're not. We're going to the lake."

"I don't want to go to the lake."

"Come on. It's a beautiful day. It'll be nice." He came over, helped her to her feet, then bent to pick up the flower petals. For a moment he looked at them, gently touching them, then he pressed them into her hand. "You know the secret to getting the answer you want with these things? Use an odd number of petals." Clasping her other hand in his, he pulled her around the counter and toward the door. There he shut off all but the display lights, turned the sign to Closed, took the Will Be Back clock off the door completely, and ushered her outside to wait while he locked the door. While he was busy with that, she unfolded her fingers and looked surreptitiously at the flower petals. There had been eight on the flower—she had plucked it bare—but now only seven nestled in her palm.

It meant nothing. He had simply overlooked the eighth petal. It had drifted under the desk or had gotten caught in one of the casters on the chair legs. He probably had no idea how many pieces he'd picked up. He hadn't deliberately counted, then spirited one away. Still, as a gentle breeze wafted around her, she closed her fingers around the petals, then slid them to safety inside her pocket.

True to his word, lunch was waiting in the pickup, tucked inside the wicker basket in the center of the seat. Two bright red napkins that she recognized from every meal she'd ever had at Antonio's were draped over the top, and a quilt was folded over the seat behind the basket. A winter picnic at the lake. It shouldn't sound so appealing, but, heaven help her, it did.

"Did any of your boyfriends take you to Hardison Lake?" he asked as they headed east out of town.

Rather than point out that she'd never had boyfriends, not really—there had only been guys that she'd dated a time or two—she simply shook her head.

"Good. Then I get to introduce you to the lake's charms myself."

"Are these the same charms you introduced Theresa Harland to years ago?"

His grin was quick and dear. "What do you know about Theresa Harland?"

"I know that you and Dan Wilson dated the Harland twins." She turned to look out the window at the flat winter landscape. "Theresa comes into the shop practically every time she comes home. She's a pretty woman. The next time she stops by, I can give her your number."

"Don't bother. I'm not interested." Turning in at the first entrance to the park surrounding the lake, he followed a narrow winding road away from the closest beaches, the ones most people frequented in summer, and instead picked a quiet spot on a long, narrow finger of the lake.

Faith opened the door and slid to the ground, then looked around. It was a pretty place, even in winter with the grass turned yellow, the trees bare of leaves and the water a cold, glassy gray. In spring or summer, it would be lovely. Remote enough for privacy, it was the perfect place, she supposed, for a carefully planned seduction or a spur-of-the-moment party for two.

So why had he brought her here?

Nick shook out the quilt, spread it on the grass near the water, then returned to the truck for the basket and her. She let him take her hand, let him lead her across the uneven ground and help her down onto the quilt. Leaning back on both arms behind her, she gazed out across the water. Back when she was in high school, *everyone* had come to Hardison Lake for one reason or another. Most of the girls in her class, it had seemed, had attended "submarine races"—always said with a wink and a giggle—with their chosen dates. More teenagers had seduced and been seduced on the shores of the lake than in all the back seats in north Texas combined.

She had been the exception. She'd never had a date in school who might have taken her to the lake, and even the more innocent activities—the summer swims, the wiener roasts and chaperoned parties—had been decreed off-limits to her by Great-aunt Lydia. The old woman had wanted to keep her from temptation, but she needn't have worried. No one had ever tempted her—no one but Nick, and he hadn't been around eight years ago.

But he was here now.

He sat down behind her, moving her hands so he could slide in close, tugging her back to lean against his chest. "Every Friday night all the grandkids spend the night at Mom and Pop's," he said, his voice a murmur near her ear. "Next spring, before it gets too warm and the lake is overrun by kids, we'll let Amelia Rose stay over there, and we'll come out here. We'll bring a sleeping bag and build a campfire, and we'll make love under the stars."

She felt a curious little tingle deep in her belly. Arousal. She was in no condition to do anything about it, but she felt it, odd, vaguely familiar, and full of promise. "Is that what you used to do with Theresa Harland?" she asked, conjuring up an image of his old girlfriend to distract herself.

For a moment he sat still, then he moved around in front of her. There was annoyance in his dark eyes, frustration in the thin set of his mouth. "Yes, I did. We used to come out here every Friday and Saturday night and sometimes in between. We would drink, get naked and do all kinds of wicked things. Sometimes we went skinny-dipping, but mostly we stayed under the covers and did things an innocent little girl like you can't even imagine." Then his voice turned hard. "That ended over sixteen years ago, Faith. I don't give a damn about Theresa now. Why do you?"

The honesty of her answer surprised him. It surprised her even more. "Maybe I'm jealous. You were with her by choice. You did the things you did because you *wanted* to.

You're here with me because you have no choice. Because you're trying to make the best of a bad situation.''

He stared at her a long time, then slowly sat back on his heels. "You're an idiot, Faith."

The flatness of his insult stung and made her scoot back a bit. "Because I want more?" she asked defensively. "Because I think that maybe, just maybe, I deserve a little more?"

"Because you wouldn't recognize 'more' if it was in your face," he said scathingly. "You think I'm here because I have no choice? Darlin', I've got plenty of choices. I can have my daughter without having to take you, too...but that's not what I want."

"You want a family for Amelia Rose," she said sarcastically.

"No, damn it!" Clenching his jaw, he looked away, staring angrily at nothing, then at her again. "I want *you* for *me*."

Faith's mouth went dry and butterflies sprang to life in her belly. That sounded frighteningly close to something she'd waited all her life to hear, something too important to take lightly. "You...want...me. For what?"

He grimaced, his impatience almost palpable. "I want to marry you. I want to make love with you and live with you and raise our children with you. I want to come home from work to you and go to bed beside you. Hell, I even want to fight with you...and I want to make up with you. We belong together, and nothing can change that—not your insecurities, not your doubts, not your damnable stubbornness. For God's sake, Faith, quit being so safe. Take a chance for once."

"I did that last February, and look where it got me," she whispered.

"Yeah, look where it got you," he agreed sarcastically. "You're about to give birth to a baby you already love more than life itself. As of tomorrow, you're going to be a part of the biggest family in the whole damned county, and—"

She interrupted him. "What do you mean about tomorrow?"

For a moment, he had the grace to look sheepish, then it disappeared and defensiveness took its place. "We're all invited to dinner at my folks' house tomorrow. Pop is going to tell Mom about Amelia Rose, and she's going to tell everyone else. Sweetheart, your secret's been shot to hell."

Feeling a sudden chill, she hugged herself. "What if they're not as pleased as you think they'll be?"

"They will be."

"But what if they're not?"

He moved closer, right in front of her, his dark gaze intense and grim. "Do you trust me at all, Faith?"

Unable to force the word past the lump in her throat, she nodded.

"Then trust me on this. They're going to love Amelia Rose, and they're going to love you."

"How can you be so sure?"

"Believe me."

"But how can you—"

"Because *I* love you, damn it!"

His tone was harsh, his temper barely controlled, but his words were the sweetest Faith had ever heard...if she dared believe them. If she dared trust him. She had just told him that she did, and she'd meant it... at that moment. No, she *did* mean it. She trusted him to be a good father to Amelia Rose. She trusted him to treat her with the respect his daughter's mother deserved. She trusted him to be there for her, to be strong and take care of her. Before she'd even fully accepted that he was going to be part of their baby's life, hadn't she admitted that he was the one she wanted with her when her labor began? He was the one she'd wanted from the very beginning to share their daughter's birth, the one she'd wanted to lean on and hold on to, the one she'd wanted to draw courage from.

Was it right or fair—or even possible—to trust his actions but not his words? To believe that he would be there when she needed him, that he would take care of her, but not believe him when he said he loved her? After all, as far as she knew, he had never lied to her. He had never given her reason to doubt him. Other people had—her parents, her grandparents, Lydia—but he never had. All he'd ever given her was a baby, a few hours of magic, a week of pleasure, anxiety, anticipation, comfort, support, concern and sweet, warm kisses . . . and the promise of a lifetime more.

Was she an idiot for wanting—for thinking she deserved—more than life had offered? she had asked earlier, and his reply had been quick, sharp and scornful. She was an idiot because she wouldn't *recognize "more" if it was in your face.*

Wasn't in her face precisely where he'd been the last week? Forcing her to see him, to acknowledge him, to get to know him. Refusing to run back to Houston and hide from the problems that had entangled his life with hers. Facing the future with more courage and willingness than she'd found. More open to the needs of their daughter and to their own needs than she'd managed to be. Offering her all the things she'd lived without so long that she hadn't even recognized them.

He was waiting, watching her with the kind of uncertainty that she'd made her very own, watching for some hint of the response he wanted. She opened her mouth to give it to him, but before she could form the words, with a great rush of warm fluid, her body delayed her.

There was no pain, just incredible shock, incredible fear. Instinctively she reached for him, and he took her hand in both of his. "Are you all right?" he demanded. "Faith? *Faith!*"

She took a deep breath, then blew it out through her mouth. "I need to go home. I need to change clothes. And then I need to go to the hospital."

"Why—" His gaze dropped past her stomach and for just a moment she saw her own fear reflected in his eyes. It disappeared, though, as he grinned that charming, brash, sexy grin that she found so endearing. "You find the damnedest ways to avoid important conversations," he remarked, getting to his feet and easily pulling her up. "Are you okay, or should I carry you?"

Placing both hands on the small of her back, she stretched to ease the low ache there. When he'd been talking about making love under the stars, she'd felt a twinge that she'd written off as arousal. When he'd said he wanted her, not as the mother to his and Amelia Rose's family but for himself, she'd felt upheavals that she'd called butterflies. Now she wondered if those had been the very first signs of labor and she'd been too naive—and too enraptured by Nick's words—to recognize them.

"Carrying me gets you into trouble," she said, sliding her arm through his and starting a slow trip across the grass to the truck. "You carried me that night last February, though only a few feet. And if you hadn't carried me into the storeroom at the shop last week, you might never have looked beyond the fainting pregnant woman to see—"

"The woman of my dreams," he finished for her.

"And you carried me upstairs last night and wound up spending probably the most boring night you've ever spent in bed with a woman."

He opened the door and started to lift her inside, but paused, holding her close, gazing down into her face. "In your bed is where I've wanted to be for the past nine months. It's where I want to be for the next ninety years."

Raising her hands to his face, she leaned forward and pressed a gentle, awkward, not-sure-she-was-doing-it-right kiss to his mouth, then pulled back. "Good. I'll try not to bore you there."

Nick stood at one end of the gurney, leaning over Faith, while at the other end, Dr. Austin and his staff were gathered. Considering that an event of such importance was taking place—Amelia Rose Russo was about to make her entry into the world—the delivery room was quiet and calm, and Faith was the calmest of them all.

Nick had never seen a woman so serene, and it amazed him. For four solid hours the contractions had been swift, the pain intense—and he had the bruises to prove it—but she had never panicked, had never given in to them. She had borne them with a strength that far surpassed his own. He'd been shaken up simply watching, knowing that she was hurting and there was nothing he could do to help.

Twenty minutes ago the nurses had moved her from labor to delivery and sent him to wash up and change into powder blue scrubs. While he was gone, the anesthesiologist had given her the spinal block she and Dr. Austin had agreed on. Now she was lying quietly—pale, exhausted, and so damned *serene*.

"I do love you," he murmured, holding her hand in his, brushing a strand of sweat-dampened hair from her face with his other hand.

She smiled in spite of everything going on around—and *inside*—her. "I believe you do." Her breath caught as she tightened her fingers around his. "You know, you're going to have to marry me."

He smiled, too, even though, with the dampness in his eyes and the lump in his throat, he felt more like crying. He'd heard much talk about tears of joy, but he'd never experienced them until now. "I believe I am. You have any plans for tomorrow?"

Her laughter was cut short by Dr. Austin. "All right, Faith, you're doing fine. Just another minute. I can see Amelia Rose's head. All that dark hair."

"Just like her father," one of the nurses remarked, and Nick turned to look, but Faith reclaimed his attention.

"There's something I need to tell you," she began, urgency underlaying the softness of her voice.

He bent to kiss her. "I know you do," he said, his mouth brushing hers with each syllable.

"I do what?"

"Love me. That's what you were going to say, isn't it? That you love me."

She touched his face, her fingers so light and soft. "I do."

"No, you save that for tomorrow. Tonight you're supposed to say, 'I love you, Nick, and I can't live without you.'"

"I love you, Nick," she dutifully repeated. "I can't—*oh!*"

Swiftly he turned toward the doctor in time to see him cradle their baby in his arms. With a laugh of pure, undiluted joy, Dr. Austin said, "Aw, Faith, she's beautiful. Look at this face." Then his gaze traveled lower, and amusement came into his voice. "Correction. *He's* beautiful. Congratulations, Faith, Nick. You have a beautiful baby boy."

Faith held the sleeping baby in her arms, gently stroking his soft black hair, his thin, rounded arm, his tiny, perfectly shaped hand. "I was so sure," she whispered. "I knew in my heart that it was a girl."

Nick shifted her more comfortably across his lap, then watched as she shifted the baby more comfortably across her lap. "Are you disappointed?" he asked hesitantly. All those baby clothes, that pretty little green dress, the name, the plans. . . .

The look she gave him was filled with astonishment. "I have a sweet, beautiful, perfect little boy who will grow up as handsome and charming as his father. How could I possibly be disappointed?"

"You wanted a daughter."

She smiled the sweetest, freshest, most innocently womanly smile he'd ever seen, and it hit him with all the breath-stealing impact of a knee in the groin. For that smile he would do anything. For that smile he would have tumbled head over heels in love with her last February...which he'd started to do anyway, he suspected. It had been a long, slow tumble, but he was there now. Head over heels.

"I wanted a *baby*," she corrected him. "A daughter would have been wonderful, but so will a son. I'm going to love having a son."

Reaching past her, he touched his fingertip to the baby's cheek. Immediately, even in sleep, he turned his head to-

ward the finger and worked his mouth a time or two before
snoozing on. "Did you give any consideration to boys'
names before you settled on Amelia Rose?"

She was quiet for so long that he tilted her head back so
he could see her eyes. There was a hint of embarrassment
and a whole lot of shyness there. "I'm disgustingly traditional, you know," she admitted.

"Nick is a fine name," he gently teased. "I've always
liked it—especially the way *you* say it. But you don't want
two Nicks in the same house, and Nicky is cute now, but
he'd resent it when he's sixteen. What name would you use
with it?"

"I thought—" She lifted the baby's fingers, tenderly
curling her finger underneath them, ever so lightly rubbing
them. "I thought we could name him Nicholas Anthony and
call him Tony," she said in a rush. "That is, if you don't
mind. If your father wouldn't mind."

"I'm sure he would feel as honored as I do." After a quiet
moment to deal with the lump in his throat, he went on.
"Speaking of my father, I'd better call him." It took a little
maneuvering, but he managed to reach the telephone on the
bedside table and punch in the restaurant number. His father answered on the third ring, and, without any other
greeting, Nick said, "Seventeen grandsons, Pop, and not
one of them named Tony. That's kind of sad. Fortunately
for you, Faith had—literally *had*—a solution."

He kept the call short, then pushed the phone away and
gathered Faith and Tony closer. "He was speechless," he
said before she could ask the inevitable what-did-he-say?
"And, darlin', leaving Antonio Russo speechless is a *big*
accomplishment."

"He's happy?"

"Proud to bursting. He and Mom will be by first thing in
the morning to tell you so themselves."

"And are you happy?"

He leaned back against the pillows. Happy? He was lying in a hospital bed with Faith in his arms and their son—
their beautiful, tiny, sweet, looks-just-like-a-Russo son—in

her arms. He was getting married—not tomorrow, he acknowledged, but very, very soon. He was in love and she loved him, too. *Happy?*

Holding his family close—*his family,* an awed little voice inside echoed—he answered in a lazy, satisfied, forever-and-always drawl. "Darlin', I'm proud to bursting."

On the other side of town, Antonio Russo arrived home four hours earlier than his wife expected him. Bearing a bottle of the finest champagne the restaurant stocked, he surprised her in the kitchen, gathered her into his arms and danced her around the room.

Laughing, she stopped his exuberant dance, but she didn't pull away from his embrace. "And what occasion are we celebrating this evening?"

"Luisa, my dear, the great love of my life, have I got news for you..."

Epilogue

Faith stopped in the doorway and surveyed the scene in the
parlor with a smile and the sort of warm contentment that
she'd been searching for all her life—the contentment she'd
found six weeks ago and would never live without again.
The drapes at the windows were open, letting light spill out
into the snow-covered backyard, and a blaze popped and
crackled in the fireplace. On the rug in front of the hearth,
five-year-old Dusty Donovan was patiently explaining the
mechanics of the quick draw to Jake Spencer, his toy gun
clearing its holster in the blink of an eye. Priss, looking
happier than Faith had ever seen her, sat nearby, her hands
folded across her swollen stomach. With a spring baby on
the way and a handsome husband like Jake, Priss's life,
Faith imagined, just couldn't get any better.

On the couch the Kincaid twins, Traci and Brooke,
crawled over, onto and around anything that got in their
way, including their adopted mother, Valerie, and Wendy.
After losing their own baby only hours after her birth last
February, Valerie and Lucas had found the twins to be a real
life-saver—and marriage-saver. They'd made peace with

themselves and with each other over Kelly's death, and their marriage was all the stronger for it.

Life had changed for the better for Wendy, too. The great husband hunt had ended with her Christmas wedding to Travis Donovan, and she couldn't have been more pleased. She doted on Dusty and had since he was a toddler, and she couldn't possibly love Travis more. They were perfect for each other.

Jenny and Mitch McCord shared the big old armchair, Mitch sitting on the cushion with his bright-eyed daughter Mary on his lap and Jenny perched on the arm, listening to the conversation between her husband, Lucas and Travis but watching Mary with a smile that any mother's heart could recognize. It was the same way Wendy smiled at Dusty and Valerie at the twins, the same way Priss would undoubtedly smile at her baby.

It was the same way Faith smiled at Tony every morning, every night, every time he caught her attention. He'd brought all the things to her life that she had expected— love, happiness, security, the knowledge that she was needed—and so much more. He'd brought her a family, not just the two of them, as she had feared, but a real family— loud, loving, boisterous, thrilled by their newest baby, just as Nick had promised, and even a little bit thrilled with her. No one had cared that she wasn't Catholic, that she'd provided food for gossip all her life, that she'd created a minor scandal with her pregnancy, that she'd presented them with the first illegitimate grandchild in the family's history or that she'd hidden the impending birth of that grandchild from them all. They had simply listened when Nick had said, "This is the woman I love," and they had accepted her.

It had been so simple. She still marveled over the ease with which they had taken her in. One word from Nick, and she'd had *family.* Parents to call Mom and Pop, grandparents, sisters-in-law, brothers-in-law, and nieces and nephews by the dozen. So simple and so precious.

Finally she let her gaze settle on Nick, seated in her favorite rocker, Tony in his arms. That big old chair was one of the best investments she'd ever made. It was part of their evening ritual: every night before bedtime, they sat together in the chair, Faith in Nick's lap, Tony in hers. Sometimes they talked, and soon they would start reading to their son, but mostly they just rocked in silence, savoring the moment.

With a soft sigh, she turned away from the door and went into the kitchen. A moment later Wendy joined her there. "Whenever you're ready for us to leave, just say the word."

Faith glanced up from the pastries she was arranging on a tray. Nick had brought them home with him after work, fresh from Antonio's, so she wouldn't have to worry about fixing anything special for tonight's get-together—and he'd done it without being asked. He was thoughtful that way. He was thoughtful in *every* way. "Why would I be anxious for you to leave?"

Her friend's grin extended from ear to ear. "Don't play innocent, Faith. You've been with Nick too long to manage. What is today?"

"Friday."

"Friday what?"

"January fifteenth."

"And what's significant about that date?"

Her cheeks turning pink, Faith tried to bluff her way through. "I don't know."

"How old is Tony?"

"Six—six weeks yesterday." Now her face was hot. "All right," she admitted. "Yes, tonight is the night." *The* night. The night she'd been waiting for practically all her life. The night that she and Nick got to forget about doctors' warnings and advice and *finally* do something in their bed besides sleep. Not that they hadn't jumped the gun a little. They hadn't gone *too* far, but they'd made a good start.

Tonight they got to finish.

"Are you nervous?"

Priss wandered into the kitchen in time to catch the gist of the conversation. "Why should she be nervous? It's not like it's their first time," she said. "Nick's out there hold-ing proof of that."

"But it's only their *second* time," Wendy said. "*I* was nervous my second time, and it was only a few hours after the first. Faith's had to wait ten and a half months—and an awful lot has happened in those months."

Faith smiled as she turned to empty some of the glasses on the counter. It *was* rather like their first time, but, of course, her friends didn't know that. She'd kept one secret from them—that Nick remembered nothing about the first time. For him, this would be his first time with her. It would be the first time they were both stone-cold sober, both one hundred percent aware of what they were doing. It would be the first time when they were both weak-in-the-knees in love.

And, yes, she was nervous. Anxious, really, more than nervous. Eager. Excited. Impatient. As a matter of fact, in-stead of serving these pastries, maybe she should simply wrap them up in pretty napkins and hand them out as she ushered everyone out the door.

Then, looking through the open doorway as she turned around again, she saw Nick talking to Tony, making the baby smile and wave his fists in the air, and she knew she could wait.

After all, she'd already waited a lifetime. What were a few hours more?

Nick had never known one evening could last so long, but finally everyone was gone. The house was quiet except for the usual old-house noises that were comfortingly familiar. He locked the door, turned off the porch light, then turned into the formal living room. Before the Donovans had left, he'd shown Travis this room and the study across the hall. Neither room had been changed—not even the furniture or carpet, he would bet—since the house was built about a hundred years ago. Both rooms were grim and bleak—though not as bleak as Lydia's room upstairs—and he and Faith had talked about doing something with them. With his background in construction, Travis had offered some good advice.

Now Nick switched off the lights he'd left burning, did the same across the hall, then started back toward the parlor. He would like to think that Faith was anticipating tonight even half as much as he was, that while he'd said good-night to their guests, she had hurried upstairs, tucked Tony into bed and was now waiting in their own bed. But he knew better.

Only one light still burned in the parlor, supplemented by the warm golden light from the fireplace. Just as he'd known she would be, she was sitting in the rocker, cradling their son, singing softly to him. As Nick moved closer, he recognized the song, a lullaby that his mother had sung to him, that her mother had sung to her, complete with lyrics in Italian.

She stood up, made room for him, then let him pull her into his lap, all without breaking the sweet, soft flow of song. "I didn't know you'd learned any Italian," he said when it ended.

"Your mother taught me." She laid her head on his shoulder. "Isn't he beautiful?"

"Like his mother."

"He doesn't look a thing like me."

She was right. As he had warned her, all Russos looked alike. There might be a slight variation in hair color or eye color, one might be darker or fairer, and, of course, they came in all sizes and shapes, but they all looked alike. "Maybe Amelia Rose will look more like you. She'll be delicate like you. She'll have your eyes."

She gave him a long, steady look. They hadn't mentioned that name much since Tony's birth. They had both been so pleased with the son they'd been given that they had more or less forgotten about the daughter they had expected. No, not forgotten. *He* still thought about her, about a sweet little girl with her mother's eyes, tiny and fragile and in need of a father's—and a brother's—protection. He had just preferred to concentrate more on the son in their present than the daughter in their future.

"You have nice friends," he remarked, rocking slowly back and forth.

"Yes, I do. We do."

A long moment passed in silence before he spoke again. "Sweetheart, I think Tony's ready for bed."

"He's been asleep right here for the last thirty minutes."

"All right. I think Tony's pop is ready for bed."

"Pop." She made the p's do just that—make a soft explosive sound. "Papa. Daddy." Smiling lazily, she leaned forward and pressed a kiss to his throat. "Want to carry us upstairs?"

His laughter was unrestrained. "Right, darlin'. Would you prefer that I carry you to bed or conserve my energy so I can make mad, passionate love to you all night?"

"I'll have you know I've lost every pound—well, almost every pound—well, more than half of all those pounds—I gained while pregnant."

Her pouty look made him grin. He'd watched her discard outfit after prepregnancy outfit, complaining all the while that those last fifteen pounds were never going to budge. Personally, he hoped they never went away. She must have been almost girlishly thin before, because now she was curvy, shapely, womanly. Now she was perfect.

Sliding to her feet, she started away, shifting Tony to her shoulder. At the door she looked back to where he still sat in the rocker. "Aren't you coming?"

He'd been admiring the view—the way her jeans fit snugly over her bottom, the way her hips swayed seductively—but now impatience pulled him to his feet. "I'll take care of the fire." That task took only a moment, then he took the stairs two at a time. He joined his family in the nursery, gave his son a good-night kiss, then followed his wife across the hall to their own room. As she stopped at the makeup table to remove her jewelry, he grinned once more. He would follow her anywhere.

Catching his grin, she feigned a chastising look. "Do I amuse you?"

"You arouse me, amaze me, astonish and astound me—and, yes, sweetheart, you do amuse me. You do everything for me. You make my life complete."

Her jewelry tucked away in its proper cases, she clasped her hands together and uncertainty—shyness—edged into her manner. "Are you nervous?" she asked curiously.

He approached her slowly, wanting to touch her, *needing* to hold her. "I've seen you naked. I've held you, touched you, kissed you. I've slept beside you every night for the last six weeks." Then he chuckled. "Hell, yes, I'm nervous. This is like our wedding night."

Their actual wedding night had been spent right in this room, with Faith just out of the hospital, sore and achy, and Tony waking up every two or three hours for food, a dry diaper or just a little reassurance. Nick hadn't minded, but he'd been disappointed for Faith's sake. She'd had dreams of falling in love and getting married, and he'd been pretty sure they hadn't involved a priest, a hurriedly thrown-together ceremony, a green maternity dress and a cranky newborn who had no doubt missed the quiet, warm security of his mother's womb. She had envisioned a romantic honeymoon someplace far from the ordinariness of home, a lovely, private week or two spent making love, indulging desires, sharing intimacies—not caring for a baby, dealing with visitors and new family by the dozen and trying in vain to find some bearable way to sit while her body healed, with making love strictly forbidden and virtually impossible.

He brushed her hair back, letting it fall over his fingers. "Someday I'll make it up to you."

"What?"

"Our wedding. Our wedding night. Our poor excuse for a honeymoon."

She looked amazed, as utterly astonished as she had the night he had reluctantly asked her if she was disappointed in getting a Nicholas Anthony instead of an Amelia Rose, and the need inside him burned a little hotter. "Our wedding was wonderful. Our wedding night was sweet, and as for our honeymoon . . . We had a whole week with nowhere to go and nothing to do but get to know our son and each other. It was perfect. It was exactly what I wanted, exactly what I needed." She brought her hands to his face, and he pressed a damp kiss to one palm. "Were *you* disappointed?"

"*No.* It was exactly what I wanted, too...but I'm easy to please. All I wanted—all I'll ever want—is you." He moved closer, slid his arms around her, bent to kiss her cheek. "And Tony." His next kiss brushed her jaw. "And Amelia Rose. And Beatrice, Carlotta, Daniel, Ernest, Frederick..."

"Now wait a minute." She was laughing as she twined her arms around his neck. "Just how many babies do you plan on having?"

"At least eight. You see, there's this old Italian tradition that the eldest son should have at least as many children as his parents did."

"Uh-huh. And no one in your family thought to tell me about it, even though your father *did* take me aside on our wedding day and announce that he wouldn't mind an attempt for another granddaughter right away."

"He did, huh? And what did you tell him?"

She rose onto her toes to catch his ear between her teeth for a kiss that made him shudder, then murmured, "Six weeks. I told him that we'd start in six weeks. That's tonight, sweetheart."

He kissed her then, his tongue sliding inside her mouth even as her hands moved inside his shirt. She was unfastening buttons quicker than his dazed brain could command his hands to move to the hem of her sweater. He'd had plans for tonight. Soft music, softer lights—candles or maybe all those little oil lamps she'd collected. Slow seduction, leisurely undressing, lazy kisses and tantalizing caresses, everything measured and prolonged, building layer of desire upon layer of need until the hunger was explosive, until they would die if they waited one second longer, until everything else in the universe ceased to exist except the two of them and their need. Their love.

So much for soft music and soft lights, he thought without regret as she slid his shirt off his shoulders. He forgot slow and leisurely as her sweater hit the floor. Building desire and need, feeding hunger... Not necessary. So late that it wasn't even possible. The arousal had sprung to life before they'd even touched, full-blown, weakening and explosive, threatening to consume them. It had been like this before, that fateful night back in February. He was sure of it. They had touched, and... Combustion. Fire. Heat. Need. Hunger. Pain. Desire. Desperation.

Magic.

The last of their clothing discarded, he lifted her onto the bed. He'd done that before, she'd told him. He moved into place between her thighs, seeking, probing, entering. For an instant he closed his eyes and held himself motionless, savoring the tight, heated welcome of her body, marveling at the familiarity of it. He'd done that before, too—had recognized this place, this woman, this feeling. What his mind couldn't remember, his soul could. What his mind had needed time to learn, his heart had known right away that February night. This was where he belonged. This woman was the other part that would make him whole. This was *home.*

Opening his eyes, he looked down at her. She was gazing tenderly, tearfully, at him. "I know," she whispered, and he knew she did. She knew exactly what he was thinking, exactly what he was feeling. "It's magic."

He bent to kiss her, then gathered her close as he began moving inside her. "No, darlin'," he disagreed. "It's *love.*"

She gave him a smile, that womanly, steal-his-breath-away smile, and corrected him with his own favorite endearment. "Same thing, darlin'. It's the very same thing."

*   *   *   *   *

The collection of the year!
NEW YORK TIMES BESTSELLING AUTHORS

Linda Lael Miller
Wild About Harry

Janet Dailey
Sweet Promise

Elizabeth Lowell
Reckless Love

Penny Jordan
Love's Choices

and featuring
Nora Roberts
The Calhoun Women

This special trade-size edition features four of the wildly popular titles in the Calhoun miniseries together in one volume—a true collector's item!

Pick up these great authors and a chance to win a weekend for two in New York City at the Marriott Marquis Hotel on Broadway! We'll pay for your flight, your hotel—even a Broadway show!

Available in December at your favorite retail outlet.

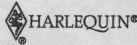 

MILLION DOLLAR SWEEPSTAKES

SWP-M96

FORTUNE'S Children™

Bestselling Author
LINDA TURNER

Continues the twelve-book series—FORTUNE'S CHILDREN—
in **November 1996** with Book Five

THE WOLF AND THE DOVE

Adventurous pilot Rachel Fortune and traditional Native American
doctor Luke Greywolf set sparks off each other the minute they met.
But widower Luke was tormented by guilt and vowed never to love
again. Could tempting Rachel heal Luke's wounded heart so they
could share a future of happily ever after?

MEET THE FORTUNES—a family whose legacy is greater than riches.
Because where there's a will...there's a *wedding!*

As seen on TV!
Free Gift Offer

With a Free Gift proof-of-purchase from any Silhouette® book,
you can receive a beautiful cubic zirconia pendant.

This gorgeous marquise-shaped stone is a genuine cubic
zirconia—accented by an 18" gold tone necklace.

(Approximate retail value $19.95)

Send for yours today...
compliments of ▼ *Silhouette*®

To receive your free gift, a cubic zirconia pendant, send us one original proof-of-
purchase, photocopies not accepted, from the back of any Silhouette Romance™,
Silhouette Desire®, Silhouette Special Edition®, Silhouette Intimate Moments®
or Silhouette Yours Truly™ title available in August, September, October, November and
December at your favorite retail outlet, together with the Free Gift Certificate, plus a
check or money order for $1.65 U.S./$2.15 CAN. (do not send cash) to cover postage and
handling, payable to Silhouette Free Gift Offer. We will send you the specified gift. Allow
6 to 8 weeks for delivery. Offer good until December 31, 1996 or while quantities last.
Offer valid in the U.S. and Canada only.

Free Gift Certificate

Name: _____

Address: _____

City: _____ State/Province: _____ Zip/Postal Code: _____

Mail this certificate, one proof-of-purchase and a check or money order for postage
and handling to: SILHOUETTE FREE GIFT OFFER 1996. In the U.S.: 3010 Walden
Avenue, P.O. Box 9077, Buffalo NY 14269-9077. In Canada: P.O. Box 613, Fort Erie,
Ontario L2Z 5X3.

FREE GIFT OFFER   084-KMD
ONE PROOF-OF-PURCHASE
To collect your fabulous FREE GIFT, a cubic zirconia pendant, you must include this
original proof-of-purchase for each gift with the properly completed Free Gift Certificate.

084-KMD-R

'Tis the season for holiday weddings!

This December, celebrate the holidays
with two sparkling new love stories—
only from

V SILHOUETTE YOURS TRULY™

A Nice Girl Like You
by Alexandra Sellers

Sara Diamond may be a nice girl, but that doesn't mean
she wants to be Ben Harris's ideal bride. But she might
just be able to play Ms. Wrong long enough to help this
confirmed bachelor find his true wife! That is, if she
doesn't fall in love first....

A Marry-Me Christmas
by Jo Ann Algermissen

All Catherine Jordan wanted for Christmas was some
time away from the hustle and bustle. Now she was
sharing a wilderness cabin with her infuriating opposite,
Stone Scofield! But once she stood under the mistletoe
with Stone, she was hoping for a whole lot more
this holiday....

 Don't miss these exciting new books,
our gift to you this holiday season!

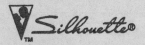